BEE ALL AND END ALL

ELLEN RIGGS

BOUGHT-THE-FARM
MYSTERIES

FREE PREQUEL

Rescuing this pup could bring Ivy a whole new life... if it doesn't kill her first.

Discover how big city executive Ivy meets Keats, her crime-solving sheepdog, in A Dog with Two Tales. Ivy Galloway doesn't know how desperate she is to escape the big city and her soul-sucking corporate career until she meets a sheepdog in need of rescue, too.

This short prequel to the laugh-out-loud Bought-the-Farm Mystery series is a page-turner for lovers of animals, humor and spunky amateur sleuths. Go to **ellenriggs.com/opt-in** and join Ellen Riggs' author newsletter to get this FREE prequel.

Bee All and End All

Copyright © 2024 Ellen Riggs

ISBN 978-1-998742-13-4 D2D Paperback
ISBN 978-1-990613-46-3 eBook
ISBN 978-1-990613-47-0 Book
ISBN 978-1-990613-48-7 AudioBook
ASIN B0CFMD5T5R Kindle
ASIN 1990613470 Paperback

Publisher: Ellen Riggs
www.ellenriggs.com
Cover designer: Lou Harper
Editor: Serena Clarke
2512230236D2D

CHAPTER ONE

The chatter under the long plastic canopy in the town square hushed when I arrived with my best friend Jilly Blackwood and octogenarian prepper Edna Evans to check out the grand opening of the farmer's market. The chilly dampness that marked the first day of spring kept most of us in parkas. Not Keats, my border collie. He had dashed out of the house without his winter coat, holding me to my word that he need only suit up in winter. Perhaps he could read a calendar now. This dog was a genius, especially when it came to avoiding outerwear.

Looking up at me, he opened his mouth in a pant-laugh. His brown eye shot warmth into me before he turned his muzzle to hit me with a bracing bolt from his eerie blue eye. It seemed like a one-two punch of encouragement combined with a warning. "Buckle up," the canine mumble that followed seemed to say. "We're in for a bumpy ride."

My eyes rose from the dog to the rows of tables, wondering what there was to worry about. The Clover Grove Farmer's Market was all that it should be, with displays of produce and buckets filled with cheery tulips and daffodils. Many in our homesteading community owned greenhouses, and I could pick out hints of mushrooms and tomatoes under the strong fragrance of homemade candles. Was I the only one who found fake vanilla and maple oppressive? The smell seemed to be hiding something. I'd learned from hard experience that quaint country life wasn't always sweet.

Today, we were here about jams and preserves, however, and Jilly had asked me to leave my cynicism behind at Runaway Farm. I'd tried shoveling it up with the manure, but we were here about that, too. It was impossible to tease apart the various strands that made up our wonderfully complex existence.

I didn't know my way around the market. Jilly, the chef at the inn we ran together, did the shopping. Occasionally, she sent me into town with a grocery list and shook her head in disgust over what arrived in her kitchen. I was distractible, to say the least. There was always something more interesting going on than groceries, although I could focus just fine when it came to enjoying the delicious meals she prepared.

"Do we rent one table or two?" Jilly asked, golden curls swishing over her shoulders as she took everything in. "One would be cheaper but I don't like the optics of selling my preserves and your manure under one umbrella, as it were."

"My black label fertilizer won't actually be on the premises," I reminded her. "Just a brochure and reference material."

"Still, it might put people off. While I'm pushing jam and chutney, you know we're really selling the inn."

I swept my arm in a dramatic arc. "Well, my fertilizer helped grow the crops that made a lot of these products possible. I have a waiting list for it. Who's going to complain?"

Edna mirrored my theatrical sweep with her own camouflage sleeve. She was wearing army fatigues, as usual. "No arguing, girls. We present a united front on the battlefield."

"Jilly and I only argue for sport," I said. "And a farmer's market is the opposite of a battlefield."

Our prepper friend yanked down the flaps on the camo hat that covered her short, gray perm. "Markets are where many battles begin. Those who control the resources control the message. I vote for a double table we split three ways. Jilly's preserves. Ivy's fertilizer. My knitted goods."

"I thought you were keeping the hats, scarves and socks for the apocalypse," I said.

She fell into step behind Keats, who was leading us on a tour around the perimeter. "It's been a slow winter for all of us. My needles were busy."

March had been a little slow, granted, but we'd helped solve a couple of murders in recent months, on top of hosting guests at the inn and welcoming several goats and sheep, courtesy of our Rescue Mafia friends from the neighboring town of Dorset Hills. We were far from idle, although Jilly had spent more time canning and I'd gained more mastery of manure management. It was nice to be doing something normal for a change.

Keats circled back and mumbled a saucy comment. Perhaps aspiring to normal was a stretch when Percy, my fluffy orange cat, rode on my shoulder like a pirate's parrot. "Never mind." I shook a gloved finger at the dog. "Normal is overrated, anyway."

"No talking to the pets under the canopy," Jilly whispered.

"Tell it to Keats," I muttered. "He's goading me."

She threw Keats a look with her piercing green eyes. "We want people to buy our stuff, and more importantly, spread the word about the inn. That means trying to fit in, not stand out."

The notion of fitting in grated on me. Throughout school and my corporate career, I had aimed to fly under the radar completely unnoticed. I'd hit close to the mark in high school and exceeded my goals while working in human resources. Now that I was back home in Clover Grove, I got noticed too often for my liking but I still didn't fit in. Some days, it was tough to be me.

Keats pant-laughed again. He knew I was happier than I had ever been in my life. My bold move in saving him from a criminal won me a head injury and the loyalty of the greatest dog on the planet. I was beyond thrilled with my farm and inn, loyal friends, quirky family, and a handsome fiancé, who just happened to be chief of police. I really couldn't and shouldn't complain.

The dog and I might have dug a little deeper into my existential crisis if Jilly and Edna hadn't been pushing forward with purpose. We'd agreed to stake out a presence here among the locals, who loved nothing more than gossiping about us. It was a new day and a new phase. No point in fighting it.

"Is it just me or is everyone staring?" Jilly asked, reaching for Percy. He dropped willingly from my shoulder into the crook of her arm, tail snapping with catitude. My fluffy feline had become Jilly's therapy animal. We took the boys wherever pets were welcome and many places they weren't. Both craved a lot of mental stimulation. If they didn't get it through positive channels, sometimes they found less appropriate outlets. Regular farm life hadn't presented enough challenge lately, so I'd need to keep a close eye on them today. Percy, in particular, loved a stage and a captive audience.

"They are staring, Jillian," Edna said, "and for once it's not at me." On top of her fatigues, she was wearing a bulky backpack that likely contained everything we'd need if the world as we knew it collapsed during our survey of the market. The contents of her "go-kit" would take us safely to one of her bunkers and there was surprising comfort in knowing that. "All eyes are on Ivy Galloway. What have you done now?"

"Nothing." My fingers dropped to Keats' warm ears. "I mean, not today. Or even this month. We've been keeping a low profile."

Keats offered a grumbled commentary about that. Aside from regular inn and farm business, we'd spent a lot of time in Thistle-down visiting our newest family members. Frost, Keats' sister from another litter, had delivered three puppies doted on by all except my dog. He far preferred *doing* to doting, and while the rest of us cooed over the perfect little creatures, Keats ran the agility course outside with Annie, his dam. Never had a litter of pups been so well loved and socialized.

Glancing down the row of tables, I looked for familiar faces and found some. Mabel Halliday was there with a collection of ceramic figures from her store, Miniature Mutts. That meant I probably wouldn't leave empty-handed. In addition to collecting living, breathing animals, I had a growing menagerie of their ceramic counterparts. The Christmas village Mabel made was still on display at the inn as spring swept in, and the replica of Runaway Farm was getting crowded. Jilly's inner hostess would usually rebel over a sprawling display so she must like it, too.

At the next table sat Teri Mason, with some of her creations. A talented and eccentric artist, she worked in various media. Her stunning portraits of Keats and Percy framed the fireplace at Runaway Inn, despite complaints from guests about painted eyes following them. I felt the same but found it reassuring to have bonus eyes looking out for the danger that arrived in our own home more often than it should.

"Something's going on," Edna said, prodding me toward Mabel and Teri. "I can feel it."

I could, too. The hum of energy felt almost electrical. If I poked my finger in the wrong socket here, I'd get a shock. And yet, I'd probably do just that. It was how I rolled.

Keats mumbled a pant of encouragement. "Do it, do it, do it." He'd found our recent period of calm interminable. In his view, a shock to the system was exactly what we needed.

"Your class reunion is a few days away, Ivy," Jilly suggested. "Do you think it has anything to do with that?"

I turned to give her a scowl, then stopped. It was nearly impossible for me to scowl at Jilly—especially not when she was smirking. "I declined the invitation, as you may recall. Put it through the shredder without replying. My stint in high school was unmemorable and I won't be missed."

Edna twirled her index finger before directing it at me. "Shredding the invite was overkill for something you claim you don't care about."

Scowling at Edna came quite easily. "I don't care. And I have better things to do this weekend than go to that party."

"Really? Because you mentioned Chief Fiancé has a training event." Edna gave an exaggerated shrug. "Well, I'm going to your reunion."

"You're going? Why?" Jilly's voice rose over mine and Edna pretended to conduct a choir with her still-raised index finger.

"More tuneful than usual, girls. Perhaps I'll let you audition for the prepper choir. We need to sing while we can. After the end times, this town will fall eternally silent." She took a long look around. "Let's enjoy the market spoils today because tinned meat and beans are tedious. I'm still trying to retrain my palate."

"You didn't answer the question." Jilly leaned over so that Percy could take a swipe at Edna. The cat was becoming an extension of my best friend, and showed the claws she never would. Jilly had claws, but they were sheathed in corporate velvet. When she scratched, no one knew they'd been gouged before they bled out.

Edna deliberately let Percy snag the fabric of her jacket. Then she eased ahead of us, reaching back to scoop him out of Jilly's arms. He'd been part of a feral colony in Edna's care at one time and they were still fond of each other. "The planning committee asked me to serve as a medic. I vaccinated most of you crazy kids and just seeing me there will prevent stabbings or overdoses."

"It's a class reunion, not a rave," I said. "Why would they need a medic?"

Edna snickered. "An ounce of prevention is worth a pound of cure. Besides, your old boyfriend is coming."

"I don't have an old boyfriend. Kellan was my one and only."

Edna laughed. "Tell it to Skiff Burger. He said he was your first love." She turned back and used her index finger again in a jaunty jab. "Your loss. Skiff's a big drug dealer now and drives a Maserati. I fancied that car myself once, but if I had that kind of money today, I'd put it toward a tank."

Jilly made an odd noise beside me. It sounded like she was swallowing something large and prickly. "Skiff Burger? Ivy, why haven't I heard about your drug dealer beau?"

Keats gave a ha-ha-ha. His spirits were rising along with his fanning tail.

"Scott Burger never stood a chance with me. He was a frequent user of recreational weed back in the day, and likely a dealer." I shrugged. "Guess I would have judged him 'least likely' to own a Maserati."

"Never underestimate a high school stoner," Edna said. "Skiff got on the weed train early and chugged north to Canada, when they legalized years ago. He beat the crowd with his start-up."

Jilly slowed to eye a table with jars of glowing preserves in red, blue and yellow. If we stopped, we'd be drawn into discussion at every table. "Tell me about sweet Skiff and your ill-fated love."

Edna's chuckle drowned out my huffy protests and I decided it was better to answer than let their imaginations wander. "Skiff asked me to a ninth-grade dance. I told him to check with Asher, who was an overprotective brother long before he was a cop. And Skiff never spoke to me again." I raised one eyebrow at Jilly, a move I learned from Kellan, who'd in turn picked it up from the owner of the local hardware store. "That's the entire romantic arc of the story. Forgive me if I failed to see it as worthy of sharing."

Jilly waggled both eyebrows back at me. "Skiff clearly remembers it differently. I can't wait to ask him all about it this weekend."

"You're going to my class reunion, too? You didn't grow up here and Asher graduated a year ahead of me." It should have been three years but he did a couple of victory laps to pick up extra credits and drag out his football career.

"I'm working, too. Mandy McCain is catering and asked for

help." Jilly headed to Teri's table. "Don't worry, I'll fill you in on what Skiff says."

Now I was trailing after them. "It's weird you two are going to my class reunion and I'm not."

"Still time to change your mind," Jilly said. "Tickets available at the door. I checked."

"I won't change my mind. I've got a busy weekend ahead. We're fencing off new pasture next week and I'm making plans to switch up the livestock. Spring is the perfect time for a fresh start."

"Just in case, I chose something for you to wear." She reached out to shake Teri's hand. They were both huggers, but there was a table of breakables between them. "Something Skiff will love."

"Nothing you can say will get me to that reunion." I crossed my arms, feeling my lips form an uncharacteristic pout. Jilly was usually on my side, whether I was right or wrong, and this felt strange and unpleasant. "Nothing."

"Maybe not me," Jilly said, releasing Teri's hand and shrugging. "But there's a higher power at work here."

"A higher power?" It wasn't like Jilly to bring religion into matters like this.

She pointed to a table down the row. "Well, not that high, I suppose. But this power doesn't take no for an answer."

CHAPTER TWO

"Darlings." There was usually an exclamation mark on the end of my mother's favorite word but today it fell flat. "What are you doing here? You never come to the farmer's market."

"Same goes for you," I said. My tiny mother was sitting behind a display of neatly folded clothing, none in her trademark scarlet. She was wearing a denim apron over a beige jacket and her makeup was equally subdued. Her products looked nothing like the bold and brash designs she typically created from secondhand clothing. "Yet here you are at a rented table."

"Just for today," she said. "I had too much stock and thought I might find new customers."

I eyed the people shuffling through the aisles with canvas tote bags. They were homesteaders, for the most part, and likely impervious to Mom's vibrant style. On the other hand, she'd clearly been working with a new muse. The skirts and dresses hanging on the rack behind her were sensible and staid. It looked like she'd deliberately targeted her product to this market instead of expecting the market to rise to her standards.

An older woman wearing a shabby trench coat stopped at Mom's table. "I heard you had aprons, Dahlia. And handkerchiefs."

Mom practically leapt off her folding chair. "I most certainly do. Potholders and dish towels, too. I'm certain you'll find just what you need." She pulled two bins from under the table and the woman in the trench coat rifled through them. Mom deftly refolded items with unvarnished nails until her client was done. "Excellent choice. Cash only, please."

As she pocketed the bills, more women of a certain age came over. The word was out about the aprons. Mom had indeed assessed her demographic. The aprons were made of sturdy floral fabric that would hide stains well. The handkerchiefs were a runaway hit, too, with customers buying fistfuls as gifts.

Edna quickly maxed out on domesticity and stalked off with Percy. Jilly waited with me for the crowd to disperse so that I could question my mother. "Aprons and potholders?" I said. "That's not overstock, Mom. What really gives?"

"If you must know, I wanted to make a little extra money. For a special project."

"Yeah? Like what?"

Her familiar coy smile returned, although it wasn't really Mom without red lipstick. "Repaying my kids for their generosity, of course."

Some of us had subsidized her during the rocky years before she turned into the dynamo she was now, with two jobs and other commissions. She was already repaying us for our investment in the salon start-up and there was no deadline. Family helped family.

"That's nice, but I'm not buying it," I said. "You'd never touch paisley unless there was a bigger reason."

"Ivy? Is that really you?" A woman's voice trilled like Mom's, but I knew it belonged to someone of my vintage. Before she learned to trill, the owner of that voice was just a stereotypical high school mean girl who made my life miserable.

I turned with trepidation and found her standing at a table on the other side of the aisle. "Hi there. It's Tamara Duke, right?"

"Hickey, now," she said, with a brilliant smile. "I married Eddy straight out of high school. And call me Tammi, since we're old pals." We had never been friends, but my lips curved into their HR uniform. Tammi was head cheerleader at Clover Grove High for three years running, and all-round queen bee. Social media wasn't a thing then, but she had myriad methods for sidelining those she deemed enemies, or simply uncool. I had avoided the worst of her wrath and credited Asher for my relative safety. He was the handsome athlete. Captain of the football team and, later, a volunteer coach who worked closely with Eddy. My brother's popularity created a fragile bubble around me that I mostly appreciated and occasionally resented.

Today, Tammi's table was covered in jars of honey in varying hues. The glassware was cute and the labels charming. The sweet, innocuous product seemed at odds with the Tamara Duke I once knew. I'd seldom thought of her since graduation but never expected to find her flogging honey at the farmer's market. She wasn't quite as pretty as I remembered but her perfect blonde highlights, sharp makeup and maroon manicure disqualified her as a genuine homesteader. Even her slightly crooked tooth—the one flaw I focused on—had been fixed. There were probably a few extra pounds on her small frame but it was hard to tell since she was wearing one of my mother's floral aprons over a down jacket.

"I see you've met my mom," I said.

"Of course! Dahlia is wonderful." Again, with the smile and the trill. Had an alien taken over Tammi's body? Was she heavily medicated? Being groomed by a homesteading cult? My experience in HR proved people didn't—and probably couldn't—change that much, even when highly motivated. The programming of childhood ran too deep.

"Thank you, Tammi, darling." Mom's voice had more juice now. The merest hint of a trill. She was coming back to life. "How lovely to see you and Ivy together again."

We had never been together, except in a classroom, and I'd always sat as far from Tammi and her squad as possible. There were three of them, all attractive, popular and cruel, just like in the movies. They differed from the cliché in one important way, however. In the movies, mean girls were usually... well, dumb. Which meant that people like me could outwit or at least evade them. But Tammi's hand was usually first to rise with the correct answer.

A sharp mind meant Tamara could appear to be a model student while still causing trouble. I aced Tammi 101 in freshman year, learning to get to class early so that I could sit as far as possible from her turf near the classroom door. Tammi was always last in and first out. It was understood.

One day, as summer break loomed, I arrived late and had to sit closer to her hive. They must have been hard up for victims because I was the most boring person in the room. There was nothing about my hair, clothing or even carefully neutral expression that would draw attention to me. It took work in the morning to erase every hint of individuality before leaving the bedroom I shared with Violet.

That day, I'd run into a problem. My only sneakers got soaked rescuing a baby squirrel from a mud puddle, leaving me to borrow Violet's black patent ballerina flats. As the tallest of the Galloway girls, I had feet to match. The shoes were a very tight fit.

Tammi noticed the anomaly instantly and whispered, "Oooh, look. *Foot fat.* Galloway's bulging right out of those fairy slippers. Let's call her Flubby Flappers."

And so they did, until something even worse replaced the nickname later.

That memory rushed back today as I stood in the aisle in front of her table. I was happy to be wearing steel-toed work boots, and even happier I had canine armor. Sensing my unease, Keats left Mom's table to stand on my left side. His lip twitched to reveal a hint of teeth Tammi would never notice and his quiet rumble affirmed my feet served us just fine.

If Tammi remembered the old nickname, it didn't show. Her blue-eyed gaze never left mine and her smile continued to blaze. "Ivy, take some honey. I'm getting rid of everything today and would love to give you some."

Picking up a jar, I admired its rich, amber color. "Why are you selling off your stock?"

"We're moving to Boston for Eddy's job," she said. "I'm out of the bee business."

Her smiled dimmed slightly, making me wonder how she felt about the change.

"Ed Hickey's a successful businessman, Ivy," Mom called over. "In case you didn't know."

I knew. Straight out of high school, Eddy opened a taco franchise that did surprisingly well for farm country. It expanded to several other towns and apparently he was ready to level up.

Jilly moved in close on my right side, suggesting she remembered my tales of high school bullying. Her smile was guarded when I introduced her to Tammi, but she was ever the diplomat. "We'd love to try your honey, Tammi, thank you. Our guests at Runaway Inn would love it."

"You're Asher's wife, right?" Tammi asked. "He was every girl's dream back in the day."

"He's a wonderful guy," Jilly said. "And Ivy's with her dream guy, too. Tell us more about your honey business, Tammi."

My old nemesis selected a few jars and handed them to us. "Take these. They're my classics. Clover, orange blossom and buck-wheat." Her smile collapsed slowly, like a beeswax candle. "Past tense, I suppose. My hives move tomorrow."

"You've sold your hives?" I asked. "I hear bees are big business now."

"Oh, yes, and my apiary is the finest in Clover Grove. Ask

anyone. But I can't take it with me, unfortunately, so I'm giving the hives to my best friend."

I cast my mind back. "Kayla Bouchard, right?"

"It's Ware, now. Kayla married a guy from Dorset Hills. She'll be excited to see you, Ivy."

I very much doubted that. Kayla had always been the backup to Tammi's queen bee, with all that the role entailed. Mainly it meant being Tammi's enforcer. If Tammi needed something done and didn't want to break a nail, Kayla stepped up. Graffiti on your locker? Kayla. Taking the last chocolate milk right out of your hand in the cafeteria line? Kayla. Evicting you from any seat anywhere? Kayla. And that was just the beginning. There was nothing Kayla wouldn't do for Tammi, including taking over an apiary, it would seem. "It's nice she's able to give your bees a good home."

Tammi nodded. "I've taught her everything I know and set her up to succeed."

"I've heard bees are challenging," I said, "and with the trouble they're facing around the world, your job is more important than ever."

Her eyes watered and her lip quivered. I had never seen Tammi experience normal human emotions and it was unsettling.

"Thank you, Ivy. I'll miss my bees." Reaching across the table, she squeezed my hand around the jar of honey I still held. "Somehow, I knew you'd understand."

"Of course." I tried to free my hand but she gripped it even tighter. After all these years, Tammi and I were having a moment over buzzing insects. No one was more surprised than me.

Except, perhaps, Edna, who'd come back from a short tour of the market with Percy. "What's going on? Are you all right, Ivy?"

"Sure. I'm just learning a little about Tammi's work with bees. I've read about the critical role they play in the ecosystem."

"Undoubtedly." Edna shot out the word like a bullet, proving she had no love for Tammi. "Enjoy that honey now, because I very much doubt bees will survive the ap—"

Jilly caught Edna's arm to cut off the word "apocalypse." Tammi was deep in her feelings about her bees and probably viewed them as pets. There was no reason to upset her more.

"Would you like to see my apiary?" Tammi was still holding my hand. "It would be an honor to give you the grand tour. Come this evening."

"Sure. That would be, uh"—I couldn't quite bring myself to say fun—"interesting. Very interesting. Maybe I'll have hives at the farm one day."

"Not while I'm allergic, you won't," Mom called from behind her table, clutching her throat with one hand. "Puffed like an adder after getting stung as a child. That's why I try to avoid being outdoors." Moving her hand to her cheek, Mom brightened. "Staying out of the sun kept me young, though. Wouldn't be surprised if people mistake me for you at the class reunion, Ivy."

So, even Mom was going to my reunion. "Maybe they will," I said. "It's been so long they might remember me as nearly a foot shorter." I hated mentioning the word "foot," but Tammi had mellowed so much she might not make the connection with my nickname.

"It was so kind of Dahlia to volunteer for reception," Tammi said. "It'll give us more time to catch up, Ivy."

"I won't be there, I'm afraid." I finally freed my hand and set the honey down so I could rub life back into my fingers. "I hope you'll all have fun." Now I could say the word. I actually did hope they'd have fun. Planning livestock relocation at home would be fun for me.

Her caramel-colored eyebrows shot up. "You *are* coming. You RSVP'd to say yes. I'm the head of the planning committee and I've kept a detailed list."

"You're mistaking me for someone else." Someone who didn't run the invitation through a shredder.

"Oh, Ivy, you're unmistakable." There should have been a smirk after a comment like that but instead Tammi beamed again and pulled her phone out of her apron. She tapped a few times and turned the screen to face me. "See? I have a screenshot."

Jilly and I leaned in to look. The checkmark on the reply was strong. Bold, even. Someone was confident enough to use a black marker. Underneath the checkbox was a list of names: Ivy, Kellan, Jilly, Asher, Daisy, Iris and Violet.

"I don't understand." I straightened up, still resolute. "But I can't come. Previous engagement."

"We've ordered meals for all of you." Tammi frowned for the first time. "You really must come."

Jilly took the phone out of Tammi's hand and blew up the image. "Look at the handwriting, Ivy."

Ah, yes. If the names had been in swirling cursive, I'd have noticed sooner. Mom's handwriting verged on calligraphy. I was about to turn and accost her when the name on the top of the invitation caught my eye.

Not mine.

Poppy's.

"Let's discuss this at home, darling," Mom said, fading into the rack of clothes behind her table. "It's a private family matter."

"I don't get it," Jilly said. "Why is Poppy personally invited to your class reunion, Ivy? She's older than Asher."

Tammi answered for me. "Because Poppy flunked a few grades." She tapped her temple to suggest my sister was stupid, or worse. Just like that, the honeyed businesswoman disappeared and the queen bee came back, with a quick, sharp sting.

"She did not!" Mom was outraged. "You take that back, Tammi Hickey. After a short hiatus, Poppy went back and finished school. I'm proud of her."

"It was a long hiatus, Dahlia. Poppy was like a grannie in our year." Tammi shrugged as she rearranged her jars to fill in the holes her gifts had left. "A delinquent grannie, but whatever."

The next round of return fire came from a true delinquent grannie. "Tamara, I suggest you avoid derogatory terms about seniors." Edna turned to rest her camouflage derriere on Tammi's table. "And I assure you Poppy isn't the dunce among the Galloways." She gave Jilly a pointed look that threw Asher to the dogs. "I commend her for graduating at all, considering what happened."

Edna's last words were a nearly inaudible mumble and I stared at her. Considering what? Poppy had trouble at school but what didn't I know about my sister? We may have finished senior year together, but she only needed two credits so I basically forgot she was there. If my sister ditched commencement, she wouldn't show up for this reunion.

Pulling a shammy out of her apron, Tammi buffed her golden jars. "Then Poppy must have been expelled. She had a rap sheet a mile long."

The last part was true. Poppy had more trips to the principal's office than the rest of the Galloways combined. That was saying something, considering Asher's record.

Edna got off the table and turned. Tammi flinched, but it wasn't my warrior grannie the queen bee had to worry about. A small frumpy hen flitted across the aisle, snapping an apron like a whip. "Stop talking smack about my daughter. Or any of my children. If you continue, I'll have no choice but to—" Mom raised the apron and Jilly pressed it down. "Call your mother. That's what I'll do, Tammi. Should have done it twenty years ago when you said Ivy had—"

"Mom, stop." The next words out of her mouth would be some version of Flubby Flappers and the nickname did not need to be resurrected.

Jilly quickly defused the situation by pulling Tammi aside to talk honey. The beekeeper's smile switched back on. Turns out it was only genuine when insects were involved.

Keats herded Edna over to provide backup to Jilly while I nudged Mom to her table. In the time she was distracted, aprons, potholders and handkerchiefs had been scattered around and she clucked in disgust as she set things right.

"Homesteaders. So rude." She counted the coins and bills people had left in a pile. "On the bright side, I have enough to cover everyone for the reunion dinner." She swept the money into the large pocket of her denim apron. "You'd better show up, Ivy Rose Galloway."

Percy picked his way through Mom's piles and she shoved him aside rather roughly. "Speaking of rude," I said, scooping up the cat. "And why would I go now? Tammi insulted Pops."

She stacked everything neatly, order restored. "Because this is important to your sister."

"Why? Poppy hasn't shown the least interest in this reunion."

"A mother knows. She's sensitive about being the only one who struggled in school."

"She struggled with authority, not academics. Your authority, to be specific. You two were always at loggerheads back then."

"Don't I know it." Reaching into her pocket, she pulled out a tube of red lipstick and applied it expertly without a mirror. Having reached her cash goals, she could go back to being herself. I wouldn't be surprised to find a red dress and heels in her purse to complete the transition from frump to fantastic. "I wasn't there for her then, so I need to be now. We all do. Something happened to your sister in school and if she's willing to face it, let's have her back."

I rapped my knuckles on the table. "Mom, look at me. Are you serious about Poppy wanting to go to this event? I'll ask her, you know."

She flashed a bright smile at the next customer, said a few kind words about how well the paisley fabric suited her coloring, and then let coins jingle in her palm. If Mom was willing to abandon her sartorial standards, she must be serious indeed.

"You go right ahead, Ivy." She bent to pull more stock out of her bins. "In the meantime, I'm going to sell every last apron I made and hire a stretch limo that holds all of us."

Keats gave a pant-laugh and even I had to smile at the thought of the entire Galloway clan surviving a ride in one vehicle, no matter how large.

"Wouldn't want to miss that circus," I said. "Count me in."

CHAPTER THREE

Tammi Hickey's house, at the end of a long, sparsely populated road, was everything I expected it to be. In other words, pretty much the same as everyone else's on the outskirts of town, only with upscale finishes. Her goals weren't lofty. She wanted to be the biggest fish in our small high school pond. Maybe that's why she wasn't enthused about moving to the city, where she'd have to work hard to stand out. She'd been coasting on her rep for over 20 years. Starting over was tough, as I knew all too well.

"Never liked that girl," Edna said, as we all got out of the truck early that evening. "She spread a heinous rumor about me."

"Do tell," Jilly said, adjusting Percy in her arms. "You're not normally bothered by gossip."

Edna smoothed her jacket with short, jerky motions. "Once upon a time I was foolish enough to care about public opinion. When I was the school nurse, a story circulated that I had inappropriate relations with Grenville Brunk. It started after Tammi found me in what no doubt looked like a compromising position."

"Right, I remember that," I said. "Grenville was buck naked in your exam room."

She turned a ferocious glare on me. "Completely untrue. He had a boil and asked me to take a look. Had I known it was on his posterior I wouldn't have agreed, nor left the door unlocked. My reputation meant everything to me then, and the principal called me into her office to account for it."

"Mrs. Gillespie?" I asked. "She was pretty tough."

Edna's face was flushed, a rare sight indeed. "She had to be, after replacing Rodney Preacher. Fiona was the youngest principal in hill country and the only woman, so I understood that. To her credit, she gave me the benefit of the doubt. Word still got out, thanks to Tammi. It was a scandal I didn't need, but Doc Grainer got a chuckle out of it. I left lancing the boil to him."

Jilly fought a grin and failed. "Was Grenville married?"

"No, he was not." Edna's voice was crisp. "And a patient is a patient, regardless of marital status. I've seen plenty of male derrieres, believe you me, and nearly as many boils."

My best friend hugged Percy closer. "Then why was it such a scandal?"

Keats stared up at Edna, mouth gaping in a pant-laugh. She shook her finger at him and sealed her lips, leaving me to do the honors.

"Grenville was a man of the cloth, Jilly," I said. "All the local ministers cycled through our school chapel, but it sounds like Reverend Brunk was the only one to seek medical assistance."

"Far from it," Edna grumbled. "They all did, and plenty of male teachers, too. For some reason they preferred me to Doc Grainer. Said I made them comfortable." She gave an uncharacteristic shudder. "I don't understand it. My desire to make people *un*comfortable was very much entrenched even then. But so it was, and I got the worst of this rumor, not Grenville Brunk. The unfairness of it still rankles and I have yet to confront Tammi about it."

"Not today," Jilly said. "We're here to sweet talk her, remember?"

Edna's slumped posture proved the wound was still raw, more than a decade later. "I thought we were here to see beehives."

I snapped my fingers to bring Keats close to my side. "Both. We'll talk honey and then ask her to lay off Poppy."

Jilly shushed us as we walked up the front stairs together. A united front, as always. "You talk beekeeping and leave the rest to me. If Tammi's all you say, we need to be very careful to avoid being stung. Or worse, let Poppy get stung."

"I don't believe for one second Poppy cares about this reunion," Edna said. "And if she did, she could handle the likes of Tammi and her worker bees."

"Pops confirmed she wants to go. And sadly, that means I have to go. Backing my sister feels like the right thing to do." I sighed over the magnitude of the sacrifice. "I'll get to the bottom of it. In the meantime, we can tell Tammi to stop talking smack."

"You mean 'gently encourage,'" Jilly said. "Trust me, I know my way around the queen bee type. You don't *tell* them anything. You've gotta *sell* the advantage of seeing things our way."

No one answered the door, but there was a car in the driveway and a light on inside. Maybe Tammi was in the basement. Or outside, getting her bees ready for their move to Kayla's house. Beckoning to the others, I went down the stairs and walked around the side of the house. The grass had deep tire grooves, making me wonder if a moving truck had already delivered Tammi's furniture to Boston.

I expected Keats to charge ahead, but he actually pressed me back.

"What's up, buddy?" Jilly asked, as she released the thrashing cat. "Percy is good to go."

"Maybe the dog's afraid of bees," Edna said. "Most sensible creatures are. Even I have reservations, as much as I appreciate their work. I've seen people die of anaphylactic shock."

Dodging around Keats, I looked back at Edna. "I did a quick

check online and learned honeybees are pretty mellow. The pussy-cats of the bee world."

Edna aimed a camo glove at Percy's tail up ahead. It was lashing ominously. "Pussycats sting. Looks like Percy is planning to do just that."

My boots picked up speed. The last thing I wanted was for my pets to be stung. Any of us, for that matter. "Tammi wouldn't have invited us to check out her operation if it meant putting us at risk. She cares about her hobby."

"She wanted us to use her product at the inn." Jilly's voice faded a little as she dropped behind. "I'm sure she knows what she's doing."

Edna caught up with me. "Tammi's the outgoing head of the beekeepers' club. Wouldn't be surprised if it falls apart after she leaves. Seems like every club is born of one person's passion and dies with them. Can't tell you how many I've seen come and go."

"Like the Bridge Buddies," Jilly called, now a few yards behind us. "I figured they'd regroup but it hasn't happened."

It was almost as hard to make Edna flinch as blush, but she did it now. The Bridge Buddies had been her friends, or what passed for friends, before everything blew up dramatically during a tournament at the inn. Normally Jilly was too tactful to mention it, which suggested the bees made her extremely uneasy.

Slowing my roll, I turned. "Are you allergic to bees, Jilly?"

Her expression was uncertain. "I had a bad reaction to a sting in Wyldwood Springs once. Then I moved to the city where things like that don't often happen. So, I don't actually know and I'd rather not find out."

"Then stay back, my friend. I'll collect Tammi and bring her to you."

"We don't even know she's out here," Edna said. "Could be a short mission."

"Oh, she's out here," Jilly said. "Percy has purpose in those paws."

There was a flick of orange tail as he disappeared behind the house. Meanwhile, Keats continued to reverse herd me, succeeding only in making me work hard for every inch gained. "She must be here, but Keats isn't inclined to take the meeting outdoors." When we reached the corner, I added, "Heard you loud and clear, buddy. We'll leave our introduction to beekeeping for another day and have a chat with Tammi somewhere safe."

His mumbled answer was surly. A "don't say I didn't warn you" kind of sound.

"I don't feel good about this." Jilly was close again. "But I won't leave Percy behind."

"Just one of many reasons I love you, bestie. Let me get the cat. I've been stung a few times since taking over the farm and I'm not allergic."

Jilly caught up with us in time to circle the house together.

I had no idea what to expect from an apiary. The word sounded elegant, quaint and peaceful. Tammi's huge backyard was none of those things. One blue hive stood against the back fence, but otherwise, it looked like a tornado had ripped through the area. Two hives had tipped and others split, leaving fragments of wood on grass that was barely beginning to green up. The sweet smell of honey hung in the air, but it felt like the wrong time for it.

"What a mess," Jilly said. "Is this because Tammi's moving?"

Edna shook her head and pointed at the tipped hives. "Looks more like the place was ransacked."

"Who'd ransack a bee yard?" I asked. "Even thugs are afraid of getting stung."

"You'd be surprised. There's a high demand for bees, especially in California for the almond bloom. Thefts are common enough to hit the national news." Scanning repeatedly, Edna shrugged. "I'm guessing Tammi was robbed."

"Maybe she went back inside to report the incident," Jilly said.

"Or pursued the thug," I suggested. "There were tracks beside the house."

"Two vehicles," Edna said. "One small enough to be a forklift."

Offloading her backpack, Edna knelt and groped in a side pocket. I figured she'd scrounge up a weapon or a canister of insecticide, but in her gloved hand was a blue velvet bag. Unzipping it, she plucked out a pipe with a burnished cherrywood bowl and a packet of tobacco.

"This isn't the time for a smoke, Edna." Jilly's tone turned prim and schoolmarmish. "We need to make sure Tammi knows her apiary's been vandalized."

"Since when do you smoke?" I asked. "Let alone a pipe."

Straightening, our friend shook off her gloves and filled the bowl with tobacco. She tamped it down with a few practiced jabs that confirmed it was far from the first time. An image of her sitting around a campfire flashed into my mind and I wondered why I'd wondered at all. Of course Edna smoked a pipe.

"It's my father's," she said. "One of the few things that survived the fire that destroyed our home. So, yes, I have a puff now and again. Not so many that my lungs complain." She grinned around the stem of the pipe and then locked her lips to suck in a few quick breaths. Letting smoke trickle from her lips, she shrugged. "Can't overdo it if I want to outrun those zombies you're always talking about."

"You're full of surprises, Edna," I said. "Can you teach me how to do that?"

"No, she cannot." The schoolmarm spoke again. "Even recreational smoking is—"

"Bad for your unborn Galloways?" Edna interrupted. "Judge away, Jillian, but I'm doing this for you."

"Really? Enlighten me."

I touched Jilly's arm. "Smoke calms bees. It interferes with pheromone reception. Their communication channel. They can't get the word out to deploy."

Edna sent a misty cloud of approval in my direction. "Gold star for Ivy Rose. If the inhabitants of the toppled hives were cut loose, you might find out if you're allergic, Jillian." She nudged her backpack with an army boot. "Fear not, I have something for that, too."

"No thanks," Jilly said. "I'll keep my status of being one of the few in town who hasn't been on the bad end of your needle."

"Suit yourself." Edna waved the pipe around and then moved into the smoky trail. "I'm going in to collect Percy."

"Huddle," I said, moving closer to her. "Keats, how about you stay back for a few minutes? The smoke is rising and you won't be safe down there."

He mumbled an "as if" and trotted toward the back of the big yard. The white tip of his tail dusted the grass, but he was clearly determined not to be outdone by his fearless feline compadre.

"Percy? Percy Bysshe Shelley!" This time Jilly's schoolmarm was shrill. "You come back here right now."

Edna was the first to spot the cat and gestured flamboyantly with the pipe in the direction of the rear fence. "Over there. Sweeping up the mess." I started to move ahead and Edna elbowed me back. "Stick with the pipe."

"Percy!" My voice overlapped with Jilly's, but it was Keats who caught the cat's attention. Two green eyes locked on the dog and then the cat went back to sweeping.

"Maybe he isn't gathering dead bees," Edna muttered, around an exhalation of smoke. "Haven't we seen this maneuver before?"

Jilly and I stopped walking for a second, but when our smoke-screen kept moving, we hurried to catch up.

"You don't think—" Jilly began.

"Jillian, I do," Edna interrupted. "I think all the time and somehow these pesky pets outthink even a brilliant mind like mine. Percival is onto something."

"Percival? Was the poet named that?" I asked.

Edna huffed briskly, releasing clouds more frequently. "You tell me. You're the frustrated librarian."

I almost laughed, despite the circumstances. "Guilty. I was wasted in HR. Should have pursued library sciences. Life in the stacks would be safer."

"Don't be so sure about that. Thelma Tilrow has war stories." Edna picked up speed over the last few yards and we followed suit. "Dottie Bridges, too. Never underestimate the ladies of the library."

"What's that white thing flapping in the bushes?" Jilly asked. "Looks like a ghost, left over from Halloween." She didn't wait for a response before adding, "I hate Halloween."

"Probably a beekeeper coverall," Edna said. "A good Halloween costume, I suppose."

Percy gave an eerie howl to get our attention. When I looked down, the first thing I noticed was Keats in a point. Not just a casual point, but an all-flags-flying stance. Then my gaze travelled reluctantly to the cat.

I was pretty sure what I would find under his scraping paws.

I just wasn't sure whom.

CHAPTER FOUR

ur boots clomped to a stop—one, two, three, four, five, six.

Edna sucked too hard on the pipe and coughed out a couple of smoky belches. "Dagnabit," she gasped. "Not again."

I assumed she meant the body Percy was burying in fake kitty litter, not the lung-clogging fumes.

The deceased—and there was no doubt in my mind they'd departed for the hereafter—was splayed awkwardly between a cute garden shed with gingerbread trim and the last hive standing. The long dry grasses from last year had shielded the body from us, despite a white jumpsuit and helmet that looked similar to a space suit, if less robust. Given who owned the property, I could make an educated guess as to the person's identity without bending to peer through the veil.

One arm was stretched to the side and one leg was bent at the knee.

All Tammi needed was blue-and-gold school pom-poms to complete her final pose.

"Tammi?" All traces of the schoolmarm had vanished from Jilly's voice. "Is it her?"

Finally, I bent over. "Think so. We'll need to move the veil to be sure."

Jilly's hand turned into a claw on my arm. "Don't disturb the evidence."

Keats mumbled a defiant retort and pawed at the netting. Percy caught the fabric in his claws and finished the job.

I dropped to one knee and stared. It was the closest I'd ever been to my old nemesis, but she was no threat to me now. No threat to anyone. Never would be again.

"So pretty," Jilly murmured. "Such a shame."

"On the bright side, she'll never call Ivy Flubby Flappers again," Edna said. "The nickname dies with her."

I straightened and glared at my prepper friend. "Who told you that?"

"Tammi herself." Edna spoke through teeth clamped on the pipe stem. "Last year at the market. Said she was going to apologize. Not sure if I buy it. Didn't seem to regret slandering my name."

"Quiet." Jilly raised her phone and backed away. "We need to call the police and report the accident."

"It's no accident, Jillian." Edna circled the body to examine the objects strewn about. "Tammi told me she had nearly a hundred hives last year. There's only one left standing, plus a few lonely bees looking for their family. Someone murdered Tammi Hickey in broad daylight to get her hives before she gave them away."

Jilly poked savagely at the phone. "We don't know that. There's not a mark on her."

"She probably didn't die of natural causes at her age." I pointed to the cat, who was still randomly sweeping around the body. "Percy seems convinced."

Smoke rose and fell as Edna nodded. "Tammi was an athlete, and bright enough, too. I thought she'd go far but she married that quarterback. Eddy's dumber than a bag of hammers."

"Smart enough to succeed in business," I said, over Jilly's

command to be quiet. It was just her normal voice. The schoolmarm had left the apiary. "I'm glad she didn't leave children behind."

"I wondered about that. Kayla has a bunch of them." Edna continued to inspect the damage. "Nadia Reddy, as well. The third wheel in their squad."

"I guess the bees were Tammi's kids. She seemed fond of them." I followed Keats around the yard, mainly to get out of Jilly's way. If there was anything worth seeing, the dog didn't point it out. "Would someone kill her just to get the bees? Can they be that valuable?"

"A healthy apiary of this size could bring over fifty grand at this time of year," Edna said. "They'll probably be heading for sunny California."

I turned in surprise. "That's not chump change. And she was just handing them to Kayla."

Edna's next exhalation was long and slow. A sigh. "I guess Tammi died fighting to make good on that gift."

"The hood in the bushes might belong to the killer." I pulled out my phone to take photos. It felt tacky, but if I intended to help find justice for Tammi—or at least her bees—propriety wouldn't hold me back. Clues didn't always just pop up on cue. Usually, we worked hard for them.

Jilly finished her call. "Ivy, don't. Tammi deserves respect."

"Tammi never respected Ivy," Edna pointed out. "Or many others for that matter. What happened isn't that shocking."

"Edna, don't say that." Jilly's phone waggled threateningly. "It's bad karma."

"I'm saying karma's probably what got her," Edna said. "But I suppose I have my share coming."

I stared around. "Doesn't she have security cameras?"

"Leave that to the police," Jilly said. "We promised not to interfere in cases like this."

"When was that?" I squinted at her. "Had I puffed some of Skiff Burger's product?"

"It was implied." My best friend's glance was withering. "After the police corruption incident. Kellan is really worried about the state of the hill country nation. You know that."

I shrugged. "Maybe I implied I'd stay out of high-level corruption, but this is just your average garden variety murder. The type that happens around here all the time. Hate to say it, but it's true."

"Well, don't say it even if it's true. What if the place is bugged?"

"Then it's a good thing Ivy didn't share how she really feels about Tammi," Edna said, her smirk appearing around the stem of the pipe.

"I detested her," I said. "Mostly for how cruel she was to others, like Mandy McCain. But if she's been murdered, we need to do what we can. My biggest worry right now is the bees. If someone was willing to kill for them, I worry the hives won't get good care."

"Beekeeping is a finicky business," Edna said. "Lose more than you keep, from what I hear, especially in severe winters. So, the common criminal probably couldn't do the job right."

Jilly patted my arm soothingly. "We have *un*common criminals here. Remember that. You've met loads of them who care more about animals than humans. This could be another."

I probably shouldn't have taken comfort from that, but I did. Just yesterday bees weren't on my radar and now I was worried about yet another creature. It seemed my compassion for the non-human denizens of our world was bottomless.

Edna waved her pipe around, leaving a thin trail of smoke. "We've got a buzzer and she isn't taking tobacco for an answer."

"She?" I asked. "How can you tell it's a gal?"

"Hive demographics. There's one queen, a few drones, and thousands of worker bees—all female."

The bee made a wide loop around all of us, never coming close enough to be threatening.

"I thought honeybees were bigger," I said. "This one isn't so different from a wasp."

"Different in temperament." Edna puffed vigorously to create a smoke barrier around us. "Never seen the point of wasps and hornets but maybe I'm missing something. Honeybees are happy to mind their own business unless people get too nosy."

"Maybe this lone bee wants us to get nosy. Her family is missing in action. She probably went out looking for early flowers and came home to find nothing. Poor orphaned Bernice."

Jilly pushed curls back from her forehead. "Here we go again. Ivy, the chances of reuniting Bernice with her hive are small."

"Minuscule," Edna agreed. "Lone bees don't last long."

"Doomed to heartbreak, probably." I reached for Keats' ears and found them waiting. "Honeybees are wired to be part of a huge system. Not functioning alone. Like humans, come to think of it."

Edna snorted. "Not *this* human. But I'm forcing myself to become more social to prepare for the end times. The more of us in the bunker, the harder I'll be to pick off."

The Edna of my youth had been so committed to pushing people away that she armed herself with syringes. She stung everyone like a bee to maintain her personal space. That prickliness began to dissipate after the Bridge Buddies' blowup and fell away faster every day. Now, if caught off guard, she'd even permit a hug without employing martial arts moves. Sometimes I wondered if having a couple of bunkers at her disposal made her freer to connect with people. They were back doors out of society if it got as ugly as she feared.

"We're in this together," Jilly said, linking arms with us as the sirens got closer. "All of us."

"Including Bernice?" I watched as the bee did an aerial show overhead. The sunset sky created a beautiful backdrop for her. Was she trying to communicate something? If so, I'd be hard-pressed to learn her language. Mammals were challenging enough to decode, let alone complex insects.

"Your ark is packed pretty tight but we do need bees." Jilly squeezed my arm. "As long as she's not gunning for me."

The bee zipped off, leaving us free to worry about the approaching swarm of uniformed officers. Asher was first to arrive, as usual, driving his SUV right around the house. He leapt out and bounded across the lawn to his wife, pulling her away from me into a big hug. "Are you okay?"

"I'm fine." She patted his back before freeing herself. "Tammi Hickey, not so much."

My brother's handsome face puckered. "Cheerleader Tammi? Never much liked her."

"Officer Galloway, this isn't the time for personal commentary."

The reprimand came from the tall, handsome man I was lucky enough to call fiancé. As chief of police, Kellan Harper was Asher's boss, but he was trying to give my brother more responsibility. Asher had shown integrity and courage under pressure recently while handling a complex case in Kellan's absence. But it was hard to believe my brother's boundless optimism and good cheer could ever be tamped down enough to make him chief material. I wanted him to achieve his dreams, but I hoped it wouldn't come at too much of a personal cost. Kellan carried a heavy professional load that cast a shadow on his personal life. The more deviant behavior I witnessed, the more I understood that. I had the capacity to carry it without cracking up but I wasn't sure about my brother.

"Right, Chief," Asher said, bending over Tammi's body. "Doesn't look like death by bee. She looks, well... perfect."

"Perfect?" Jilly asked.

He threw his wife a guilty grin. "Not Jilly Galloway perfect. But high school prom queen perfect. They have a best before date. You're timeless."

Kellan shook his head as he walked over and touched my arm. "You all right?"

I nodded. "Looks like someone vandalized Tammi's apiary. We ran into her at the farmer's market this morning and she said she was giving her hives to Kayla Bouchard tomorrow. She's moving to the city with Eddy."

"You came to say goodbye?" Kellan asked. "I thought you hated Tammi."

"Hate's a strong word," I said.

Edna managed to snicker while drawing in a hearty puff of tobacco. "You used it earlier."

Keats joined her with a pant-laugh. He enjoyed seeing me get flustered around Kellan.

"I said detested. There's a difference, at least in my mind." I shot a look at her and then Keats. "I did detest Tammi in high school."

"Back when she said you had fat feet?" Asher asked, not even bothering to fight a grin. "Flubby Flappers, wasn't it?"

"Never mind." Jilly slapped him lightly. "Ivy's feet are perfectly normal."

"Pretty near as big as mine," Ash said. "I can see how they'd catch Tammi's eye."

My glare shifted to him and intensified. "Are we really going to talk about my shoe size now, Asher? There's a woman lying dead at *your* feet."

"I argue it's relevant," Asher said. "I know you and Tammi threw down at the market earlier. Someone told me when I ran over to grab lunch. I'm guessing you finally confronted her about foot shaming."

My ears grew hot and the shame felt as real as it had in that classroom of long ago. Maybe Kellan hadn't noticed that my feet were on the large side. Maybe Kellan wouldn't be able to unsee it after this. He'd asked for my hand in marriage without understanding that his future children might inherit these feet. His feet were average and proportionate to his height and build.

"Officer Galloway, I'd thank you not to perpetuate that foot shaming now," Kellan said. "My fiancée's feet are all that they should be and I'd like you to focus on the current situation."

"Chief, did you miss the part about Ivy and Tammi arguing?" Asher asked. "Maybe she came here to settle the score."

"Seriously, Asher?" Jilly's inner schoolmarm returned in full force. "Are you suggesting your sister—my best friend—killed her high school nemesis over foot slagging?"

He seemed to shrink a little in his uniform. "No, I guess not. Lots of people were slagged worse by Tammi. The suspect list is going to be long."

Edna gestured at Asher with her pipe. "Ivy wasn't the one throwing down with Tammi, young man. It was Dahlia."

My brother shrunk even more. Pretty soon he'd be so small his uniform would fall right off. "Mom? Why?"

"Because Tammi dissed Poppy right to our face," I said. "Mom is set on Poppy getting to the class reunion. Remember she graduated in my year after her, uh, hiatus."

"Expulsion, you mean," Asher said.

"The point is, Pops had the guts to come back to school and today Tammi made some caustic remarks that set Mom off."

Kellan rubbed his forehead. "Please tell me Dahlia didn't threaten Tammi."

"Only if you count a brisk lashing with an apron as a threat," Edna said. "I do."

I waved for her to simmer down. "Mom's done worse. Said worse. She just wanted Poppy to enjoy the reunion and was selling aprons at the market to pay for our tickets. We're going as a family to support Pops."

"There won't be a reunion until this is resolved," Kellan said. "Are you even sure it's foul play? Asher says she looks perfect."

Edna aimed her pipe in Percy's direction. "The cat has spoken. You'll see soil, leaves and a few dead bees scattered over the deceased."

Kellan stared at Edna as she inhaled deeply enough to sputter.

"What's with the pipe, Miss Evans? The camo isn't enough to set you apart?"

"It's about the bees," I jumped in. "There are some strays left from what appears to be a hive heist and smoke keeps them from communicating the alarm message."

He signaled everyone to move away from the body and then texted on his phone. "We'll get some professional beekeepers here to secure the scene."

"Until then, you can borrow my pipe, Chief," Edna said. "No need to thank me."

Kellan ignored her. "Jilly, maybe you could tell me more about what happened at the market. I'm guessing you'll be the most objective."

Keats herded Jilly and Asher over to Kellan and then pressed the rest of the officers back around the side of the house. One flash of his blue eye told me the move was less about their safety than about creating an opportunity for me to do something.

"Edna, lower your weapon," I whispered. "Bernice is back and she's repeating a flight pattern. I could swear it looks like an arrow."

"Dagnabit, Ivy, you can't follow an insect's lead on a whim. It'll get you stung."

"Technically, I'm following Keats, who's following Percy. The cat has the best vision of all of us."

Percy turned to give me a green-eyed glance and I turned to find another set of green eyes. Jilly gave a subtle flick of her fingertips to tell me to go ahead. She'd keep the officers distracted for a few minutes. "Be careful," she mouthed.

"I'm always careful," I mouthed back, and we both smiled. It was almost never true and never ceased to amuse us.

"You know there could be a murderer lurking around here," Edna said. "I left my pack near the hives but don't worry, I got you covered."

I used my arm as a shield to force my way into bushes so dense even Keats struggled. Percy darted through without trouble, hopefully keeping at least his ears on the honeybee. "There's no murderer. Not right now, anyway. The boys are enjoying this too much."

"I'm not, particularly. While I'm no shrinking violet, the idea that there could be displaced bee colonies around gives me pause. Luckily the light is nearly gone and they're quiet after dusk."

"We've stumbled into worse." I held back a branch for her as she emptied her pipe, ground the ashes with her boot, and then slipped it into one of many pockets.

"Fire retardant fabric," she noted, following again. "And for the record, I'm not sure we've stirred up worse than bees. Too small to shoot."

"It'll be fine. We're almost there, anyway."

"There being...?"

The bushes had disgorged us into a meadow that would soon be in bloom. Percy was looking at the sky and making staccato cheeping noises, as he did with birds. He moved in what seemed like a complicated choreographed dance as he followed a bee I couldn't see. "Wherever Bernice wants us to go, I guess."

"Ivy!" The bellow was faint and faraway, but the impatience in my fiancé's voice covered the distance nicely. "Where are you?"

"Just over here," I yelled back. "Nature called!" I smirked at Edna and added, "Not entirely untrue."

She shook her head. "He sounds cranky. You'd better get off the pot."

Percy stopped dancing and started scraping, while Keats lifted one paw in a point.

"Not again!" I walked over to them, switching on my phone light. "I hope this isn't a double homicide."

"Probably just dead bees," Edna said, clomping after me. "Who knows what the killer did to them?"

It wasn't bees.

Nor was it a body.
But it was bloody.

CHAPTER FIVE

I bent over till my face was just a foot from the sweeping paws. "What is that?"

Dropping to one knee, Edna directed her flashlight at the object for a closer look. "An old, rusted smoker. Most beekeepers use them when working with hives." She pointed out the parts. "The flammables go in the cannister, and the smoke comes out through the cone when you press the bellows. More effective than a pipe, obviously."

For some reason, the smoker reminded me of a genie's lamp and I felt a sudden urge to rub it and collect three wishes. My first would be to reverse what happened to Tammi. Failing that, I'd wish to catch her killer quickly so that Poppy could go to the reunion and work through her regrets.

Keats mumbled an opposing view in my ear. He didn't want this new puzzle to be solved too soon. He was already having fun and more would surely follow as we searched for the missing hives and helped to sort out what befell Tammi.

I sighed. My intentions were good, but maybe I should wish for something easier. Something warm and fuzzy. A wallaby, perhaps, whose big feet would desensitize me to mine.

Or I could wish for smaller feet in the first place.

"Ivy?" Edna nudged my shoulder. "Are you in shock?" She slapped her pocket. "Got a little something to perk you up. I don't consider it illegal if it's for medicinal purposes."

"I'm fine. Or as fine as anyone could be after finding their high school nemesis dead." I stood up and let Edna steady me. Maybe I wasn't quite as fine as I claimed. We'd seen a lot of people pass, but Tammi was the youngest and fairest of them all. She should have had decades ahead to atone for her misdeeds. If her apiary was any indication, she was well on the way. "This thing looks like a genie's lamp. It doesn't seem substantial enough to kill someone."

"The metal cone is sharp. With enough force, it could get the job done."

"Still, I doubt it would have been anyone's weapon of choice. I'm going to guess Tammi surprised someone in the act of stealing her hives and the person acted on impulse."

"Why didn't we see more blood?" Edna asked. "Was it trapped in the hood?"

Looking around for Keats, I shook my head. "Dunno. Maybe they moved her."

Kellan's arrival with a high-powered flashlight put an end to our speculation. "I see you've finished relieving yourself. Something I never endorse near a crime scene, incidentally."

I gestured to the smoker. "Bernice led us to the murder weapon."

My fiancé peered around. "Bernice?"

"The orphaned bee. I call her Bernice." I said it with a sheepish smile.

Edna patted my arm rather gently, for her. "It wouldn't be a hill country crime if Ivy didn't develop a crazy crush on a critter."

"We've barely met," I said. "But I do feel for this little buzzer who lost her family. The hives may be destined for California, Kellan. They pay big money to pollinate almond trees this time of year."

Edna caught Kellan's eye and they seemed to have a silent exchange, because he dropped an arm over my shoulder and squeezed. "Hopefully Bernice will be taken in by another family. You feeling okay, honey?"

"Right sentiment, wrong endearment," Edna said. "I'd also avoid 'sweetie,' out of respect to the bees. You could go with 'dear,' which is dated, or 'babe,' if you want to stay current."

"Or darling," I added. "If you want to sound like Mom."

Kellan flinched. "I don't. How about I stick with 'Ivy'? However, the question stands. Are you feeling okay?"

"Yeah, I guess. It's just that Tammi was my age. Too young for this to happen."

"I know. That's always hard to see." Duty and compassion battled in his eyes, but he found a ready solution. "Deputy Keats! Attention, please. I need you to dial up the love for Ivy today. This one hit close to home."

Keats offered an irritable mumble as he came back from searching the perimeter. He was in crime-solving mode and switching hats to emotional support was difficult. But as always, he stepped up to the task and offered me his ears. His next mumble was kinder, with only a hint of "buck up."

Squatting, Kellan said, "What is this thing?"

"A smoker," I said. "Beekeepers use them to keep the bees calm. Notice the blood. I'd guess it was Tammi's, even though we didn't see any."

"It's there, and plenty of it." Standing, he gave me a look. "That's all I'm saying. You're too close to this crime, Ivy. People saw you and Dahlia having words with the victim just hours before her passing. I need you to go home. And I need you to keep your mother at home."

"Young man, we've known Tammi all her life," Edna said. "We could be of great assistance."

"And I'll be glad to hear about your memories when the time is right. Currently, the time is only right for keeping a low profile."

I grabbed Edna's sleeve and started pulling. "Okay. Got it, Chief. I'll go put my livestock to bed."

There was plenty of time before evening chores and he knew it. His expression turned wary. "You're giving up, just like that?"

"I want to hang with Poppy while we muck out stalls. Her interest in the reunion has me puzzled. There's more to this story, I'm sure of it, but I need to get her alone and let the manure work its magic."

"Not buying it, Ivy," he called after me. "And there's zero magic in manure."

Grinning over my shoulder, I called back, "You proposed in manure, Chief. That's as magical as it gets."

My goal was to throw my fiancé off the scent and it worked a charm. His lips closed into a straight line, no doubt because the police officers assembling near him in the field were fighting grins.

Dropping Asher's arm, Jilly joined me. "That wasn't respectful to either Tammi or Kellan," she chided, as we made our way back to the truck.

Keats swished around all of us with a flourish of his tail. My lighthearted exchange with Kellan showed the dog I was back on track. Once again, he had work worthy of his genius.

"Jilly, you're right," I said. "But I hope what I do next will help get Tammi the respect she deserves."

CHAPTER SIX

Mandy was locking the door of the country store when I drove into the parking lot just over an hour later. "I didn't expect you till morning," she said, backing up to let me inside. "I planned to bake something special for you."

"No need. My sweet tooth is out of commission after finding Tammi Hickey in such a mess."

She made a show of peering out the window. "Is the sky falling? I've never known you to turn down baked goods, before."

Keats escorted us both to my favorite stool and I set Percy's carrier down. Mandy signaled for me to release the cat. Normally he stayed contained to prevent anyone complaining about long orange hairs in their confections. Tonight, she was willing to take the risk. A murder sent all good people looking for a pet to hug.

"I could hardly eat a bite of dinner," I said. "But I suppose I can find room for dessert."

"I've got just the thing. It'll stick to your ribs." She disappeared into the kitchen and came back carrying a plate with an enormous serving of bread pudding. Holding a steaming pitcher of sauce over it, she said, "Say when." Her eyes widened when I let the liquid pool to dangerous levels. "There's bourbon in there and you're driving."

"If I get tipsy, I'll give Keats the keys. He's always wanted to drive the truck. Am I right, buddy?"

His goofy smile confirmed it.

"You'll give *me* the keys," Mandy said. "I've taken a few lessons on a standard transmission. I'm thinking of getting a sportier ride."

Now *my* eyes widened. "Mandy McCain, are you trying to shock your former classmates?"

"The ones who deemed me least likely to accomplish anything in life? It wouldn't be hard to surprise them."

"It wasn't that bad." I sliced into the pudding with my fork. "Or if it was, no one included me in the loop. My social currency was very low, as you know."

"My nickname was Skelebore, Ivy. A combination of skeleton and boring." She crossed her still-slim arms and stared at me. "Bad enough?"

"Harsh, yeah. Mine was Flubby Flappers. Later evolving to Froggy Flappers, after I asked to opt out of dissecting amphibians in biology class."

"Not great either." Mandy slid onto the stool beside mine and welcomed Percy into her lap. "How did we survive those piranhas to become the upstanding citizens we are today?"

"As the old saying goes, what doesn't kill you makes you stronger." I swallowed a mouthful. "This delicious treat is similar."

A smile flitted across her thin, pale face. "I hope to win a few points with it at the homecoming party tomorrow night. I'm catering that, too."

"Homecoming party? Why didn't I hear about it?"

Her pale eyebrows soared. "You weren't invited?"

"Nope. I guess I'm still an outcast. Anyway, I doubt Kellan will allow reunion events to go ahead after what happened. With Tammi's record of bullying, it'll take time to rule people out."

Mandy sighed. "Figures. I stocked up for it. Maybe someone will do the right thing and confess. My money's on Kayla Bouchard Ware."

"Kayla? Why? They were always best friends."

"Frenemies, more recently. Kayla was in here making snide remarks about how Tammi ran the bee club. I expected a blowup, but nothing like this."

I swirled another forkful of pudding in the sauce as I pondered. "What motive would Kayla have for what happened? With Tammi leaving, the keys to the queendom were hers. There was no reason to steal the hives when Tammi was entrusting her with them anyway."

"I don't know much about bees, and I refused to carry Tammi's honey in the store. As if I could forget how she treated me. She wouldn't have dared propose it when..."

Her voice drifted off and I finished her sentence. "When your grandmother was alive." It might be the only time I ever spared a kind thought for Myrtle McCain, but she could certainly put someone in her place. She had almost put me in my grave.

"Yeah. That's the only reason they didn't brand me. They still wanted to shop here."

I shuddered, and Keats whined as he moved between us, offering his ears as comfort from a disturbing memory. Tammi and her crew liked to ambush girls in the restroom and threaten to burn them with cigarettes. Once they blocked me in a stall and discussed it for so long I had to use the facilities again, and more urgently. "Asher was my get out of jail free card. They loved and feared him in equal measure."

Our fingers touched briefly on Keats' head. "And yet we never reported them," Mandy said, cradling Percy in her other arm.

"Because there were punishments worse than branding, even before social media. Teachers didn't care as much about bullying then. Now it would make a great exposé. Hopefully Justine Schalow will do something useful for a change and cover it in the paper."

"She's away this week," Mandy said. "Sniffing out a story on political corruption, or so she said before leaving. Personally, I'm glad she's gone." She pulled her hand away from the dog and shoved fine, dirty blonde hair out of her eyes. "And I'm glad Tammi's gone, too. There. I said it."

I sighed, unwilling to voice such words aloud. "Moving to the city probably would have been enough, though. In time, we'll shake off those memories."

"I doubt it. Nearly every day I ran home from school with a full bladder because I was afraid to use the restrooms. You never knew which one they'd stake out."

I started to slice another bite but set my fork down instead. "Couple times I climbed up on the toilet seat and held my breath so they'd think the stall was empty. Things got better in high school when you could predict their schedules."

"Exactly." Mandy hugged Percy with both arms and he didn't squirm. "Cheerleading practice was the only time I ever felt I could straighten up. I was always hunched over. Trying to be invisible."

We sat in silence for a moment, perhaps mourning the carefree school experience we never had. Percy gave an eerie meow that sounded like sympathy, but Keats took the hem of my jeans between his teeth and gave it a shake. The dog's message was clear. Enough ruminating. Tammi was gone, and her reign of terror needed to end, too. Even in memory.

I considered pushing the dessert plate away and then decided to finish. Every bite of bread pudding was about taking back my power and appreciating Mandy's. "This is so good. When the class gets together, they'll see how talented you are, Mandy."

"Thanks." She found a little smile as my fork flew. "Talk to Kayla, okay?"

"I will, but I can't see why she'd do something like this. Unless they had a last-minute dispute about bee accommodation, or something like that."

"Tammi would have tried to control every last detail, I'm sure.

Kayla's a good place to start, anyway. If the homecoming party happens, you can poke around there. Consider yourself invited by the caterer."

Keats gave my cuff another tug but I wasn't quite done. "Did you know Scott Burger has been saying we were a thing? The nerve!"

Mandy laughed. "I'm sure you never had eyes for anyone but Kellan."

"Never." A big bready mouthful muffled the word. "Not even for Kellan, to be honest. If he hadn't won the right to ask me out, I'd probably be single till the bitter end. Only I wouldn't be bitter. My life is as full as my stomach."

"*Won* the right?" Mandy pushed a spoon toward me so that I could better tipple the sauce.

"Drag race with my brother, according to Kellan. Asher refuses to confirm or deny. Probably scared of what Jilly would say."

"That's so romantic." Mandy pressed a hand to her heart. "I wish someone would drag race for me."

"Get yourself that sporty ride and I bet it happens."

Keats mumbled advice not to get sidetracked.

Looking down at him, Mandy nodded as if she understood perfectly. "Ivy, you should talk to Finch Pefferlaw."

I stopped scooping sauce. "Finch had a beef with Tammi?"

"Just hearing it secondhand. He's in the bee club, too."

"Huh. Wouldn't have taken Finch as a joiner. Has he softened around the edges?"

Mandy laughed. "He has warmed up a bit since his farm started doing so well. Surplus produce has to go somewhere and their stall at the market was popular."

That warmed my heart. "He uses my black label manure, you know. Color me proud."

"Head over and deliver his next load."

I pushed the empty plate away, regretting the last few mouthfuls. Bread pudding started as a light caress and ended with a gut punch. "Hope he has a load of intel for me. Although Finch is a reluctant gossip."

She walked me to the door and kissed Percy on the head before slipping him back into the cat carrier. "Tell Finch there's shelf space here for his honey. I didn't dare take on a competitor when Tammi was alive for fear of reprisals. She was a major hub for gossip."

I stared at her from the open doorway. "Without Tammi the town's social structure might collapse."

"The queen bee is dead," Mandy said, gently pushing me outside. "Let the fight for the throne begin."

CHAPTER SEVEN

The brilliant man I'd been lucky enough to win—and be won by —was sitting in a squad car outside the barn when I finished my chores the next morning.

He got out, dropped a kiss on my cheek and gave me a weary smile that told me he'd been up all night. "Figured I'd get the jump on you before you started your illicit investigation."

I snapped my fingers to call Keats away from the sheep pen, where he was practicing his mesmerizing stare. He did it every morning to maintain mastery. One day those sheep might be loose and he would be ready. But now, I needed his help to evade being herded by a certain authority figure. "Can't pull the wool over your eyes, Chief. But I'm just here doing my farmer thing."

"With no plans to visit Mandy for pie and gossip?"

I rubbed my belly, which was still complaining about the volume of bread pudding the night before. "Absolutely not. You couldn't pay me to eat pie right now." I tipped my head. "Are you paying? Want me to find you some leads in Mandy's fine pastry?"

He shook his head. "I'll find my own leads and keep my weight down. Gotta fit into my tux at the wedding."

Leading him to the fence, I leaned against it. "So jealous. You press your tux and you're done. Meanwhile, I have to try on fifty white dresses in front of witnesses to prove I made a deliberate decision."

"You'll make a snap decision," he said.

"Of course I will. It'll take me two seconds and then another two hours for everyone else to be satisfied I know what I want."

His smile perked up a bit. "Glad to see you're getting into the right mindset. So many decisions ahead."

"Can't we just run away together? Jilly and Asher had a big wedding. People got their fix."

"Sure. Your truck or mine?"

I rolled my eyes. "Nice try. You don't have a truck, and mine isn't worthy of a bridal breakaway."

"Well, think on it. And while you do, you can promise me you'll stay out of my investigation of Tammi Hickey's murder."

"Didn't I already promise last night in the field? Or did I just wish I had when I thought the smoker was a genie lamp?"

His eyes glazed with fatigue and confusion. "What a waste of wishes. You could have wished for a sexy car to elope in."

"Instead, I wished for a wallaby. And smaller feet. No wonder Edna thought I was in shock."

The mist of fatigue cleared from his eyes. "The shock has passed. I can tell you're gearing up for new sleuthing escapades."

I shook my head. "I only want to help with the bees. Any idea where they landed?"

"Not yet." He ducked his head suddenly. "What was that?"

"You mean 'who.' Bernice came home with me. The bee who led us to the smoking gun. Pretty much literally in this case."

His eyes closed and he sighed. "Not again."

"What? A bee's never followed me home before, at least to my knowledge. They're smarter than people think, though. Capable of recognizing facial features, for example. I guess I left an impression."

"You always do." His eyes were still closed. "And if you're backing this busy bee—"

"Bernice. And I am."

"—then we're bound to lock horns." His eyes opened. "At the risk of mixing metaphors."

Keats mumbled an order to get a move on it, which meant nips would surely follow. I might as well come clean. Or at least, cleaner. "Look, I wanted to help bring justice for Tammi. But then I remembered just how horrible she was in school. Did you know she burned girls with cigarettes as a reminder to curtsy when she passed? You'll find plenty of people have the round Tammi 'brand.'"

His handsome face paled. "Is that a joke?"

"I wish it were. Ask around when you're asking around. I only escaped because of Asher's golden shadow. So I'll stick with the real gold—helping the bees."

"The golden shadow didn't help Poppy?" Kellan's expression was wary now, as if he sensed he was being sized up for ambush. He was. The dog's blue eye said attack was imminent.

"It only works for younger siblings. Tammi probably stuck with slander for Pops. My sister got suspended for fighting a few times."

"Fighting boys, as I recall."

"Mostly. She punched out of her league, and I don't know why she didn't kick the stuffing out of Tammi." I plucked a piece of wood off the fence beam that would otherwise impale me one day. "If you're here to talk to Pops, you're out of luck. She got Dad to cover her shift last night and is late today."

"I'll track her down." He glanced up at the house. "Need to talk to your mom, too."

"Mom and Poppy are dead ends, Kellan. How about Tammi's husband? Eddy always seemed slick."

"Asher said the same, but Ed's got a clean record. Seemed legit heartbroken about what happened. They were about to start a new life together."

"Is Eddy's alibi bulletproof?" I asked. "It's usually the husband, right?"

"On TV, maybe. When has it been the husband in Clover Grove?"

I thought back. "Too early for a pop quiz. Haven't had enough coffee. But I'd take a close look at Eddy. Maybe he wanted to leave his big fish in the small pond."

"It wasn't Eddy and don't go bothering him, Ivy. He's grieving. And innocent."

Pushing it a little, I asked, "Is that what the security feed said? Because there's no way Tammi would have fifty grand worth of bees without cameras."

He rubbed his eyes before admitting, "They were turned off. Shame, as footage would make my life a whole lot easier."

Time to back off my beleaguered beloved. "Sounds like you need another coffee too, Chief."

"That I do." Kellan managed to drum up a smile for me. "Listen, would I be here interviewing your mother if I thought I could pin the murder on the husband?"

"Good point. You'd save your strength for less wily suspects. But Mom didn't get anywhere near that apiary. She'd never risk being disfigured by stings."

"We'll see. Dahlia always knows more than you'd think." His smile turned coy. "More than she tells you, anyway."

"Is that true?" I was indignant. "I'm her favorite daughter. Right after Jilly."

"Most of it is gossip no one wants to hear. She'll slag Kayla and the other bee-witching cheerleader."

"Nadia Reddy. And I heard what you did there. You'll be punning like crazy after a coffee."

Kellan began moving sideways, perhaps unaware of the sheepdog energy at work. Keats wasn't touching him as far as I could tell. The dog was gently air-pressing my fiancé toward a rather large puddle. "And with that, I'd better head up to see Dahlia. Get the worst done first."

"What a terrible thing to say about your future mother-in-law." Grinning, I snapped my fingers to summon the dog. "Well warranted, though. I was surprised she went all mama bear on Tammi. There's more to this Poppy story than we know."

He scowled at Keats and sidestepped the puddle. "What's on for you today?"

"Feed store first. Then I'll collect the mower from the mechanic. Lawn's starting to green up already."

Keats resumed his chief-herding project. Kellan moved away from me, perhaps only vaguely aware of his journey to the porch. "That's it? Errands?"

"If the weather holds, I'll probably mend the fence later. The goats tried to bust out yesterday. Had to stick them in the new pasture for now."

I was trying to lull him with mundane farm tasks and it seemed to be working. "I could definitely use a coffee," he said, as Keats air-pressed him up the stairs. My fiancé looked vaguely confused, perhaps over the growing distance between us.

"I can smell a fresh pot brewing. You'll need it to stay ahead of Mom."

He snapped out of his trance when his fingers touched the door-knob. "What about this bee?" he called. "Bernice."

I made a show of looking around. "Gone. I think she's a scout bee. They're proven to have the highest need for novelty in the whole hive. And I've got a lot more facts where that came from, so... bee-ware."

He winced in the same moment the door opened. Jilly welcomed Kellan inside and released Percy, who raced down the stairs to join us. The cat's enthusiasm was too obvious, and it made Kellan glower through the screen. Then he started moving backward with jerky hops as the inn's polished hostess towed him toward the coffee he craved.

"To the truck, boys," I said, walking so fast it was nearly a run. "Pretty soon Kellan's going to be a whole lot sharper, so we'd better get bee-zy."

Keats gave a canine groan and I shrugged. "Too much? Too bad. I'm just getting started."

CHAPTER EIGHT

K eats pawed at the glass until I pressed the button to lower the passenger window. Then he took a long, deep snort that sounded more like contentment than a clue. He was glad to cast off the shackles of the farm dog's mundane life. I felt a familiar flutter of excitement, too. We were free. We were on a mission together. It didn't get much better than that.

"Will we ever settle down?" I mused aloud as we headed for town. "We've got ants in our pants. Or bees in our bonnets."

Keats poked his nose outside and let his mumbled answer drift away on the breeze, while Percy rolled onto his back and groomed his cream-colored belly.

"We're living our best life, but I do regret it comes at someone's expense. I never liked Tammi but her moving would have been enough. Dying was too much. Now I have to feel bad for someone who caused bladder problems for a lot of girls. I still don't like using public restrooms and it's her fault."

Keats pulled his muzzle inside and gave a mumble of indifference. He didn't know Tammi enough to care one way or another.

"It seemed like she'd become a valued member of the home-steading community. As mean as she was to me and others, she probably didn't deserve to be smacked with a smoker." I patted the back of my head. "Her hair was always her pride and joy. She'd be so mad it was a mess when she passed."

I turned right as we drove into town, and then right again to take the route less traveled. All the shops on Main Street would be buzzing with gossip. I wanted to avoid it and exploit it at the same time, and that meant choosing my moment. If I parked on a side street, I could pop in and out of stores on foot and catch the story as it snowballed. Bits of gravel and trash would stick as it grew, giving us hints and clues.

At the last stop sign on the side street, I stalled the truck. Thankfully, that wasn't a daily or even weekly event anymore. I could go a whole month without so much as a stutter.

Unless there was a bee in the cab. Then all bets were off.

A small gold-and-black missile had flown past Keats' nose and circled my head. Percy reached up to swat at it.

"Stop, Percy." I fanned my right hand in hopes of sending the bee back out through the passenger window. Someone honked behind me—a little too hard, considering it wasn't a major intersection. I gave the sheepish "just a second" wave before rolling down all four windows. "Go away, little bee. This is too close for comfort."

The bee didn't go away. Instead, it buzzed overhead in what appeared to be a tight figure eight pattern.

"Is that you, Bernice? If so, I'd thank you to keep your stinger holstered. We're investigating what happened to your family, I promise."

The figure eight tightened even more, bringing the bee uncomfortably close to my ear. She had four windows to choose from yet decided to stick around and make my heart race.

The driver in the red hatchback behind me lay on the horn again and I turned the key in the ignition. With the bee still doing her circuit, I could barely keep the truck lurching forward.

Keats mumbled an order to focus and I nodded. If I didn't stay cool, we'd get rear-ended. The driver behind us honked yet again. The lady at the wheel was in a big hurry.

"She's the one you should be bugging, Bernice," I said. "So rude. It's a side street. And a school zone."

My elementary school sat well back from the curb, and despite the circumstances, I smiled. I had good memories of my early years in the classroom, where it was safe to be a keener, and even rewarded. Back then, I didn't mind raising my hand and participating. In sixth grade, however, Tammi transferred here from Dorset Hills. I began growing and shrinking at the same time. By high school, I was the tallest girl in class, and as close to invisible as I could manage. Some days I got my wish and no one acknowledged me from the first bell to the last.

I turned into the school driveway, just to get the red hatchback off my tail. "See, boys? This was the school that made me who I am today. I had some good teachers who nurtured curious minds. High school beat me down, which made me a perfect corporate HR drone. But then the real me came back when I got clobbered rescuing you, Keats. The genie is out of the smoker again."

Keats suggested with a mumble that we revisit my golden age when the black-and-gold insect moved on.

"Point taken." I cruised slowly past the front door and back out to the street. In my last year here, Mom drove me to school in her yellow sedan, Daffodil, a forerunner of Buttercup and just as embarrassing. Even then, Mom could barely navigate the drive-through without knocking over a student. It took a lot of badgering before she agreed to drop me down the street so I could walk back. By middle school, I dumped her completely and rode my bike.

Another mumble brought me back to the present. Keats raised his paw in a point just in time for me to see the bee fly out the rear passenger window.

"Whew! I'm all about helping critters but that was far too close for comfort." I rolled up all the windows. "If any bee wants an audience with us, it needs to be outside." Driving down the block, I pulled up near Clover Grove Public Library. "I wonder if that really was Bernice. It worries me that a lot of her buddies could be homeless right now. The thief left in a hurry and damaged some hives."

The red hatchback that had been riding my bumper was parked right in front of the library. A woman with gray, backcombed hair rushed up the ramp. She ducked and dodged as if something was after her.

Like a bee, perhaps.

"Bernice," I muttered, getting out of the truck. "I didn't mean that literally. Since when does a bee take orders from a hobby farmer?"

Keats and Percy jumped out after me, and the dog gave a neutral rumble.

"You're right. I suppose there are plenty of disenfranchised bees at the moment. It was a coincidence." The woman flung back the door and it stayed open long enough for her pursuer to join her. "Bad call," I said, following. "Dottie Bridges doesn't like critters in the library."

I knew that because the librarian routinely tried to ban the cat and dog from the premises. She had never really recovered from the time I took a donkey and miniature horse into the stacks, but we were friends now. I happily included her in our holiday get-togethers, along with her best friend and my absolute favorite librarian, Thistledown's Thelma Tilrow.

Catching the door before it closed, I heard Dottie say, "Get that thing out of here."

I assumed she'd already seen me, but the woman with the big bouffant was blocking Dottie's sightline.

"It's just a bee, Dorothy, and it's not mine," the woman said.

"If it was 'just a bee,' why did you sprint in here like the devil himself was after you? You're a beekeeper, Fiona Gillespie. You know how to handle them."

Mrs. Gillespie, the high school principal, patted her hair gingerly, as if to make sure no winged insects had lodged there. "That one joined me in the car and was very persistent. The first rule of beekeeping is to stay alert."

Dottie grabbed her cane and hoisted herself off her stool behind the checkout desk. I suspected it was more of a prop now, or at least a precaution. Like Thelma, she moved with more ease every time I saw her. Perhaps they'd found a limited edition book containing the secrets to age reversal.

Mrs. Gillespie looked nearly as old as Dottie but I knew the principal was about a decade younger. Though past retirement age, she continued to run the school with an iron fist, according to my eldest sister, Daisy. My nephews, two sets of twins, had frequent flyer points to the principal's office.

As Dottie moved around her desk, she spotted me. "Ivy, what have I told you about bringing pets in here? Are you deaf or just dumb?"

"Dorothy, hush," Mrs. Gillespie said, bobbing under the circling bee. "You can't say things like that anymore. Besides, Ivy Galloway was the brightest student in her year, although she went to great effort to hide it and refused to collect awards."

"Get too big and your head is chopped off," Dottie said. "They call it 'tall poppy syndrome.'"

"Now, Poppy Galloway was another matter," Mrs. Gillespie continued, holding out her hand to me. "And Asher. It's hard to believe all those apples fell from the same tree."

I smiled as I shook her hand. "The Galloway tree is full of surprises. It's nice to see you, Principal Gillespie. I credit your grammar lessons for my corporate success in HR. No one could write a dismissal letter like me."

Dottie gave a derisive snort. "That's your claim to fame?"

"I would imagine that's a red herring, Dorothy," the principal said. "Ivy wants to distract you from the fact her pets have skulked into the stacks."

"There was no skulking about it," I said. "Keats and Percy love it here, just like I did, back in the day. And if you don't mind my asking, Mrs. Gillespie, why were you laying on the horn earlier? It made me so nervous I stalled the truck."

The color rose in the principal's sallow cheeks. She had been attractive enough 20 years ago and could still fit into the mustard tweed suit I considered her uniform. The backcombing was new and I wondered if she was compensating for thinning hair. Abundant locks were an advantage she'd always had over the "boys' club" in hill country's school administration. "Oh, was that you? I was running late and got a trifle impatient."

"Late for a library visit? You must have something very special on hold."

Keats came back and sat beside me, taking the principal's measure. He directed his blue eye at her and mumbled something.

Mrs. Gillespie turned slightly, perhaps trying to avoid the sheep-dog's probe. "I stepped out for a meeting during first period. Must get back before the bell."

She started to ease away but Keats circled around to bring her back. Our business was not done. The bee seemed to share the same view, as she was still dive-bombing the bouffant, much to Fiona's dismay.

Dottie threw me a line. "The Bee a Good Citizen Club is meeting in the back. Fiona's a longtime beekeeper. I suppose she's gunning for president now that there's a vacancy."

The flush in the principal's cheeks deepened. "Dorothy, hush. We're gathering quickly to pay our respects to Tamara Hickey, that's all. Club leadership is a topic for another day, after things settle down."

"I assumed Kayla Bouchard was stepping into her shoes," I said. "Those two were always so close and I wasn't surprised to hear

Tammi was conceding her hives to her bestie. Well, if I'm honest, I was surprised they were beekeeping at all. I wouldn't have seen that coming in high school. It's a leap from cheerleading, pardon the pun."

"Strange things happen to young people when they stay in a small town," Dottie said. "I figure it's best for them to leave and join the real world for a bit, and then come home when their brains mature. Like you did, Ivy."

"On that we agree, Dorothy." Mrs. Gillespie patted her hair cautiously. "Ivy's such a boon to Clover Grove."

If I hadn't been watching the principal closely, I might have missed the twitch of her lip. Keats saw the slight sneer, too, and mumbled something insolent. Despite her kind words, Mrs. Gillespie wasn't my biggest fan. She was hiding more than a bald spot or a honeybee under her bouffant.

Muffled voices rose at the back of the library. If it was the beekeepers, they had an odd way of paying respect to their permanently departed leader.

"Tell your crew to keep it down, Fiona." Dottie pursed her lips in the standard librarian pucker of disapproval. Thelma had it nailed, too. "The preschoolers are coming in for reading club and I don't want them distracted. You know the importance of early literacy."

"Absolutely." The principal's retreat was succeeding now, although she probably didn't expect company in the stacks. Keats decided we would escort her to her meeting and circled to keep his little herd together. Looking up, I saw Percy running a zigzag pattern on top of the non-fiction stacks, probably chasing the bee.

Mrs. Gillespie and I bumped elbows and shoulders as we made our way past the romantic poets.

"Are you looking for some light reading?" the principal asked, trying to slide around me and failing. Keats slipped ahead on my right and pressed her back. Watching me jockeying for space with a woman I once feared and respected was probably entertaining for my clever dog. He enjoyed puncturing myths and misbeliefs, and I was beginning to sense Mrs. Gillespie was never what I thought. "You were the rare teen who enjoyed the great poets."

"Still do." I glanced up at the cat, who hooked a book with his claws and knocked it down a few yards ahead of us. "I've named some pets after my favorites. Percy. Keats. Lord Byron."

"Those distinguished men of letters would appreciate the honor." Mrs. Gillespie gasped as another book came crashing down. Percy was adding obstacles to Keats' herding challenge.

I accidentally jabbed the principal in the rib cage with my elbow and she gave a startled squawk. "Sorry, ma'am, sorry."

"Ivy Galloway." Her voice became imperious. "Would you like to explain why you and your pets are accosting me?"

"The pets are excited, ma'am. Maybe there's someone in your meeting they're eager to see."

"I doubt that. It's a small club, no matter how hard we try to boost our numbers. Someone's always leaving from natural attrition or politics."

"Politics? What kind of politics?"

We finally reached the end of the row and emerged in the open space near the meeting room. There was a small table with four chairs, where I'd liked to study. It was usually vacant because people probably felt smothered being surrounded by so many books. To me, it was a warm embrace of wise words.

Principal Gillespie didn't answer my question. She rested her left hand on the door handle and I noticed the rings she used to wear were gone. It had been a glittery stack of diamonds and I remembered thinking it must weigh her down. Perhaps Mr. Gillespie had left or passed away. He used to run a physiotherapy clinic in Dorset Hills.

The door opened with a push from the inside, shoving the principal back a little. "Fiona, finally!" someone exclaimed. "Come in. We have a mess to clean up."

She slipped inside and slammed the door shut before I could join her.

Keats grumbled in annoyance and another reference book toppled, barely missing my head.

"It's okay, boys," I whispered, hoping to overhear the discussion inside. "I saw what you wanted me to see."

The honeybee evidently thought so too, because she nearly clipped my ear as she headed back in the direction of the front door.

Dottie didn't look up as she checked out someone's books. "You're taking the bee, Ivy?"

I appreciated her confidence in my abilities, even if I didn't share it. "Apparently."

"Good. Then you can apologize to Alfred, Lord Tennyson later. Percy broke his spine."

"Sorry, Dottie. I think he nailed Emerson, too."

Her eyes drilled into my own spine as I left, and I made a mental note to donate my personal copies to her collection.

"When will we ever have time to read poetry, anyway?" I said aloud as we hurried to the truck.

Keats' verdict was a decided "never," and I was inclined to believe him.

CHAPTER NINE

There were many long and twisty lanes into farm properties around hill country, but the entry to Finch Pefferlaw's had to be the most forbidding. He'd cleared trees to create sharp turns that made navigating difficult in summer when the foliage was thick and nearly impossible in winter when the surface was icy. I considered it the equivalent of a moat outside a rather humble fortress. Finch was a refugee from the city who embraced self-reliance and living off the grid. When we first met, he was openly hostile. Later, he added a fierce mastiff for backup. While I liked to think we'd forged something approaching mutual respect over my black label fertilizer and other encounters, he wasn't fond of me and I didn't expect a warm welcome.

That's why I hadn't come alone. An intrepid sleuth knew when to bring backup.

"Dagnabit, Ivy, surrender the wheel if you can't make these turns," Edna said from the passenger seat. "The driving conditions are fine."

We'd had heavy rain for a couple of weeks and there were deep ruts in the mud. "Fine for an armored tank," I said. "Do you have one of those?"

"I wish. Don't think I haven't priced them. There's no better vehicle in an apocalypse." She cackled as the truck's wheels spun and the engine roared. "Gear down."

"I'm already in tractor mode." I blew strands of hair out of my eyes, feeling cool beads of perspiration form on my forehead. The only thing I hated more than a driving challenge was having witnesses.

"Maybe we should finish on foot," Gertie Rhodes said, from the back seat. Her knee-length braid was coiled in her lap over a ratty brown poncho and under a rifle named Minnie. I'd thought about letting my hair grow, too, but a long braid would be heavy and an occupational hazard on the farm. Further, Jilly would strangle me with it. We'd slid as far from our polished Boston styling as she was prepared to go, but I admired my octogenarian friends for letting their freak flags fly.

"Can't without leaving Keats and Percy," I said. "Jaws would go after them, and you'd never shoot a dog."

"True. I'd sooner shoot Finch. If I depart this life without ever firing on an animal, I can look my maker in the eye and call it good."

I struggled to reconcile my prepper friends' eccentric beliefs and behaviors with religion, but both attended church regularly. What's more, Edna always swapped out her camo for a nice sweater and slacks. Gertie still wore her poncho, but Minnie waited out the sermon in the van. When the service ended, the two old friends shared refreshments with the congregation. Afterward, they shook off the chains of conformity with target practice and a fencing duel, followed by a hearty dinner.

I knew about their routine because they usually showed up at the inn tired, dirty and hungry. Jilly never turned them away. The resident chef cooked for an army on Sundays and happily fed whoever appeared. Buckley Brackens, another octogenarian prepper, was a regular. Wendel Barrick and Rickie and Madge Merriweather often made the trek from Thistledown for a good meal and spirited conversation. If Kellan and Asher were working, the conversation was even more spirited. The tales told pushed the boundaries of the law and credulity, yet I suspected most were true.

Edna and Gertie leaned forward now, as if to help me push the truck out of the sludge. Keats and Percy grumbled as Edna squished them in her lap, but our combined effort seemed to do the trick and I managed to get the truck rolling down the last stretch of the lane.

Unsurprisingly, Jaws had alerted Finch to our arrival and they were waiting outside. The huge, jowly dog barked and slobbered at my window until I raised my eyebrows at his owner. Finch would let the intimidation play out as long as he liked and all I could do was wait. Eventually, he'd call off the dog because he valued my fertilizer. The thought made me smile. When I left my corporate job, I couldn't have imagined manure would be a marker of my success.

Today, Finch snapped his fingers to silence Jaws in short order, proving he actually wanted to talk to me. I rolled down the window a few inches and said, "Hey, Finch. Missed you at the Bee a Good Citizen meeting today."

His dark eyebrows drew together in a heavy, straight line. "What meeting? It was canceled because of what happened to Tammi."

Edna leaned across me to shoot him a smirk. "Young man, I feel for you. People cut me out of things all the time. I'm sure it has nothing to do with our sparkling personalities."

"They're jealous," Gertie said, poking her head between the seats. "Or afraid."

"Both," I said, letting Keats get into my lap to exchange growls with Jaws. "But the meeting was in progress when I was at the library, Finch. Fiona Gillespie was there, as well as Delsie Stubbing, the school librarian, and Clint Sever."

"The science teacher?" Edna asked. "I thought he got packaged out."

"He did, according to Daisy, but he must have an apiary." I raised my eyebrows at Finch again. "You would know."

The recluse farmer was giving a passible impression of a librarian's pucker. "Yeah. Most of them have bigger bee yards than mine."

"Bigger ambitions, too, if they're shutting you out of the committee," Edna said. "What did you do to annoy them?"

"Exist?" Finch gave a barking sound that passed for a laugh. "I was there to learn about bees. There's only so much you can pick up from books and websites. This winter I lost three out of five hives and it was..."

His voice drifted off and I supplied a word. "Devastating?"

"Something like that." His voice was gruff.

That sentiment was the reason I knew Finch and I would someday become more than frenemies. On previous visits, he'd shown he was attached to his livestock and they didn't grace his dinner table. While he wanted to know he could survive a crisis, he wasn't hardcore. Starling, his wife, gave out free bean recipes at the farmer's market. Jilly had tried some of the dishes and we found them simple and tasty. As the Pefferlaw family was still growing, budget-friendly legumes made good sense.

"It doesn't pay to get too attached to livestock," Edna said. "Bees probably qualify."

I pushed Edna back. "It's wonderful that Finch is trying to learn more about apiculture. It benefits the entire community."

"Is it true that someone stole Tammi's hives?" he asked. "You know I hate gossip more than swinepox, but I'd be sorry to hear that rumor is true."

"I'm afraid it is. We know the hives were destined for Kayla Bouchard and didn't make it."

"The Hickey yard was a wreck," Edna added. "I hate to think what happened to those bees."

Finch winced. "Shame, that. Tammi had great lines and a way with bees. Hadn't lost a hive in five years. I asked to train with her, but it didn't happen."

"Tammi was head cheerleader and prom queen, Finch," Edna said. "She didn't have time for the likes of us."

"We got along just fine." His eyebrows told a different story—one of disdain mixed with a dash of confusion. "I mean, there was always more going on in that group than I could understand. Even Starling couldn't make head nor tail of it and she's better at these things than me."

"Every group in town is like that," Gertie said. "Full of subtext and intrigue. It's always a popularity contest and this time you had high school politics, too."

"We can't blame pom-poms for what happened," I said. "I could tell Tammi really cared about her bees."

"Don't sound so surprised." Finch's lips tipped up. On another man it would be a grin.

"I was surprised," I admitted. "Tammi had a miniature poodle in middle school she didn't treat well. Sometimes it would lie down on the sidewalk and she'd drag it along like a stuffed toy. I tried talking to her about it once and the next thing you know someone had painted my head onto a poodle body on the gymnasium wall." I waited a beat and added, "It was a good likeness." Everyone laughed, including me. "One night, Asher and I snuck into the school and painted a black sheep over it. As far as I know, it's still there. Guess it was a portent of things to come. I need a black sheep on the farm."

"You are the black sheep," Finch said, nudging Jaws aside and leaning against the truck. "And Tammi spoke highly of you, so I'd say you won the round."

That gave me pause. "Really? She wasn't always that nice. I guess beekeeping was changing her."

He shrugged. "Maybe. Bees have complex social systems and I think she liked that. She tried to explain some of the dynamics to me." Raising a palm, he skimmed his unruly thatch of dark hair. "Went right over my head. Made me doubt my potential."

"Young man, you're too sensitive," Edna said.

Finch gave his barky laugh again. "That's not something I hear often. As in, ever."

"Plenty of ordinary people manage hives and produce honey," Gertie said. "Including my husband, Saul. He kept his eye on the big picture and let the details take care of themselves. Neither of us ever understood human social behavior, let alone insects."

Finch rested his hand on his big dog, who leaned in for a scratch. Jaws put on a savage show, but he was also a family dog. "Joining that club was a stretch for me. I tried hard to Bee a Good Citizen but if they didn't include me today, I guess I failed."

Shaking my head, I rolled down the window a little more. "I doubt that's it, Finch. They probably wanted to talk about something you wouldn't like. Any idea what it was?"

His eyes glazed for a second as he pondered. "There's been a lot of bickering since Tammi said she was leaving. She passed the torch to Kayla but others wanted a shot at the club presidency."

"Fiona Gillespie?" I guessed.

He nodded. "Clint Sever, too. They both said they had more time for the role than Kayla. She has four kids and a business to run. There was a contender from outside Dorset Hills, too." He rubbed his head again, harder. "Seemed like I was the only one there just for the bees."

"And that's why you weren't invited today," Edna said. "You weren't playing the game, Finch."

His already small eyes squinted. "I'm smart enough to stay out of a game when I can't understand the rules."

"Then you're smarter than most people," Edna said. "There will be zero tolerance for such shenanigans after the end times. Players will be the first to fall."

"But we'll need honey," Gertie said. "So keep those hives going."

Finch nodded, his heavy brows still nearly joined over his nose. "I like beekeeping. But this confirms clubs aren't for me."

"You can learn everything online," Gertie said. "Saul did just fine that way."

"Finch is off the grid," Edna reminded her.

"Not *that* off the grid," he said. "Besides, the library has free access."

I stuck my head out the window. "I don't suppose you'd consider staying in the club to figure out what they're doing?"

He snorted. "Do I seem like a mole to you? Anyway, they're already cutting me out."

Edna tried a different tactic. "You don't seem like a quitting man, Finch."

"You don't know me at all." He pushed off the truck and folded his arms.

"We know you love animals," I said. "Maybe you could do this for the bees. They deserve better than what happened at Tammi's apiary. Who knows where they are now, and how many even survived?"

"What if they come after yours next?" Gertie said.

He bent over to stare into the truck at her. "Then they'll meet a mastiff, followed by my rifle. Ladies, I'm nobody's spy. I report only to me."

Edna shrugged. "Can't fault you for that. It's a quality I admire."

I summoned what I hoped was a pleasant smile. "Finch, could I ask you a favor?"

"Nope. I don't ask favors and I don't grant them."

"All I want is to meet your bees. Tammi offered to show me her apiary, and never got the chance."

He shook his head. "Again, nope. Staying out of this one."

Edna leaned on me again to glare at him. "You're already in it, lad. But don't believe me. The police will show up to question you before long."

This unpinned his eyebrows and they rushed the short distance to his hairline. "Cops? Why? All I did was join a club. Not against the law."

Gertie chuckled. "Against the laws of common sense for people like us."

"I'm not like..." He pulled himself up short. "Anyone. I live by my own rules."

I fluttered my fingers out the window, earning a growl from Jaws. "But bees have rules. Lots of them. And maybe by understanding them, I could help figure out what happened."

"Help her help the bees, Finch," Edna called. "The benefit is getting the cops out of your hair."

He pulled a heavy leather leash out of his coat pocket and hooked up the mastiff. "But will it get all of you out of my hair?"

I waited till he'd backed away before cracking open the driver's door. "I could say yes, but would you believe me?"

"No one around here believes a word you say." He signaled for the pets to stay in the truck. Keats had decided of his own accord to sit this one out, anyway. "I do believe you have the best interests of animals at heart."

I jumped down and grinned at him. "Good enough for me."

CHAPTER TEN

Jilly pressed her golden curls against the truck's headrest and gripped the handle on the door until I slowed down. "That good, huh?"

"So good, my friend. I wish you could have been there to see inside the hives. The way they move around is—"

Her head tilted sideways to send a cool, green-eyed glance my way. "Ivy? Not a fan of bugs, remember?"

"Bees aren't regular bugs, Jilly."

"No, they're bugs who sting. In other words, worse than your average housefly, and I already get you and Asher to escort those from the house."

Keats gave a mumble from her lap that seemed to suggest I pick my battles. Bees weren't the hive to die on, at least not with Jilly.

"Fine. It was fascinating and we'll leave it at that."

She continued to look at me but the intensity faded. "How'd you get Finch to agree to show you the ropes?"

"Easy. We're besties now." We both laughed. "Well, not even close, but I think we've come to a bit of an understanding. Underneath his gruff exterior is an animal lover and I can work with that.

It's people he distrusts. With all that's going on in hill country, it's no surprise."

Now she turned her eyes back to the road. "We still trust people."

"Not all people. Just the good ones. And under that cynical crust, I think Finch is one of them." Keats mumbled again and I translated what I thought he was saying to Jilly. "Some of the crustiest people are the most sensitive and that's probably why they end up off the grid. I feel bad for Finch because the one time he joined a group, he got burned. It'll be hard for him to trust again."

"Did he like showing you around his apiary?"

"I think so, yeah. By the time we were done he was barely clashing with Edna. It helped that she was actually interested and asking the right questions." I glanced over at her. "But now we're heading into a job for Superfriend."

Jilly laughed. "I hope I live up to the hype."

"The bar is high, yet you always surpass it." I made a turn onto the highway that led to Dorset Hills. We weren't going that far, but it was the better route for avoiding traffic and detection. "I wish I'd known in high school there were friends like you." Keats had his nose out the window but his mumble was clear nonetheless. "You're right, buddy. I needed a good dog and a good friend of the human persuasion. Instead, my posse consisted of the romantic poets and a few fine novelists."

"Didn't your family count for something?" Jilly twisted her hair into a loose knot and sighed. "I was practically estranged from mine in school. But yours is different."

"They had their own lives. Poppy was a dropout with a massive chip on her shoulder. Daisy fell in love and married young. Iris and Violet were busy 'finding themselves' after graduating. That left Asher, who was incredibly popular and the life of every party. He did try to include me but I couldn't handle the pressure. I think we were both happier when I found my fictional crew in the library." I took my eyes off the highway for a second to look at Jilly. "Regrets? Not a one. It was time well spent. In addition to the literary greats, I read every issue of National Geographic and a lot of detective novels. They prepared me for what we do today."

Jilly's lip twitched. "Which is?"

"Pursue justice for animals and the good people of Clover Grove." I left the highway at the second exit. "And sometimes the bad ones, since it's hard to tell the difference. We're on the side of the underdog."

"And underbee."

"Underfox, underparrot, underrabbit and sundry other under-critters."

She plucked Percy from her lap and held the cat to her chest. The dog was getting excited, and his white paws were dancing and catching Percy in the fancy moves—probably quite intentionally. "And how might we be doing that today? I notice you like to wait till we're nearly at our destination before telling me in case I refuse."

"Am I really that transparent?" There was a small strip mall with a few shops on the side of the road and I pulled into the parking lot.

Jilly scanned the shops. "Maybe not. I can't see you being interested in sporting goods, a manicure, new flooring or yarn."

"That's where you're wrong. I have a yen to crochet."

The double yelp of laughter from her and the dog made me happy. Humor in hard times was a huge help in keeping me grounded.

"I don't believe you, Ivy Galloway. You don't sit still long enough to do crafts."

"A girl can change." Putting the truck in park, I checked my hair in the rearview. "On that note, how do I look?"

"You care less about how you look than you do about crafting. Ivy, what's going on? You're worrying me."

"Relax, my friend. I may be a bit eccentric, but I still care about what people think of me. At least, a few of you." I beckoned and got out of the truck. "Today, an old injury is aching, like my bum ankle on a damp day." We met at the front of the vehicle and I looked down. "Do these boots make my feet look fat?"

Realization dawned in Jilly's eyes. "Ah, Kayla Bouchard. She works at Stitch and Miss."

"Owns it. And we're here to share our condolences over the loss of her longtime leader in Clover Grove society."

"Oh, great. I wonder if Edna packs a flask in the go-kit."

"I didn't see one," I said, leading her to the store window. "But there's a pipe if you think tobacco might help."

"Good icebreaker, I suppose, but I'll pass."

I stared at the window display of rather gaudy sweaters and shawls. Despite my inability to sit still and focus, I'd always had a fascination for needlecraft. The idea of making hats, sweaters and mittens appealed to me and would probably be good for my busy brain. For the moment, I settled for buying gifts from a couple of fine yarn artists in town.

Stitch and Miss had a different aesthetic. It was like someone had gathered a bunch of scraps and cobbled them together in big, loose stitches. The hill country climate would make these items impractical, no matter the season. Perhaps, as with high school, what was "cool" didn't need to make sense. Sometimes, it was about cachet versus crochet.

The stenciling on the glass showed Kayla Bouchard Ware had cropped her maiden name to an initial.

"Kayla B. Ware," I said aloud. "Clever. If these are her original designs, though, I'm not buying."

"Not to my taste, either, but what do I know? I've never been crafty."

"We're crafty in an entirely different way. Sleuthing is an under-rated art form."

Keats herded us to the door, tail waving merrily. He was looking forward to this, possibly because Jilly, normally so calm and collected, was fidgeting with her purse. She clicked the snap half a dozen times, and then picked Percy up from the sidewalk.

"You want me to make small talk about crochet?" she said. "Just so you know, I'd rather pursue someone in a golf cart, climb into a cemetery or any of the other crazy things you've made me do." She stroked the cat so firmly he gave a snippy meow. "Except the crocodile episode. Crochet beats crocs, I suppose."

I considered mentioning the croc had been a gator but decided against it. Turning with my hand on the doorknob, I grinned. "This visit has you in knots, Jilly. Why so triggered by crochet?"

She let out a small groan. "Gran. Every gift for every occasion is handmade and in no way suited to my personality. I love her, so I have to fake it." Pushing my hand away, she opened the door. "I'll face those knotty demons and fake it today, too. For the bees."

"For the bees," I said, entering the store ahead of her.

"Ivy Galloway, what a surprise!" Kayla Bouchard Ware was holding a basket of colorful skeins of yarn and didn't look surprised at all. It was actually hard to tell how she was feeling because her eyes were so puffy it looked like bruising. I almost wondered if she'd been stung, but the tissues sticking out of her pocket suggested she was just grieving hard. "You look great."

"You, too," I said, before introducing Jilly. While Kayla had never been as pretty as Tammi in school, she'd aged well. The blonde highlights were gone, likely sacrificed to the demands of the family in photos on the shelf behind the cash register. With a natural hair color about the same as mine, it would have been hard work to stay blonde. "I like your hair."

"Thanks. Yours is nice, too. A ponytail is so practical."

It was probably a dig, but I didn't get a good look at her eyes before they dropped to my feet. Maybe it was old habit, or maybe she was deliberately playing on my insecurities to gain the upper hand—or foot, in this case. Either way, I felt teenage Ivy stir uneasily and knew I had to act quickly to regain my equilibrium. What use were big feet if they didn't keep you steady?

Keats leaned into my leg to give me more strength to face the past. "I see you're admiring my boots, Kayla. Steel toed and rock solid. I get a discount at the hardware store and could hook you up."

Jilly dropped Percy and grabbed my arm in the Blackwood pincer. She was giving me a little yarn, but not enough to hang myself.

"Work boots aren't required in a business like this," Kayla said, lifting a black ankle boot and angling it toward me. "These do the trick. Italian leather."

"Still a size six? That's amazing after six children."

Her mouth dropped open. "Excuse me? Your feet don't grow from childbirth. And I only have four."

The Blackwood pincer closed hard, but a mumble below urged me to clear the teen toxins out of my system. Kayla had trapped me in bathroom cubicles several times at Tammi's command. Once, I missed history class and had to slither under a bank of stalls to make it to math.

"Still, it was a lot to carry," I said. "A solid work boot takes you from playground to bee yard."

Kayla set the basket of yarn on the floor beside her sharp boots. Then she straightened and smoothed her sweater. The colorful patchwork cardigan was probably a work uniform rather than a legit style choice. The more she resembled her customers, the more yarn and other products she could sell. Kayla had been a chameleon since sixth grade, disguising her true self to stand behind Tammi. Would that change with the queen bee gone, or was it too late for her to develop a personality all her own?

"What do you want, Ivy?" she asked. "You've gone out of your way to avoid us since you came back to Clover Grove, and now you're here in my store. I doubt you've developed a sudden interest in crafts."

I stared around and my eyes landed on a fluffy orange investigator on a long shelf near the rear of the store. "Don't be so sure. I'm super interested in what you have back there."

Keats herded Jilly and me past Kayla, his black ears flattening in judgement of her. They perked right up again as we stood in front of the shelf. Arranged in two rows was a veritable zoo of crocheted animals. There were cows, horses, sheep, chickens, goats, donkeys, a swan, a llama, an alpaca, and many others in the row behind. Percy swatted a stitched orange cat off the shelf, where it landed at Jilly's feet. She picked it up, automatically cradling it in the crook of her arm, just as she would the ginger marauder himself. He stuck his paw between sheep, hooked out another figure and flung it in my direction. I caught it and stared at the black and white crocheted dog with one blue button eye, and one brown.

"What on earth...?" Jilly began.

Kayla tried to grab my crocheted dog but the real one fended her off with a mumble that verged on a growl.

Meanwhile, I lifted my hand and started naming the animals on my farm and others I'd supported along the way. On a lower shelf sat a veritable fluffle of colorful crocheted rabbits. Opal and her friends had certainly caught someone's imagination. "Did you make these, Kayla?"

She ran a hand over her impeccably flat-ironed hair. "Not me. My daughter, Linzy. She loves animals."

"You mean she loves *my* animals," I said. "Pretty near every creature I've ever owned or helped is sitting here. It's a Runaway Farm tribute band."

Jilly set crochet Percy on the shelf and collected the real cat while doing her own inventory. "No Picasso," she pronounced. "He was easy to miss."

"Which one is he?" Kayla asked. "Linzy will want to know."

Jilly gave me a chance to answer before saying, "A small friend who's moved on, now."

I wasn't sure what to make of the collection and tilted the crochet dog in my hand to look at the flesh-and-blood version. Keats let his mouth drop into a happy pant, unconcerned. In fact, the mumble that followed suggested he was flattered by this crafty attention. To me, it felt more like an invasion of our privacy, such as it was. Kayla B. Ware hadn't welcomed me home, or even acknowledged my existence when we passed in the street or the grocery store, yet she was clearly watching my every move. One day, when the time was right, she'd find a vulnerability bigger than my feet to exploit.

"Linzy is talented," I said, at last.

Kayla pressed her lips together and shrugged. "I suppose. I don't always understand her and we're quite different."

Jilly summoned the blazing smile that won over the most cynical executives. "You're running a yarn and craft store and Linzy's creating some wonderful pieces. Sounds like you have plenty in common." She picked up a three-inch long, crocheted yellow-and-black insect. "Your little bee didn't stray far from the hive. Maybe she'd like to visit Runaway Farm."

Kayla and I glanced at each other, startled. I liked kids, but I wasn't thrilled about having a former foe and her progeny on my turf.

"Linzy would love that," Kayla said. "She's asked a hundred times."

Jilly's smile amped up another notch. "We'll make it happen. Won't we, Ivy?"

"Sure. After the dust settles." Keats gave a pant-laugh and I realized how that might sound to Kayla. "Not Tammi's dust. I'm so sorry for your loss, Kayla."

She snatched the dog from my hands and put it back on the shelf. "My heart is broken. Tammi and I were best friends for so long."

If her heart were truly broken, she'd been hiding it well thus far. Puffy eyes aside.

I took the little bee from Jilly and examined it. "You enjoyed beekeeping together?"

Kayla took the bee from me and set it beside the dog. "It was Tammi's passion. She didn't have kids, so she threw herself into it. Between my family and the store, I couldn't do much until recently."

"She was training you to take over her hives." I picked up the bee again. "You're probably the only person she trusted. I could tell how attached she was to them. We spoke in the farmer's market yesterday."

"I know, Ivy. She said you were asking questions and I told her to be careful. When you stick your nose in, someone ends up dying. Now look what's happened." She took the bee back and this time, held onto it. "I wish Linzy would find another hobby. Her interest in you is unhealthy."

"There's nothing healthier than a hard day's work on the farm. Turning manure into designer fertilizer makes me happy."

Her eyes narrowed and instead of intimidation, I felt... pride. Knowing that Linzy admired me despite Kayla's disgust was very heartening.

"Back in school, you didn't have a sense of humor, Ivy," she said.

"I did, but I was too scared to speak. You, Tammi and Nadia and the rest of your crew beat the humor out of some and burned it out of others."

Kayla opened her mouth to light a new fire but Jilly beat her to it. "We're here to talk about bees, remember? Something we all care about. Kayla, you must have felt honored when Tammi chose you to step into her shoes."

"Of course. Yes."

Keats raised his paw to point out the silent "but" hanging in the air.

"An apiary is a big responsibility and Tammi had a lot of hives," I said. "Must have felt a bit overwhelming."

Kayla rolled the crocheted bee between her palms. "I suppose. My youngest is a toddler and the thought of having nearly a hundred hives behind the house worried me. Plus, bees are delicate. I didn't want to let Tammi down." She put the bee on the shelf. "Especially if she ever came back."

That put a different spin on things. If Tammi were only giving Kayla temporary custody, it would have increased the pressure to do right by the bees. Maybe she had arranged to have them "stolen" to get off the hook. "Sounds like Tammi was handing you the torch, including leadership of the bee club, and yet you didn't really want any of it."

"It's not that I didn't want it. Like you said, it was an honor."

"And a lot of work with a young family," Jilly suggested.

"My husband is away on business a lot. He says beekeeping is stupid and honey is overrated." She glanced around the store before setting the bee on the shelf. "He thinks knitting and crafts are stupid, too."

My heart softened as I thought about how supportive Kellan was of my interests, all of them more eccentric than beekeeping and crochet. "That must be hard. Did you think about offering this honor to someone else who had more capacity? Tammi was your best friend. She would have understood."

Her expression turned sour. "I hinted and she wouldn't hear of it. She was planning to come back every few weeks to check on things. Keep the club stable." Her eyes stayed on the animal gallery. "I doubt they'd have let me keep the role till Tammi's first visit home. People resented a newbie sailing in and getting so many thriving, productive hives."

"Mrs. Gillespie?" I asked. "Must be hard when the principal takes a stand against you. She still scares me."

Kayla finally found a weak smile. "I'm used to her now. Tammi and I joined the reunion planning committee and got on her good side. She still didn't like us."

That was a mark in Fiona's favor. "And she wanted the hives?"

"Lots of people did. Tammi made good money the last couple of years. Very good money. And didn't lose a single hive. She was a bee whisperer." Sighing, she examined the crocheted bee again. "And look what happened to her precious bees on the day I was taking them. If she were alive, she'd—"

"Swat you with her pom-poms for blaming yourself," Jilly interrupted. "This had nothing to do with you. Tammi would know it was a plot."

I nudged the front row of farm animals aside to look at the others. "Why didn't the attacker wait till Tammi left for the city?"

"We have a security system. My husband's hobby is collecting antique cars." Under her breath she added, "Not stupid, apparently."

"It sounds like the robbery was actually timed to beat the move."

"Probably." She turned and shrugged again. "I've shared all of this with Chief Harper, Ivy, and he told me not to talk to you."

"I bet he did. But we both know you're doing it for Linzy."

"For my daughter? Why would you say that?"

"Because she cares about animals, including bees. I bet she's as upset about their loss as she is about Tammi."

For the first time, Kayla's dark eyes watered. "More. Linzy can't stop worrying about those bees. Are they homeless? Cold? Starving? So many questions and no answers." Kayla handed the bee back to me. "Maybe you can answer them. I think she's counting on it."

"Does this one have a name?" I asked, waggling the bee.

"A name? No."

"I bet it does. You're worried Linzy will turn out like me."

Crossing her arms, she scowled. "Ivy, every mother in town is worried their kids will turn out like you."

Keats took a lunge at her smart boots that she easily sidestepped.

Jilly made the next move. "Kayla, Ivy's a hero who's solved plenty of crimes to keep kids and animals safe."

Crossing in front of Kayla, I grabbed another critter. "Look at this! I've dreamed of owning a wallaby."

"Dream bigger," Kayla said. "It's a kangaroo."

"Gosh, no," Jilly said. "They're ridiculous and fighty. We can't handle that."

Kayla shrugged. "There's more where that came from. Things with wings. Things with spines. Things with fins."

"I've gotta talk to this kid," I said.

She took back the kangaroo. "Save the bees, Ivy. And come to the class reunion."

"I'll consider the reunion if you promise to be nice to my sister."

"Poppy?" She flapped both arms to waft us to the door. "I was more scared of her than of Mrs. Gillespie. Happy to avoid her."

I stopped in the doorway. "Call off your backers, too. You're the queen bee now, Kayla B. Ware. If you want me to help save Tammi's bees, promise you'll start a new, kinder era."

Keats circled her legs and applied some fang to Italian leather. "Sure, whatever." We stepped outside and Kayla added quietly, "For the record, it's Bernice."

I turned. "Pardon me?"

She pointed at the crochet bee in my hand. "Linzy named her after my great aunt."

The door closed behind us and I turned to Jilly. "Isn't that strange? I chose the same name."

My best friend just smiled. "Coincidence works in mysterious ways."

"I guess, yeah. How is it I can like that kid and hate—"

Jilly cut off the last word. "We don't hate anyone except killers. Is Kayla one of them?"

Watching Keats and Percy frolic ahead of us to the truck, I shook my head. "Not according to them. But I'm reasonably sure Kayla still kills reputations."

CHAPTER ELEVEN

S utton, my favorite nephew, clutched his belly and groaned on the faux leather sofa in the reception area outside Fiona Gillespie's office. Then he gave a wracking shudder and writhed, before rasping, "Help me. Help. Me."

Keats' mouth dropped open in a pant-laugh. He was enjoying this fine performance by a young actor whose previous ambition had been to become a grease monkey. Like his twin, Weston, Sutton's true gift was auto repair and an abiding love of motors would save him from the dissolute life of the child star.

Well, that and his lack of theatrical talent.

I should have given more direction when I texted to offer him the role. He'd taken "act sick and call me to pick you up" as "depict your deathbed scene."

"Ivy, thank goodness you're here. I was about to call 911."

Mrs. Gillespie came around her desk and stood in the doorway of her office. It looked exactly as it had during my tenure here, with the addition of a few more plaques and awards. Like the best educators, she was committed to continuous learning and had three master's degrees. None, luckily, in theater arts.

"Sutton will be fine, ma'am, I'm sure of it." I sent Keats over to collect my nephew. "Did you eat something nasty, buddy?"

Pushing himself up on one elbow, Sutton nodded. "Couple tuna sandwiches. Few days old. Thought they'd be okay in my locker but then my friends complained about the smell. Couldn't let them go to waste."

The principal's shudder was only slightly less robust than Sutton's. "Head home before all that comes back, young man."

Sutton took his cue. Covering his mouth, he sprung upright and then ran out of the office. "Gonna hurl."

"Oh my," I said. "Daisy will flip. She's a stickler for hygiene."

Mrs. Gillespie nodded. "Always was. Did you know she used to stay behind and help the janitor of the day? Miss Flicken worked into her seventies and Daisy couldn't bear to see her mopping alone."

"Aw, that's my sis. She pretty much raised the rest of us and her reward was a quadruple dose of hooligan."

"The older twins aren't so bad, but the younger two..." She patted her bouffant hair. "They've aged me prematurely. That's saying something given how many students have passed through these doors."

"Oh, I know. I feel for Daisy. That's why I offered to pick Sutton up today. Anything that makes her life a little easier. She's earned a break."

The principal stared at me over her glasses. They were dark and heavy on the bottom and rimless on the top. It was as if her raptor eyes needed support and freedom to fly at the same time. I suppose someone in her position had to take in everything at once.

"So, you're not here to question me about Bee a Good Citizen?" The raptor eyes narrowed. "Kellan said you might, and that I should resist with all the strength I've gained from dealing with manipulative students."

"Manipulative? Did he use that word?"

Her thin lips quirked. "I may have misheard. Your brother said, 'twisty.' That I know."

I couldn't help smiling myself. "Did you ever think Asher would end up a cop?"

"Not in my wildest dreams. But unlike some of the teachers, I sensed he'd do something worthwhile. I imagined a sports commentator, or even a gym teacher."

"A teacher? Ash?"

"Sure. Don't underestimate your brother. He still coaches football when we're in a bind. Asher's kept a few kids out of trouble and he'll make a great dad someday." My expression must have softened because she smiled. "You're never too old to learn something new about your siblings, Ivy."

Keats poked me in the shin and mumbled audibly. "Yeah. Right," I said. Mrs. Gillespie's eyebrows rose, probably wondering whether I was responding to her or the dog. "Speaking of siblings, can you tell me more about Poppy's time here? I was surprised that she wants to come to the reunion."

It was like a veil dropped over the raptor eyes. "I'm sure she'd be happy to share. You girls seem close. I admire Poppy for taking extra credits online. Do you know if she has plans for higher education?"

Now she was testing me. "Still weighing her options. Working at the farm is probably making education look good."

"She was a bright student. Not like you, but very capable. And artistic."

"Artistic?" My voice sounded false and Keats poked me in the shin to remind me of my HR training. "Yes, she does have quite an eye."

"For a while she was never without her sketchbook and then, one day, it was just gone."

I leaned against the receptionist's desk, since no one was using it. "I'd forgotten. That probably happened around the time she was expelled. Someone said she was wrongfully accused of something and should lodge a complaint with the school board." Edna had merely passed along a rumor but it was worth lobbing out there.

The hint of a smile was gone now. "There's a statute of limitations and it's long past."

"If there's one thing I learned in corporate HR... it's never too late to make a stink."

Fiona's squint came back. "Why are you really here, Ivy?"

My HR smile unfurled like the school flag rising. "The upcoming reunion made me nostalgic. I just wanted to come in and take a look around." Keats and I lifted our noses together and took a deep breath. "You know what I smell?"

"Manipulation?" she asked, the glint behind her glasses returning. "Sneakery? That was something else Asher mentioned. Evocative, but not a real word."

"Books. The library door must be open. Do you mind if I poke my head in while I wait for Sutton? It's next to the boys' room."

"Not at all." I moved to the door of the reception area and she followed. "I'll come with you."

She was a worthy adversary. Understandable, given decades spent outsmarting adolescents. Still, Fiona was no match for my dog, and as we left the principal's office, he moved into position between us and eased her further away. The halls were quiet but that would change when class let out in 25 minutes. Judging by the swaying white tuft on Keats' tail, it was enough. Time to let the dog take over.

He shot me a look with his blue eye and mumbled something like, "Leave it in my capable paws."

Mrs. Gillespie's head swiveled in my peripheral vision, perhaps trying to get a read on the dog. While she was as good a student of human nature as I was, hopefully I had her beat when it came to animals.

"I always knew you'd go far, Ivy," she said. "The corporate career I expected. But the rest, well... I admit I was surprised."

"Farming? Me, too. I never liked getting my hands dirty. And now..." I waggled my fingers and sighed over the state of my manicure. "Lost cause."

"I was speaking more of your work in the, uh, community."

Her heels clicked over the speckled floor. When I was 16, I knew every splotch. Now there were new generations of unsightly stains. Rather like the town itself.

"I was probably voted least likely to take down a criminal. And yet here we are."

Percy leapt from my shoulder to hers, and she gave a squeak of alarm. "Where did he come from?"

"Lost track of him earlier. Percy loves exploring."

While she tried to shoo the cat off her tweed shoulder, Keats slipped away. Around the corner there was a loud, metallic crash.

"Lionel! No!" Mrs. Gillespie sputtered the words and shifted her heels up a gear. Percy held on for dear life as she pulled her phone out of her skirt pocket and rounded the corner swiftly.

Lionel Stansbury was a founding father of Clover Grove and a proponent of education throughout hill country. Many schools had busts of him. It shouldn't have tipped so easily, but when Keats put his mind to something, it usually happened.

Slipping into the library, I took stock. There was no one behind the desk but I heard hushed voices in the stacks. If memory served, they were deep in the 600s, somewhere near animal husbandry and well before home economics. I headed into another aisle that had once held a meager selection of psychology and self-help books, now grown immensely. Would students really take on the challenge of improving themselves before their brains matured in their late twenties?

A movement overhead told me Percy had left the principal and joined my cause. Moreover, he was not alone. His eyes were trained on the ceiling and I saw something small buzz past. At the end of the row, the cat stopped and crouched, tail lashing. Library ambushes were among his favorites. He could get the aerial view with minimal effort, while keeping his fur pristine. Cats were masters of energy conservation.

I slowed to let the worn carpet swallow the thud of my boots and immediately recognized the voices. One belonged to longtime school librarian, Delsie Stubbing. She had seemed old when I was in school but was likely in her sixties now and looked about the same. If Dottie and Thelma were any indication, she had at least two decades of service ahead of her.

The other voice was male and it sent a flash of annoyance through my chest. Clinton Sever had been my science teacher for two years. He turned down my requests to skip the dissection segments of the curriculum, despite my offers to do special projects that would have been quintuple the work. It was probably the only time I ever took a stand in school. I saw no reason to kill frogs or anything else and go poking around. Even then there were alternatives in video. At worst, one rat could die for the sake of our education.

Mr. Sever not only declined my request, he also mocked me repeatedly in class about my delicate sensibilities. That in turn opened the door for Tammi and her squad to ridicule more than my feet. "Frog-lover," they'd whisper. Sniffing loudly in the hallways, they'd ask, "Do you smell formaldehyde?" Eventually my nickname evolved from Flubby Flappers to Froggy Flappers and stayed that way until Kellan and I started dating. No one guessed he'd end up police chief then, but his solid sports career, solemn demeanor and good looks were enough to make the mean girls stutter in confusion. I liked to think it was the first time they questioned their judgement and hoped it paved the way for other victims.

Keats poked me in the leg to jar me out of my reverie. Then he lifted his paw to point to the row behind us. Seeing movement, I applied my eye to a crack between books. Sutton grinned back at me. "What are we doing?" he whispered. "Spying on old man Sever?"

I held my finger to my lips and turned back to my investigation. Meanwhile, Sutton stealthily retreated and joined me in my row. For a kid closing in on six feet, he had moves.

We seemed to be joining Delsie and Mr. Sever mid-conversation. Unlike Delsie, Clint Sever looked every bit of his age. His hair had long since departed and he clearly never worried about sunscreen. Gravity—or sheer cussedness—pulled his lips into a permanent frown. And yet, he had once been handsome enough to break a heart or two on the faculty, including that of his Spanish teacher wife.

"You know I can't let you check out books, Clint," Delsie said. "You're not on the faculty anymore. Try the public library."

"I don't want Dottie Bridges knowing my business," he said. "Besides, I volunteer in shop classes here. If I oversee circular saws and motors, I can handle a book."

"Why not just use the computers?" she asked. "Our print reference material on apiculture is out of date."

"Beekeeping hasn't changed, Delsie." His voice was as mocking as it had been when I tried to wriggle out of dissection. "And you can't trust anything on the internet."

"The best and most current information is online," the librarian persisted. "You just need to be judicious."

"I'm not leaving a digital footprint. When I quit my job here, people said some terrible things."

Delsie's fingers clenched around a fat reference book as if she were holding in her thoughts. Finally she set it down and let go. "Clint, you didn't quit, you were fired, no matter what package they gave you. Everyone knew your business and it didn't take a digital footprint. But enough time has passed that you have a fresh start."

"There are no fresh starts in this town," he griped.

It was one thing we agreed on. I doubted there were many.

"Takes five years tops," Delsie said. "You keep a low profile and pop up doing good works and the slate wipes clean. Don't ask me how I know."

Clint laughed. "I know how you know but I remember everything, and so do most people. Just let me take the book. It's the best reference going."

"You'd do better asking the bee club for help. Isn't that the point of it?"

"I lost two hives over the winter and I can't risk looking sloppy when I'm gunning for president."

"I thought that role already belonged to Kayla Ware."

"That girl never even looked into a hive until a few months ago. What does she know about beekeeping?"

"She was groomed by one of the best," Delsie said. "At least according to Fiona. Tammi had a gift and she passed her knowledge to her best friend."

Mr. Sever rolled his eyes. "Neither was in it for the right reasons. Those girls always had ulterior motives. Never met a bigger pair of schemers, and I've seen a lot of kids come and go."

Fine, I was wrong. We shared two views in common.

"They were a handful," Delsie said. "Along with Nadia Reddy. That poor girl was always running to keep up with Tammi and Kayla. She's started beekeeping to stay relevant."

"Yeah. I couldn't help but wonder if she took the queen bee out of the equation to move up the ranks faster."

"Clinton Sever." Delsie shook her finger. "Don't say things like that. Books have ears."

Sutton and I froze in our row, but Keats just opened his mouth in a silent pant-laugh.

"Everyone's speculating," Delsie continued. "And if you're so worried about gossip, you should wait a while to start talking about your run for club president."

"I'm only talking to you, my old friend. Kellan Harper will get this sorted out soon enough. Never thought that kid would amount to much, given his rough start in life. He surprised me. Galloway, too."

Delsie laughed at that. "I figured Asher would end up driving a truck. A big rig, if he found the right girl and settled down. Color me surprised."

Anger welled up in my chest and the nerves in my legs twitched. I wanted to charge out and confront them. Support came from the usual source, Keats, but also an unusual one. Sutton pressed his lips to my ear and said, "Forget it. People say worse about me and I'll prove 'em wrong."

"I meant the Galloway girl," Clint said. "Which one is the troublemaker?"

"Ivy," Delsie supplied. "She was fine earlier but went rogue. Some of the others... well, I figured they'd be bagging groceries or worse. Galloway is a hard name to climb out from under."

I never thought my nephew would be the one holding me back from actions I'd regret. His grip was harder than Jilly's and his words more pointed. "Who cares? They're losers."

"Losers," Clint said, making me think he overheard. "Especially the middle one with colored streaks in her hair."

"Poppy, although she's toned down the dye lately. The others turned out okay, considering. But the next generation is even worse. Fiona says two janitors quit because of the twins' graffiti. Couldn't keep up."

"The boys likely have brain damage from the paint fumes," Clint said. "Irreversible."

Keats kept busy circling both Sutton and me to hold us in place. My nephew's face turned scarlet under his freckles.

Delsie finally handed Clint Sever a book and started leading him away. "It's not paint, it's genetics. Fiona also said that Daisy—"

Sutton was listening closely now, but a scrabble from on top of

the metal stacks drowned out the librarian's words. Percy leapt from one bookcase to the next, until Delsie and Clint went after him into the poetry section.

It gave me breathing room to get my nephew out of the library, past the group kneeling beside the bust of Lionel and out the exit to the back field.

CHAPTER TWELVE

I held the door open a crack until Percy joined us, leaving the dog to manage Sutton, who was determined to go back.

"What was she saying about my mom?"

Keats drove us around the side of the building to an area that used to be called the "smoking lounge" when smoking was permitted on school property. "Who cares? They're losers, remember? There's no finer mother than Daisy, and if you don't see that now, you will."

The color faded from his cheeks, leaving them pale under the freckles. "Mom's solid. Especially considering Dahlia."

"Exactly. Call her Grandma. She's ready now. Or just Nanny."

He rolled his dark eyes. "Nice try. Dahlia scares me a little, you know. Wild card. But she's all right. Knows how to handle a car."

I let my hair loose and shook it out. The ponytail was giving me a headache, or at least contributing to the one Delsie and Clint started. "Sutt, don't let your grandmother drive. Her license was revoked because she hit so many stop signs."

"That was before. She's getting better all the time. You'll see."

"What I'll see is Kellan having a heart attack before I can marry him. Is that what you want?"

Deploying the age-old art of distraction, he herded me into the smoking area, which had a roof that sheltered it from wind and rain. Since it was off limits for smoking now, it had taken on a new life as a makeshift art gallery. My nephew waved one arm around to show it off. "See? This is where I got my brain damage."

When Delsie and Clint mentioned graffiti, I expected the usual tagging or slogans that were lost on my generation. What I saw instead was genuine art. At least, it was art to me, because it was a veritable zoo.

"Wow! Sutton, is this what I think it is?"

He pointed with a flourish. "Alvina. Florence. Drama Llama. Clippers. Archie. Veronica. Picasso. Duncan." He rhymed off the rest of the crew, grunting in frustration when he reached a blurry spot. "They scrubbed Wilma again. Don't know what they've got against pigs."

The only animals he didn't name were an oversized black-and-white dog and an orange cat who sat square in the middle of the gallery. The inspirations for them were staring up at their likenesses, and Keats mumbled approval. The paint was vibrant and their eyes neon.

"This is awesome!" I nearly dropped my phone because I was so eager to get the gallery on camera. "Sutton, *you're* awesome."

"Can't take all the credit. Lots of hands and lots of spray cans. You're a legend in town, Aunt Ivy."

The "aunt" was rare, but I didn't let it go to my head. "I had no idea you painted. I thought you were just an artist with cars."

"Both are arts," he said. "Not everyone agrees. For now, I just make art on the side."

"On the side of buildings, you mean."

"Exactly. Even more after today. The janitors basically gave up when we started the farm art project. Maybe they like it."

"Your mother won't. Defacing property is still against the law."

He shrugged. "She already knows."

"Daisy knows about this?" My voice showed my shock.

"Sure. Weston and I drive her over whenever a new pig goes up. Ultimately, Wilma will prevail." Grabbing my elbow, he pulled me close to the wall. In the corner was a bird I took to be an emu. It wasn't as finely rendered as the rest, but still had a flair to it.

"Elaine?" I asked.

"Look at the tag," he prompted. It wasn't a name or initials, but a white flower with a yellow center, dropping a few petals.

"Daisy." My sister was tagging the school building with the sons she herself had called delinquents. I shook my head as we turned away. "Seriously? I don't even know my own sister."

He skipped like a kid, which also surprised me until I realized Keats was motivating his pant cuffs. "Don't worry," Sutton said. "She'll come back to clean it off. The buzz lasts a couple of days and then the urge to purge builds up."

I glanced over my shoulder as we left. "No cameras?"

He squealed a little as he hopped. "None working. We're picking up tech skills to help the family business."

Crooking my eyebrow, I asked, "Which one?"

"Vigilantism, next generation." He ran a few paces, turned, and aimed some martial arts kicks in my direction. He added a flurry of air punches for punctuation. "You're getting old, Ivy. Can't keep this up forever."

I felt tired just watching him and for a moment I doubted my capacity to raise kids, let alone continue to put criminals away.

Keats turned his teeth to my cuffs and I found a pocket of energy. Spinning, I aimed a kick at Sutton's butt and sent him flying. "Take that from an old gal."

"Lame," he said, jumping up and kicking me in my own butt.

I staggered forward until my hands landed in grass. "Hey. Respect. I've got something you'll never have, kid."

"Oh, yeah? What's th—?"

The word was cut off with a shrill scream. This time he was spinning with a border collie attached to the butt of his jeans.

"The best dog in the world, that's what." Percy sprung onto Sutton's shoulder and went for the ride, too. "And the best cat." Pushing myself to my feet, I laughed as I ran ahead to the parking lot.

The next generation of Galloway blood had a lot going for it. All I had to do was make sure they all graduated on the right side of the law.

CHAPTER THIRTEEN

A bee zipped back and forth as I mended the fence of the goat pen that afternoon. Aerial acrobatics began as I walked to the truck, suggesting I was heading in the right direction.

"Sorry, Bernice, you've got to cool your wings. I'm not doing this without Jilly."

My confidence had ebbed, despite the fun I'd had with my nephew at the school earlier. Hearing what my former teacher and the school librarian thought about me and my family stuck a knife deep in the part of me that never quite graduated, let alone evolved into the owner of Runaway Farm and Inn. I wondered if we all had parts that never toughened up. I had no problem dispatching criminals but what those two said about us was criminally harsh, especially when their mission was to shape young minds. No wonder so few people who left Clover Grove came back. If it hadn't been for my twin loves—books and Kellan—I probably would have been permanently disenchanted, too.

Of my family, only Asher had really found himself here. The rest were still searching, perhaps partly due to a lack of inspiring role models. That could make all the difference in a kid's life.

"It almost makes me want to teach, boys," I told Keats and Percy as I let them in the truck. "My plate's already too full, but I'm going to see what I can do. If Asher volunteers at school, I can, too. Better yet, I can enlist some of my friends in town and beyond. They inspire me and they can inspire kids. I'll speak to Mrs. Gillespie again when this is over."

Jilly overheard at least some of my monologue as she joined me. "'This' being the murder investigation?" she asked, walking around to the passenger side.

"Exactly. Then you're going to show off your chefly skills in the family studies class."

"Happy to do it," she said, climbing in and buckling her seatbelt. "We could also speak about our work experience to the business class as well."

"Great idea. Some people will thrive packed into a corporate tower, unlike me."

"Better fit for most than farm life, I expect." Jilly let the pets settle on her nice coat with a resigned sigh. Every day she wiped it down with a lint brush, but fur was a constantly renewable resource. "Maybe you can interest some in manure."

I turned the key in the ignition. "Most students here probably grow up around manure. Sometimes you need to get away to appreciate it. Maybe we could do a little outreach to expats. See if we can attract talent back here. Dorset Hills is doing something right. Lots of people stay and new blood is always arriving. We're the dud of hill country."

Jilly laughed. "If Clover Grove was a dud, land prices wouldn't be so high."

"Homesteaders like Finch Pefferlaw are driving costs up. None of our own stick around." I glanced at her before letting the truck roll forward. "Okay, some do. Kayla B. Ware has a business. But Tammi was leaving and I'm surprised it took her so long."

"And now we're visiting the third ranked bee?" Jilly asked. "Is there a fourth?"

"Not anymore. Nadia Reddy moved up from fourth place in tenth grade after another girl got expelled and was sent to live with an aunt. I don't think the others fully accepted Nadia. Just my impression."

"But they remained friends?"

"Delsie, the school librarian, said Nadia took up beekeeping to 'stay relevant,' so they must have kept the love alive. Figured she might have a lead on who'd want to kill Tammi. Or maybe she finally blew up from trying so hard and did it herself."

I looked up at the arching sign over the lane. Runaway Far, it said, since the "m" had rusted out. That's exactly what I wanted to do from high school politics.

"Has Kellan spoken to Nadia?" Jilly asked.

"Not sure. He's been working nonstop and the list is long. I figure it's reasonable that I'd want to chat with an old schoolmate."

"Someone you've shown zero interest in seeing since you came home?"

I smirked. "Takes time to get around to everyone. Besides, Nadia got more interesting when I learned she likes bees. I normally prioritize people who prioritize animals. You know that."

Jilly rolled down the window for Keats and he stuck his nose out to draw in a gusty snort. "Someone's enthusiastic."

"Bernice wanted to get going, too."

She turned and gave me a suspicious look. "Is that bee in the vehicle?"

"Technically, yes, but not in the cab. I saw her crawl through a slit in the cover over the bed. Scout bees can cover a good distance, but I guess she decided to conserve energy."

"So, what's our cover with Nadia?"

"I'm thinking we could ask her about supplying local honey for the inn. Tammi wanted to supply us and her hives were lost before Kayla took ownership. That makes Nadia the next logical choice."

Jilly tried to get the pets to settle but they were full of beans.

Keats was stepping on Percy and the cat was biting the dog's paws. "I'd rather support Finch, for what it's worth."

"He isn't producing enough yet, although he wants to grow."

"What about Fiona Gillespie? Or the retired teacher?"

"I'd buy watered down grocery store honey over theirs after what I saw today. I'm disappointed in Mrs. Gillespie. She sets the tone for the school, faculty and even former faculty."

Jilly patted my arm. "I'm sorry you overheard that, and especially Sutton. I've always thought this town underestimated the Galloways. Now that I'm a Galloway by marriage, I take it personally."

Keats pulled in his muzzle long enough to mumble something that sounded like, "Their loss" and also, "They'll be sorry."

"So, we're ambushing Nadia at her home?" Jilly asked.

"If necessary. But first we'll try her at work, where she can't turn us away."

"Oh, dear. I hate the workplace ambush. Two in one day is ambitious."

"This should be quiet. Even restful."

"Restful? What kind of job does Nadia have?"

"Not the kind she wanted, that's for sure. She dreamed of being in theater and had a couple of lead roles in school plays. She wasn't great, but I've seen worse."

"I suppose there isn't enough local theater in hill country to make a living," Jilly said.

"There are a few small theaters across the region but they're mostly shuttered." I glanced at her with a smile. "Remember our plan to bring culture back? Still a worthy goal, but in the meantime, people with dreams like that need to move. Or, in this case, put them to bed."

We pulled up beside Highway Mattress and Appliance, and Jilly laughed. Getting out, we walked the short distance to the door, only to find a small cardboard sign dangling there that read "Closed."

I never took signs at face value. Not when I had two genius pets to tell me the sign meant nothing. Keats went into a point and Percy jumped onto the windowsill and dug at the glass with both paws. His claws were sheathed and slid soundlessly over the pane.

Joining him, I peered inside. "There she is. On one of the mattresses."

Jilly picked up the cat but his paws continued to swish in the air as she lowered him to the ground. "Is Nadia okay? I'm not sure how to interpret Percy."

"I believe he's saying she's not dead, she's resting." I continued to stare inside. "Yep. Her hand moved."

"She's asleep on the job?" Jilly sounded horrified.

"Honestly, I'm not one to judge. I've crashed in the hay to catch forty winks. It'd be hard to pass up a dozen mattresses when business is slow." I looked up and down the highway. "I'm going to guess it's usually slow, at least on a weekday."

I walked over to the door and tried the knob. It opened easily and thus we truly gained the element of surprise. Nadia didn't stir until orange fur brushed repeatedly against her face. Then, she merely pushed the cat away, eyes still closed. Percy gave her a moment to reconsider and then seized a bit of skin on her arm and gave it a shake designed to kill a mouse. He had ripped me from sweet slumber that way and I knew only too well how it felt.

"What the—?" Nadia propped herself on one elbow and stared from the cat to me. "Froggy? Is that you?"

"I think you're still dreaming, Nadia," Jilly said. "This is Ivy Galloway and I'm Jilly Blackwood."

She sat up, brushed long, light brown hair out of her face and squinted. "Froggy, what are you doing here?"

"Why is she calling you that?" Jilly asked.

"Long story. It was one of my high school nicknames, unfortunately."

"Froggy Flappers," Nadia said, swinging her legs over the side of the bed. "I heard you like breaking into places. Stealing a mattress isn't as easy as you think. They're heavy and floppy. Or flappy, for you."

"The door was unlocked," I pointed out.

Jilly drew herself up to her full height. "We run an upscale inn and have no need for these. Especially the used showroom model."

Nadia's face may have flushed a little but the light was too dim to be sure. She hadn't been easily flustered in the old days. Now she smoothed her hair as she got up and walked to the counter. Hitting a light switch, she turned to stare as a bank of fluorescents flickered on. While yoga pants and a tight top showed she'd kept her cheerleader figure, time hadn't been as kind to her face. It was as if her harsh personality had permanently surfaced, displacing the glow of youth.

"What do you want, Frogs? I was told not to talk to you."

"Told by whom?" I let my eyes drift up and confirmed Bernice had joined us. She was exploring the showroom at cruising speed.

"Principal Gillespie called me to her office," Nadia said with a smirk. "First time in a while."

"Why would she do that?"

"I'm on the planning committee for the reunion." Walking to the door, Nadia removed the closed sign and hung it on a nail. "She said the best way to keep the reunion on track is to let Chief Harper do his work without your interference. I never understood what Kellan saw in you, Froggy." Her eyes dropped again. "I mean, has he seen your feet?"

Keats skulked up and lunged at Nadia's sneakers. She dodged the move easily, proving the fogginess of naptime was gone.

"You're being rude," Jilly said. "We came to talk to you about supplying honey for our inn and all you can do is slag Ivy."

"Not interested," Nadia said. "In you, Ivy or your la-dee-da inn." Keats lunged again, and she added, "Or your pets. Talk about rude."

"Keats." I snapped my fingers. "You are being rude to Nadia."

"He's rude to everyone," she said. "Thinks he's all that."

Keats' mouth opened in a self-satisfied pant and he came to lean against my leg. "He *is* all that. And for what it's worth, Kellan said my feet were all they should be. I'm a tall woman and tiny flappers wouldn't carry me."

"I heard you were kicking your nephew behind the school. Someone's got it on video."

Heat rose in my cheeks. "We were roughhousing. As family does. How's your little brother, Nadia?"

I'd heard he spent some time in jail and her expression confirmed it. "Unless you're here for a mattress or appliance, I'd like you to leave."

"Does the owner know you sleep on the product?" Jilly asked. "Sneakers and all?"

"Yep, because I am the owner, along with my husband. It's a professional perk. This has been a tough week, Froggy's Friend. I lost *my* best friend this week."

"I know," Jilly said. "We were sorry to hear about Tammi."

"Were you, though? Everyone said you and Ivy went right over to pick around in Tammi's yard. Stole the smoker passed down by her grandfather."

I wanted to laugh but swallowed hard instead. "We went over because Tammi offered to show us around her apiary before the hives went to Kayla. There were so many I figured she would split them between you. After all, you three were inseparable."

Her defiant gaze shifted as the dart hit home. "I figured so, too, and I've been beekeeping for years, unlike Kayla. But Tammi had her reasons, I guess."

Jilly's heart softened first. "Kayla's property is a fortress and Tammi worried about her bees. I'm sure it was nothing personal."

The kindness hit Nadia's shields and deflected. "What do you know about friendship? It's complicated."

"I know enough," Jilly said. "Ivy and I have been besties since college. Now we run our inn together."

"La-dee-da and good for you, Froggy's Friend. Things weren't always easy here, but I stood by Tammi no matter what. Kayla, too." She went over and perched on a mattress. "Now it's all gone."

"Hardly," I said. "You still have Kayla. You still have your bees."

She peered at her fingernails and I saw she still chewed them. I shuddered, remembering scabby fingers threatening me with a cigarette butt. "I'm selling my hives and getting out of the business. Too risky."

Bernice landed on the mattress, although Nadia wasn't aware of it. "How so? I hear bees are easy to manage with the right tools of the trade."

"It's not about that. Hill country bees are hardy and valuable. Tammi's hives were the best of the best and I have some of her lines." Bernice flew to Nadia's shoulder now. "They might come after me next so I'm getting out while I can."

"Anyone would be worried," Jilly said, making a brushing motion on her shoulder. "You should probably lock the door here when you're resting."

"Or get a rude dog," I suggested.

Nadia glared at us as she got up, and the bee lifted off before we had to tell her it was there. Walking back to the counter, she grabbed a shammy and then moved to a row of refrigerators. She started to buff stainless steel, and said, "Can you go? I'm busy."

Daisy would have been appalled by Nadia's lackluster technique, which left even more streaks. There was an art to polishing and my sister had mastered it.

"Tammi wouldn't want you to give up on your bees," I said. "Especially not if they came from her lines."

"Her bees really are the best. Mild mannered and huge honey producers. Plenty of us got started with her nucleus colonies and if she didn't like you, they cost a bomb." Nadia's shammy circles slowed even more. "But I never really wanted to keep bees anyway. It was just something we did because of Tammi."

I followed her and hopped onto a washing machine across the row. "I get that. You and Kayla probably did a lot of things you didn't want to because of Tammi."

"Maybe." Nadia turned quickly and from closer range, I saw her eyes were puffy and bloodshot. She was just as emotional over Tammi's loss as Kayla. "But I was lucky to be on Tammi's squad. It made me who I am today, Froggy. Think about that."

I did think about that as I glanced around the showroom. How much had Tammi's squad passed up because of their limiting beliefs about being backup singers to the star? The false prestige they had in high school may have kept them from achieving their authentic ambitions.

"You were a good actor in school," I said, welcoming Percy into my lap. "Did you ever pursue it?"

Shaking her head, she went back to buffing with a little more gusto. "It would have meant leaving and we committed to stay."

"You and your husband?"

"No, Tammi and Kayla. We were a team. Promised to stay till the end."

Keats' paw rose in a point and Percy trotted off in a zigzag that said he was tracking the bee. Bernice was accelerating from her slow cruise. All the critters were picking up on a vibe.

Hopping off the washer, I moved to Nadia's side of the aisle and leaned against a stove. "But Tammi was leaving Clover Grove."

"Yeah. Exactly." Her tone was flat and she moved to another fridge, further away.

"That must have been hard for you," Jilly said. "Best friends are forever." She smiled at me. "At least they are for us."

"We were going to chat online every day," Nadia said. "But it wouldn't have been the same. Kayla was too busy to hang out."

The small effort of buffing seemed too much and I sensed Nadia's despair. She had planned her life around the squad and now it had fallen apart.

"You must be questioning a lot, today," I said. "But disaster can mark a fresh start. A chance to do things another way and learn about yourself. That's how it happened for me and I've never been happier."

Moving even further away, she frowned. "I've heard about your bafflegab, Frogs. It won't work on me. Tammi was an awesome friend and we would have aged out at Sunny Acres together if not for..."

Her voice cut off abruptly and Keats' paw came back up.

"If not for Tammi breaking the squad vow?" I suggested, sending the dog to bring her back.

"Not Tammi." She dodged Keats and moved away again, not realizing that Percy was following on top of the fridges. "She was loyal. To us. To her bees. To the club."

Percy gave a couple of sweeps of a front paw and I heard the hint of claws on stainless. "What about Eddy?" I asked. "The taco king. Was she loyal to him?"

Reaching up, she snapped her shammy at Percy. That would have annoyed me if the cat hadn't leapt lightly away to the next fridge. "Of course she was. She wouldn't invite that kind of scandal. Her business depended on—"

"The good graces of the rumor mill?" I interrupted.

"I guess. We were part of the fabric of Clover Grove. For better or worse."

"For better or worse," Jilly repeated. "Did Tammi's husband stray?"

Nadia shot a glare her way. "No one knows what goes on in someone else's marriage, do they?"

Jilly laughed. "Everyone knows what goes on in mine. We live in Ivy's home. With her mother upstairs, her father nearby and sisters running in and out."

"Then you know how hard it is." Nadia flicked her shammy in our direction.

"I wouldn't have it any other way," Jilly said. "For lack of a better word, I belong to a hive now. We work hard together and achieve more for all."

"Dahlia's the queen of your hive. I'd question your lines before having kids." Nadia's snicker earned her a nip in the calf. Keats only liked snark if it was coming from him.

"We're happy in our little community," Jilly said. "It would rock us to the core if there was infidelity."

Nadia's buffing was getting erratic and I sensed our time was short. "It sounds like Tammi's husband ruined everything."

"Basically, yeah. He was the one who wanted to move to the city. Tammi had to give up her hives, her honey. It broke her heart. *Our* heart. We only had the one, you see."

For the first time ever, I felt compassion for Nadia.

"I'm sorry for what happened, Nadia. But there are so many amazing people in Clover Grove. I've made lots of new friends since coming back."

"I don't want your pity, Frogs. I had it all and now I don't." She whipped her shammy at me but it fell a foot short. "Why would I *ever* want to be like you?"

The comment didn't hurt me at all. I was thrilled with where I'd landed and nothing Nadia could say would shake that feeling.

Percy took umbrage for me, however. Or perhaps for himself since she'd targeted the shammy at him first.

His backside came up, his tail lashed, and then... he launched.

CHAPTER FOURTEEN

"That scream was very satisfying," Jilly said, as we drove away. "And I didn't even know Nadia in high school."

"Agreed." I reached out to pat Percy, now curling up in Jilly's lap. "I'm so glad the cat just glanced off her head, though. Why give more ammo to the rumor mill?"

We were headed toward Thistledown now for some puppy therapy, after a long day that had brought us no closer to finding the bees. Like most of our circle, we were entranced by Frost's pups but the mama herself was getting fed up. Maud Gentry, her breeder, said Frost wanted to get back to regular programming. Raising the next generation of amazing dogs didn't fully exploit Frost's extraordinary talents.

When I stopped patting Percy, Jilly took over. "Nadia deserved that for calling you Froggy, if nothing else. What's so wrong with not wanting to dissect animals?"

"Tammi and crew dissected *human* animals without sedation, let alone formaldehyde. Yet I was the wimp for taking a stand on pickled frogs." I cringed. "That doesn't sound right."

Jilly's hand was too forceful on Percy's fluff and he objected with a grumpy meow. "All this coming from someone who sleeps on the job. Outrageous."

"Like I said, I've been guilty of that myself. Sometimes I steal a nap in the truck, too." I tried to slow her hand before Percy took matters into his own paws. "Not while driving."

"It sounds like Tammi's husband stepped out on her. Do you think Kellan knows?"

"Probably. That kind of news comes up fast around here. But he said Eddy had a good alibi. There was no reason to kill Tammi when he could have just packed up his tacos and left her here to be the wronged wife."

"Maybe he didn't want to split their assets. Tammi didn't have a day job."

"But she was making good money from her apiary, selling honey, wax products and bee nucleus colonies." Keats mumbled and I touched his side. "Besides, our critter team hasn't led us in that direction. Bernice would know Eddy."

"Aren't you giving the bee too much credit?"

"Nope. Research says they recognize faces and get used to the people around them." I mentally reviewed what I'd learned. "Bernice must be a mature bee at the peak of her game. Apparently they start out working inside the hive, and then gradually move to trash removal, guarding and finally foraging and scouting for new hive spaces."

Keats mumbled a short comment that sounded like "Boring."

It was far from boring and further, it made me think about the life cycle of our high school bees. Tammi had unsuccessfully tried to transition from queen to scout level, and Kayla was likely a forager. Poor Nadia seemed perpetually stuck in guarding, just a short step up from the trash removal stage of high school. I had been the trash itself, I supposed.

"Keats isn't satisfied with the quality of suspects, so far," I said.

"Either that or he's enjoying himself and doesn't want the investigation to end too soon."

The dog shot me a chilling blast of blue eye, as if to punish me for impugning his integrity. As much as he enjoyed solving a mystery, I'd never known the dog to drag it out just for kicks. That could put others at risk. Wanting to savor every moment of the search wasn't the same thing.

Jilly shifted restlessly in her seat. "Kellan's still looking, so I guess we are too. Asher said they questioned Mrs. Gillespie and that Kellan never liked her." Percy got frustrated by her absentminded stroking and slipped into the back seat with an irritated meow. "Sorry, buddy. Guess I've got a head of steam. Why doesn't Kellan like the principal?"

"Fiona hauled him in a few times for things he didn't do. But she missed some things he did do." I grinned at my friend. "Like drag racing with Asher. Underage."

"On school property?"

"Not that I know of, but Ash 'borrowed' cars from the school auto shop on occasion. I heard it first from Sutton."

"He shouldn't be telling the twins stories like that. They get into enough trouble as it is."

"Oh, I know. Asher said he always left the cars in better condition than he found them. It romanticizes the 'honor among thieves' idea."

Keats mumbled something cheeky and I pressed my lips together.

"You're worried about the example *you* set the boys, aren't you?" Jilly asked.

I nodded. "It bothered me to hear there's a video of Sutton and me roughhousing. They'll say I'm training him for crime-fighting. Daisy won't like it."

"Daisy's tagging the school with graffiti. I don't think she has a leg to stand on."

That made me laugh. "Guess it's in our genes. This desire to make our own rules. It's a wonder I survived in corporate as long as I did."

"And no surprise that you finally imploded and became a vigilante."

I left the highway and entered the outskirts of Thistledown. "That's what Sutton called me, but I don't quite see it that way. There's no glamor in what we do and if he gets the wrong idea, he'll end up in danger."

"If he's tagging with his mother, driving with his unlicensed grandmother, and repairing stolen cars with his uncle, the horse has probably left the barn," Jilly said. "Training him might be the smartest thing to do."

My phone rang and I half expected it to be Daisy, ready to lambaste me. But call display showed a name I never expected.

"Hey, Finch." I pressed the button to put him on speaker. "So, you joined us on the grid. Welcome to the new age."

"I'm calling with a tip, Ivy. Don't annoy me."

"I live to annoy you. If it costs me a tip, I can make peace with that."

"Okay, then. Hanging up in five—four—three—two—"

"Fine. I'll stand down. What's the tip? And more importantly, why are you giving it to me and not Chief Harper?"

"I hate having the police in my business. And I don't trust them to do what's right for animals. Or in this case, insects."

"Ah, bee business. We've got Bernice with us, by the way. The bee who joined me at Tammi's."

He sighed. "Do you have her in a jar? Your purse?"

"Nope. She lets herself in and out of the bed of the truck. I guess it's her hive away from home."

There was a pause on the other end. "I don't know why I asked. Or why I called you for that matter."

"Because you're counting on me to help with this bee tip, and who else is driving around with a bee on board? At least, a willing bee. Someone has thousands of unwilling bees around right now. Maybe not in a truck. A garage, more likely. Or a barn."

"Millions." The word boomed out over the speaker. "And some of them are loose."

"Loose? Why would someone set valuable bees loose?"

"I expect they freed themselves when they didn't like their new accommodation. They took their queen and vamoosed."

Jilly spoke up and she sounded nervous. "What makes you say that?"

"Hang on. I'll show you."

There was a ping on her phone and then another, and another.

"Is Finch actually texting you?" I asked. "Like a modern man?"

He gave an exasperated grunt. "I have kids, Ivy. I try to keep their exposure to this foolishness to a minimum but no one living in Clover Grove goes without a phone these days. We're one call from oblivion."

"You sound like Edna. She's already declared dibs on you after the apocalypse, by the way. Says you're an asset to any bunker."

Jilly stretched out the image with her fingers. "What am I looking at, Finch? It's blurry."

"Because they're moving," he said. "Those are two different swarms, and there's a third."

I pulled onto the shoulder to give the matter my full attention. "A swarm? Is that when the whole hive relocates?"

"Yeah. Usually the queen and most of the bees park somewhere relatively safe while scouts find a new home. It's not that easy to meet the criteria for a hive. It can take days."

Jilly handed me the phone and I stared at the images. There was a large group of bees covering the top rung of a fence and another in a low bush that still hadn't leafed up. "Are they dangerous in this state?"

"They won't attack unless provoked. But thousands of bees can be dangerous, sure." His voice was anxious. "They're exposed and at risk. Any idiot with a hose could take down the entire colony. A tragic end in an instant."

"People get scared and don't know any better," Jilly said.

"Yeah." Finch sounded weary. "Might have done the same myself when the kids were young and I knew less. The bees just want to be left alone and are easily enough captured by someone who knows how."

Ah-ha. I could hear where this was going. "Finch, I'm not a bee rescuer. You're the expert on all matters bee."

"Not yet," he said. "I'm a relative novice. That's why they shut me out of the club."

"That's not why they shut you out. You're too honest. One of the good guys. No one in Clover Grove wants someone with integrity in a club."

His grunt sounded like a combination of amusement and frustration. "Which is why I didn't go to them, although they'd be happy to claim Tammi's hives. I figured you'd know someone reputable who could handle this. It's not that hard to get a swarm into a hive box. Some people even have vacuum devices."

"But that rescue could attract attention from the wrong people. It's early for swarming so someone will make the connection to Tammi's bees."

"Exactly. And like I said, I have kids. I don't want those sorts of people visiting me. Even with Jaws on security."

Keats poked me in the hand with his nose and I nodded. "Got it. We'll take care of it, Finch."

"We will?" Jilly's voice was shrill.

"We will," I said. "With help. Where are they?"

"Near Thistledown," he said.

Checking my mirrors, I steered the truck off the shoulder and onto the highway. "We're in the vicinity. Could you be more specific?"

"My brother lives on a farm thereabouts and he saw them. We'll be in touch soon, but don't implicate him, Ivy. Please."

Finch sounded vulnerable himself, and I knew this was important to him. He was doing the right thing but it came at a cost. "I'll try to keep this quiet. I promise."

There was a long pause and then, "Be careful. These bees are going to be disoriented in their new surroundings. Disoriented means unpredictable."

"Don't worry. They won't even know I'm around."

Keats mumbled mockery as I hung up and Jilly shook her head. "That's a big fat lie, isn't it?"

"Probably." A slight tremor ran through me as I took the last turn. "What are the chances anyone we know has a bee vacuum?"

CHAPTER FIFTEEN

"I have a bee vacuum," Gertie Rhodes said, as she jumped out of her van with Edna. They'd parked beside the red schoolhouse that held the Thistledown Public Library. "Found it in the garage with some of Saul's things. Never could bring myself to clear everything out."

"Awesome. Did you happen to find beekeeping suits in there, too?" I asked.

"Just one, still in the package. Saul believed if you were gentle with the bees, the bees were gentle with you." Minnie twitched under the ratty brown poncho, suggesting Gertie wasn't convinced. "His hands were covered in bees when he was working and I couldn't bear to watch. He'd hum to them. Don't know if it helped, or he just enjoyed his work."

"Bet Saul and I would've gotten along great." I loaded some of their gear into the back of my truck, after looking for signs of Bernice. She was easy to miss. "If he hummed to bees, he was one of my people."

"Saul knew how to shoot a gun and a crossbow, and was adept with a sword, for a large man," Edna said. "He drove everything from a big rig to a motorcycle. Do you still think he's one of your people?"

I glared at Edna. "What's got your jumpsuit in a twist? Saul sounds like a good guy, that's all."

"I'm pointing out areas where you could improve before—"

"The apocalypse, I know. One thing at a time. After we rescue swarms of honeybees, we'll talk about my advanced training. For what it's worth, I wouldn't say no to a Harley."

"Yes, you would," Jilly said. "Your many livestock need you alive and mucking stalls. Can't do that if you break in pieces under a Harley."

"Such a killjoy, Jillian," Edna said. "I had a Harley once and drove it all through the southwest. Best trip of my life."

I laughed. "Guess you really know you're alive when the wind's blowing through your perm."

"Or your braid, right Gertie?" Edna grinned at her friend. "You and Saul did some long rides."

Gertie's smile faded. "He liked it more than I did, at least until he got piles. Couples do need to compromise."

"We know all about that," Jilly said. "Especially when couples live in a communal setting."

"Like a hive?" Thelma asked, coming down the ramp from the library. Normally she was in a tweed skirt with lace-up Oxford shoes during library hours. Today, she'd turned the sign to "Closed" and changed into a pantsuit and sturdy boots. I assumed she'd decided to come with us, but the pantsuit didn't seem quite right for bee rescue, either.

Jilly nodded. "Exactly. We were just saying as much to Tammi's friend Nadia."

Edna's pout told me why she was so cranky. She felt left out that we'd gone gadding without her. Some visits were best kept to a small team, but I understood why it bothered her. Sometimes she was missing pieces of the puzzle, yet I still expected her to bail me out in the clinch.

"We'll fill you in later, I promise," I said. "The important thing is that we have a lead on the bees."

Keats was pouting, too, and he herded Gertie around with unnecessary flourishes. "What's wrong with him?" she asked, leaning down to direct a stare into his eyes. Surprisingly, it worked to back the dog off.

"He's not looking forward to this adventure. The sheer volume of Apis mellifera Finch mentioned made us all quail." The cat meowed a complaint from Jilly's arms. "Well, not Percy. He's confident in his bee-charming skills."

"I'll put my money on smoke," Edna said, patting the pocket of her jacket, which presumably held her father's pipe and tobacco.

"And me on the vacuum," Gertie said. "Let's stun them and suck them to safety."

"Don't underestimate a good beekeeping suit and gloves," Thelma added. "I borrowed a few from Wendel, Rickie and Madge."

"Aren't they coming?" My voice betrayed my nerves. I'd counted on plenty of experienced backup.

"Definitely," Thelma said. "But we decided it's best to divide and conquer since there's a mile between the swarms."

Finch's brother had reported several more now, spread across a four-mile radius. At the moment, only two were on his property.

"Good idea," Edna said. "How many vehicles do we have? I'll break us into teams."

"Wendel is already on the road with Maud and Frost," Thelma said. "Rickie and Madge borrowed a truck and are on their way, too."

"We need a plan." Edna was getting crankier by the second. "You don't just deploy helter-skelter."

"It's okay, Edna," I said. "We'll text as we go. They know the area and they know bees. The sooner we secure these swarms in boxes, the better. I'm grateful to all my friends for coming out for a project like this. Especially when the bee thief is likely a killer."

The gratitude softened Edna's expression. I knew she was uneasy unless she was in full control, and there was no controlling every element of this mission.

Thelma patted her stiff, roller-set curls. "Ivy, you and Keats are with me, if you don't mind."

I glanced over at Jilly. "Fine with me," she said. "Percy and I will go with Edna and Gertie."

Splitting up made sense now, especially when the swarms could relocate at any minute. Finding them wouldn't be easy in an area as heavily forested as Thistledown.

Keats grumbled as he rounded Thelma and me up. He was confident in his ability to find bees. If we got within range, they would have a distinctive sound, and possibly even a smell the dog could detect.

I expected him to usher us to my truck, but instead he looked to Thelma, who jerked her thumb toward the rear of the library. Following her, I asked, "Did you bring your Land Rover?" I wondered if that meant my truck couldn't handle the terrain. Would she expect me to drive her new vehicle in difficult conditions, or was Edna right that Thelma was a crackerjack driver?

"I did, but I have another vehicle more suited to the job." Pulling out a silk kerchief in muted earth tones, she tied it over her curls. The beauty of the roller set was that it held up well under adverse conditions. If our upcoming quest needed extra armor, that didn't inspire confidence.

Nor did the sight of the oversized van parked in the garage out back. The building was painted white with red trim, complementing the library itself. The van was white, too.

"Is that a double decker?" I asked. "It's tall. And long. Like a minibus."

"I suppose, yes. It's a specialized vehicle." There was a lilt in Thelma's voice. "I suspect you're going to like it. I certainly do."

Now I was curious. Walking into the garage, I turned on my

phone light and read the painted lettering on the side of the van aloud. "Thistledown Library Bookmobile." A smile spread over my face so fast that my eyes nearly squeezed shut. "Oh my gosh, Thelma! It's a bookmobile! A van full of books! Does it still have books? Is it operational? Do you take it out?"

She laughed. "That sounded like an even split between exclamations and questions. The short answer is yes, I take this baby on the road." She patted the hood fondly. "Not as often anymore, because there aren't enough clients to make it worthwhile to close the main library. But there are a few diehard readers who can't make it this far and as long as they're reading and I'm driving, I'll deliver."

She pressed the key fob to unlock it and I slid open the side door. The smell of books wafted out and enveloped me in a comforting hug. There was more than a hint of mildew, but I pulled in a deep, satisfied snort.

Keats snorted, too, but it sounded more like jeering than joy.

"How do you decide what books to carry? Of all the books? It must be so hard to choose." She hit a button to lower a couple of steps, but I hopped inside without using them.

Grabbing a hand grip, Thelma followed on the stairs. "A little hope and a lot of experience," she said. "There are so many books I want people to read but they never will. It doesn't make sense to use up limited shelf space. There are perennial favorites among romance, mystery and thriller genres. But there's a surprising appetite for nonfiction. Even in this digital age, most of my remote clients like to hold print books in their hands."

"And smell the paper." I pulled out a book and rifled the pages, snorting again. "The perfume of heaven."

She laughed, but *with* me, not *at* me, unlike Keats. "I agree, but my main travel collection does get a little damp and musty."

Keats gave Thelma a brisk poke in the pant leg to get her moving. With anyone else, it would have been a nip, and I silently thanked him for holding back. Thelma was hardy but she wasn't a prepper like Edna and Gertie, who either had thick hide or hardy pride and rarely objected to being treated like sheep.

"I suppose we should get going. You and I could talk books all day, Ivy."

"Books and animals. My two favorite subjects." I followed her out and she closed up the van. "Thelma, I love the bookmobile, but why are we taking it to collect bees? Both of us have vehicles that might be better suited."

She walked around the van to the driver's side. "I have my reasons and I'll explain on the road."

The van was long but drove like a dream. As Thelma steered it down the main street of Thistledown, pedestrians smiled and waved. One child blew kisses. It was like being on a parade float and Keats perched very happily in my lap to enjoy the view.

"Thelma, bringing books to the people makes you a hero in my eyes."

She inclined her stiff curls slightly. "Thank you. In many towns, libraries struggle to stay relevant. Our clientele tends to be very young or very old—those without money and transportation. The very people who need books most. So I did what I had to do, including asking people for funding. A wonderful gentleman with a passion for old westerns bought this van with cash. He's an advanced senior with poor vision and more money than he'll ever need."

I loved that this octogenarian was still on the road doing good work. She was indeed a skilled driver, who piloted this big machine along small side streets with ease until we got on the back roads, which were barely wide enough for two vehicles to pass. Luckily, we didn't meet anyone else as we headed deeper into the country.

"Do you know where these swarms are?" I asked. There was so much texting going on I was already out of the loop.

She shook her head. "Not precisely, and two have moved, based on my private intel."

"You're getting intel? From whom?"

"Finch's sister-in-law, Binty, is on my regular route. I reached out when I heard about the swarms. Told her I'd drop by with some books and find out more." She turned long enough to wink. "Binty loves the classics. She's worn the covers off Pride and Prejudice, even with library binding. Designed for heavy use."

"I like her already. Wouldn't have expected that, since she's married to Finch's brother. Are they homesteaders, too?"

"Indeed. Jay Pefferlaw comes into town as little as possible and the kids are home-schooled. I don't know what happened to the brothers to turn them against polite society."

"Society isn't always polite in these parts. I'm glad they value books and education."

"Once in a while they come in for a library event geared for kids, and it feels like an honor." She turned down a lane that wasn't nearly as twisty as the one at Finch's, thank goodness. Still, she had to pay close attention. "I dread the drive in winter, but tea and cookies always await."

"What do you make of all this, buddy?" I asked Keats. "Are we on the right track?"

He mumbled an affirmative and pounded the dash with his paws until Thelma stopped him from dinging her vinyl.

A few more twists and the house came into view. It was painted a beautiful blue and meticulously maintained. There wasn't much in the gardens yet, but a dozen planters sat waiting.

A huge brindle mastiff ran down the front stairs and for a second, I thought Finch must be visiting with Jaws. The man who came out on the porch looked just like his crusty brother, with only half as much thick dark hair. It was still plenty. The Pefferlaws were a hirsute lot.

The dog was a lighter version of Jaws, too, in both color and personality. It gave a few deep barks and then whined at Thelma's door.

"Persephone and I are good friends," she said, reaching into her pocket and pulling out a handful of liver treats. "I make sure dogs never stand in the way of readers."

"Persephone? That doesn't sound like a Pefferlaw type of name."

She laughed. "Jay calls her Peeps, which suits her. She's a sweetheart."

Jay Pefferlaw gave a half smile as he opened Thelma's door and offered his hand to help her down. They really were the gentler version of the Clover Grove Pefferlaws. "Hey, Miss Tilrow. Thanks for coming out. Binty has the kettle boiling."

"How wonderful," Thelma said. "Could you grab the basket from the back? I found some books for everyone."

"I wish you wouldn't bring books for me," he said. "I don't have much time for reading but if I crack the cover I get sucked right in."

Keats evaluated Persephone before jumping down. The bigger dog inspected him gently and turned her attention back to Thelma's treats.

Meanwhile, a small, pretty woman in overalls like mine had appeared on the porch with a baby girl on one hip and two young boys behind her. "Thelma! So good to see you."

"I brought Sense and Sensibility today," Thelma said, after introducing me. "I checked your record and it's been eighteen months since you last borrowed it."

A flush raced into Binty's cheeks and I hastened to put her at ease as we climbed the stairs. "I've read it a dozen times and used to cycle through Austen on the regular. I don't read as much anymore."

"Because you're fighting bad guys?" Binty asked, smiling.

I touched my head. "It's more about the concussion I got two years ago. Reading still gives me a headache. I had to take up more active hobbies."

Jay followed with his hand on his tall dog's head. "I've heard about your fertilizer, Ivy. I was jealous of my brother's garden last summer."

"Happy to hook you up, Jay. With Finch and I being so close, how could I say no?"

He joined me on the landing and gave me a friendly shove. "My brother tolerates you. That's high praise."

Thelma went inside with Binty and the kids but I sensed Jay wanted me to hang back. "Can you tell me about the bees?" I asked. "Finch sent me photos of swarms but that's all I know."

He nodded, checked the door and then beckoned. "Want to keep the kids out of the way. Those boys are into everything. Worse than we were at that age."

Leading me around the house, he passed the barn and walked out into a field that would turn into a lush meadow in a month or so. On the far side, we found a very large clump of bees covering a fencepost.

"They're fanning," Jay said. "So the queen's there. I'm guessing thirty thousand or more." He pointed into the next field. "There's another over there even bigger."

I pulled out my phone. "Let me call my friend. She has a bee vacuum and we'll get them relocated."

He caught my hand and the curt shake of his head told me he was more like Finch than I originally thought. "No circus, Ivy. Swarming bees don't venture too far from their hive. Catch my drift?"

I didn't, at first, but Keats mumbled something that connected the dots for me. "Ah. You think the bees stolen from Clover Grove were stashed close by and you're worried your neighbors could be in on it."

His next nod was equally curt. "Travis is keeping an eye on things."

I figured Travis was another dog with more of an edge than Persephone, but a man in a plaid jacket waved from across the field and then headed our way. He was bearded, attractive and likely in his early forties. He was also very well armed. A rifle was in easy reach and a pistol stuck out of a holster at his waist.

The white tuft on Keats' tail waved modest approval as Jay introduced us to Travis Wigg, whose nod was also curt.

"Thanks for keeping an eye on the bees," I said. "I know they're vulnerable and we want to rehome them as soon as possible." I glanced at Jay. "I suppose you and Finch will say no, considering their provenance?"

"Hard pass. How about you, Travis?"

The taller man shrugged. "Sure. If it's okay with Harper."

"You know Kellan? We're, uh..." My voice faltered. Normally I wasn't shy about dropping my relationship status but these guys were men's men. They didn't want to hear about my romance.

Travis saved me with a smirk. "Yeah. I know Kellan. And your brother. I live further down the range and can keep these bees off the radar."

I had half a dozen questions to ask but I doubted they'd be well received. "I just want them to be safe. And as happy as bees get." I looked up as a lone bee arrived and flew a tight figure eight over my head. Had she stowed away in the bookmobile? "There's Bernice. Maybe one of the swarms is her family."

The silent exchange of glances between men told me my weird was showing. It caused some heat to rise from my flubby flappers, moving as slowly as Thelma's bookmobile.

"Bernice?" Travis asked. His eyebrows made me wonder if he was a Pefferlaw cousin.

"Yeah, Bernice," I said, owning it. If he was as familiar with my menfolk as he seemed, he probably knew what I was about. "She was foraging when the heist happened at Tammi's, I think. Now she's staying with me until we find her hive."

"Wow. Your brother's not wrong," Travis said.

"He might be. Asher's a little hit and miss when it comes to accuracy."

He shook his head, this time seeming a trifle bewildered. "Let's get started. As soon as we get this lot into a hive box with their queen, they'll settle right down."

"My friends have a bee vac but Jay won't let me call them," I said.

"No worries, I got it covered." Travis had an air of confidence. "Used to own bees. Moved away for a bit and rehomed them."

He walked back into the field to collect a hive box and canvas bag filled with tools. "Jay, can you hold Ivy back while I do this?" He winked at me. "Bernice, too."

"I'll take care of myself, thank you very much," I said.

"Suit yourself. Bees can only sting once. How many do you want to kill?"

I detested this guy for figuring out how to handle me so easily. I hated being handled, especially by lumberjack types. "Keats, you watch him," I said. "We may need to repeat this operation."

"Keats, buddy," Travis said. "I hear you're smart enough to keep your lady out of trouble when needed."

The black-and-white traitor actually pant-laughed, which made the men laugh, too. "What is this? Bro code?" I demanded.

"Just following the chief's orders," Travis said. "I called him about this. Did you?"

I stared at him with what I hoped was a chilly gaze. "You think very highly of yourself, Mr. Wigg. I hope you can handle a swarm."

He stopped joking around when he finally got down to business, and in the end, I was grateful to be sidelined to watch.

Travis put on a baseball cap, which turned out to be the full extent of his uniform. He set the hive box on the grass near the fencepost holding the swarm and lit his smoker. After that, he spread a piece of white tarp on the ground right up against the post. Giving the bees a few smoky puffs, he used a brush to gently sweep the clump down the post with feathery movements until the majority dropped onto the tarp. He collected stragglers and then shot a few more puffs at the far end, which got them moving in the direction of the hive box. Then he bent over and watched the small entrance. "Good. There's the queen running over her loyal subjects and leading them with pheromones. We'll leave them to populate the hive and go grab the other one."

The next swarm was even easier, because Travis was able to cover the swarm with a bucket and trim the bushes until the swarm dropped inside. Then he repeated what he'd done with the tarp, the hive box and the smoke.

"That's it?" I asked, when he came over.

His smile was genuine. "Yep. They're calm, they're happy, and I'll have honey to spare this year. Just need to leave enough time for the strays to catch up."

"Let's grab a coffee at the house while we wait," Jay said.

Keats raced around us in circles as we headed back. He was mumbling up a storm but I couldn't pick up half of it. I figured he was relieved he didn't need to do anything heroic. That made two of us.

"What's with your dog?" Jay asked. "Peeps doesn't chatter like that."

"Just excited, I guess. He loves new adventures."

Travis was still smiling. "Harper brags about him all the time. You'd think he was marrying the dog." I stared at him, and this time my gaze really must have been chilly. "Sorry. That came out wrong."

Keats ran up, poked me in the leg, and mumbled an order. That one I got.

Turning away from Travis, I directed a question to Jay. "Could you tell me a little more about your neighbors?"

"No." The answer was fast and left no room for debate. "I don't bother them and they don't bother me. The very definition of good neighbors."

"So good they steal bees?" I asked. "And maybe kill people to get them?"

Travis raised his hand to interrupt the exchange. "Got an idea. How about we leave all that to Harper? No wonder your brother complains about you."

Keats came up beside me and mumbled a warning not to take the bait.

I took the bait.

"What is Asher complaining about to a complete stranger?"

Travis shrugged. "I'm not a stranger. To him. Or Harper."

"Or me. Or Finch," Jay added. "Travis is Binty's brother and a talented craftsman. He's done some woodwork at Kellan's house. I'm sure you've seen it."

I racked my brain. "There's a lot of wood and I'm not there often. Kellan doesn't like pet hair."

"Then he must have loved it when you were driving around with a goat in the cab," Travis said. "There would have been some hair then."

"And the mini horse," Jay said. "Didn't you get an alpaca into the truck, too?"

"Not at the same time, if it happened at all." I was so flustered I really couldn't remember the details about Alvina.

"The dog is saying yes," Travis said.

I shook my finger at Keats. "The dog is saying nothing... to you. What he really wants is for you guys to stop trying to decoy me and explain how the bees ended up here."

Two sets of shoulders went up in unison. "Your guess is as good as mine," Jay said. "Probably better."

"Probably better," Travis agreed. "Harper says she fires out guesses like a broken slot machine and comes up gold the odd time."

"Gambling is a dangerous hobby," Jay said, giving me another shove to take the edge off. "That's why I stick close to home. Less temptation."

"A guy could lose his shirt," Travis said. "Ask me how I know."

I wanted to do just that, but I started with the obvious question. "Is there a casino in Thistledown I don't know about?"

Broad shoulders shrugged again. It looked too choreographed. As if they were in on a secret with Kellan and Asher.

Keats must have thought so, too, because he did a couple of arcs behind the men to drive them up the stairs and gave each of them an entirely unnecessary nip.

It didn't get me closer to information but it was balm for my wounded pride.

CHAPTER SIXTEEN

I waited till Thelma steered the bookmobile onto the main road before grumbling, "I didn't get a thing out of those guys. They ganged up on me."

"To keep you safe," she said, accelerating gradually. "For Kellan and Asher."

"Who've been talking smack about me to complete strangers. Honestly, I expected more of Kellan." Keats mumbled from my lap. "Asher, not so much."

She adjusted her kerchief for maximum coverage as I opened the window. "The bees are safe and that's the most important thing, right?"

"Definitely. Travis can give them a good home. He has a secure bee yard and is well able to defend them. But we have no idea why the swarms ended up near Jay's house and many colonies are still missing. Including Bernice's family. They can't be too far away. When bees leave their hive they usually don't fly more than a mile before gathering. The police might be able to find all the others if they act quickly. Otherwise, the thief could get on the road to California."

"It can't be easy to find a safe space for that many hives," Thelma said. "Regardless, we didn't leave empty-handed. Sometimes things are said over a pot of tea and an exchange of classic books."

A grin spread over my face as I turned to look at her. "You got a lead from Binty?"

"Possibly. We were talking about the neighbors and she mentioned there are several vacant lots in the area. One property belonged to BiBi Adcock, who passed away last year." She waited a beat and added, "Her maiden name was Bouchard."

"Bouchard! As in Kayla Bouchard, before she slimmed that down to the initial, 'B'? Was this her grandmother?"

"I believe BiBi was the sister of Kayla's grandfather. If it hasn't been sold, the property is still in the family and your old classmate, Kayla, may have chosen to hide the hives there."

"Why would Kayla need to steal and hide the bees when Tammi was giving them to her anyway? Unless Tammi changed her mind at the last minute and Kayla wanted them more than she let on."

"Questions we can't answer today, I'm afraid."

I ran my hands over Keats, feeling the energy percolating under his sleek fur. He was primed for more action. "How about we drive in that direction and see if Keats can find more swarms? He knows exactly what to look for, now."

"Where's your little bee friend?" Thelma asked.

"Not sure." It was true, but I had given her the opportunity to fly into the back of the van with the books. There was mesh screen between the library and the cab, so I wasn't worried about the bee joining us up front.

Thelma piloted the bookmobile around the next bend and then turned off into a lane that initially looked too grown over for the big vehicle. Rolling the window down, I peered up and saw plenty of branches that had been recently bent or broken. We weren't the first to force our way through.

Keats panted heavily on my lap. It felt like more than the usual excitement. We were onto something, but unless I was much mistaken, it wasn't all good news.

The lane was shorter than Jay Pefferlaw's and we soon emerged into a clearing. The squat old house in the middle seemed to droop in despair of ever getting the repairs it needed. It had been loved once, judging by the dry, dead lilies and rosebushes, but time had been unkind.

"Always makes me sad to see an abandoned house," Thelma said. "I hope to transition the library and my home into new hands before they fall into ruin. Then I can go knowing they're cared for and loved. It looks like Bibi Adcock didn't get that chance."

It made me sad to hear her speak that way, but not every octogenarian wanted to live forever, like Edna. Having a backup plan wasn't a bad idea.

"If you sold, where would you go?" I asked.

She must have heard the sadness in my voice because she put the bookmobile in park and turned to me before answering. "I have no living relatives that I care to remember, so I looked for a good retirement community. Believe it or not, there's one down near Wyldwood that has its own freestanding library. The homes range from apartments to bungalows and you can choose your level of service. I figured I'd make likeminded friends there, so I put my name on the list."

"Already? Thelma, you're still going strong."

"And the wait-list is long. I can turn down an opening if it comes too soon." She patted my arm. "Don't worry, Ivy. I'm not going anywhere just yet. But I want to make my own choices as long as I can. I enjoy my life and I feel good about the contribution I've made, but I've always liked to leave a party too early."

Keats mumbled something that sounded both respectful and impatient. Maybe he understood Thelma was communicating something important, but he also wanted to keep our own party moving.

The old woman nodded. "I hear you. Better to chat back at the schoolhouse. There are bees to save."

We got out of the van and I barely had time to crack open the back door for Bernice before Keats went into a point. His hackles were down and he actually seemed to shrink a little. That told me the issue was probably bees. He didn't need to like every species we were called to help.

I walked in the direction he indicated and then stopped to listen. Over my head there was a quiet drone that I could feel as much as hear. Thousands upon thousands of bees had gathered on a broken branch at least 20 feet above us.

Far closer to me, a lone bee swooped and dove, before doing a figure eight. Bernice, no doubt, and since she didn't approach the swarm, this colony likely wasn't her family, either.

Pulling out my phone, I took some photos and texted Gertie. This was a case for the bee vac and a long ladder.

"Contrary to what some people think, I know my limits," I said, beckoning to Thelma before following the dog into a smaller and even more overgrown lane. "Bee detection is where I draw the line right now, especially since I left the equipment in my truck."

Keats mumbled agreement as he moved easily under branches that pushed his human companions back. His next comment was brusque, but we really couldn't go any faster.

Luckily, Keats went into his next point soon after. A swarm had coated the fork of a tree. They looked less formidable than vulnerable. It would be so easy for the wrong person to eradicate a thriving colony. Three days ago, these bees were living a pampered existence behind Tammi's house and producing wonderful honey. They were rudely ripped away from that life and then seemingly chose to move on of their own free will. I had to make sure they got a safe and happy landing.

Untying her kerchief, Thelma graciously sacrificed it to the cause. "Mark the hive for the team."

Thanking her, I tied the kerchief to a branch. "Anything more, Keats?"

There was something more, that was clear. The dog's paw was up, but so were his hackles.

"That doesn't look good." Thelma's voice was a whisper.

"To the bookmobile," I said, firing off a last text. "Discretion is the better part of valor."

Thelma swatted at branches that seemed intent on snagging her exposed curls as we hurried back to the clearing. I took a second to let Bernice into the back of the bookmobile before jumping into the passenger seat with Keats. There was no sign of anything amiss but the dog continued to indicate a problem.

"I'm worried about leaving the same way we came in," she said, turning the key in the ignition. "It's a single lane. If we bump into someone we'll be stuck. This beast is far from nimble."

Keats' paw came up again and he leaned over to claw at Thelma's side of the dashboard, mumbling instructions.

"Go around the house," I said. "There must be another way out."

Maneuvering the big van through the overgrowth wasn't easy, but if Thelma was flustered, it barely showed. It reminded me of the time she sat at her library checkout desk with Keats in her lap as an armed killer paced and ranted. Only one curl flipped out of place.

Today, the branches had overturned two curls and I couldn't help but wonder if they represented her state of mind. "Glove compartment, Ivy. Open it."

I expected to find a weapon. Instead, there was a stockpile of silk scarves in various colors. Choosing the most subdued pattern, I handed it to her.

Easing off the gas, she wrapped her hair with practiced ease and tied the kerchief in place. Then she rolled down her window and nodded for me to do the same. Keats stuck his nose out and swiveled, taking in all the smells. His faint, high whine told me we weren't alone.

Reading his cues, I navigated for Thelma as we took a series of small lanes through the vast tract of property. "It's like the back country trails in miniature," I said. "Everyone wants an escape route."

Someone was following us, at least according to Keats. I couldn't see or hear anything, but I was worried. This hulking white vehicle meant our pursuer would have the advantage.

"I was just thinking the same about the back country," Thelma said, pressing the pedal down slightly. "I'm no stranger to those trails."

"You take the trails?"

"Not often anymore, but there were times it was necessary."

I took my eyes off the path ahead to stare at her curiously. "In the bookmobile?"

Her kerchief bobbed. "Not this one, but the previous two took a beating. Happily, I was never unlawfully detained in the line of duty."

Keats' ears came up long enough to offer one quick pant-laugh. It was heartening to see he could enjoy Thelma's tale amidst a new one in the making.

"Why on earth would someone chase a bookmobile? You're a public servant doing good deeds."

"You'd be surprised at how hot under the collar people get about books. One irate father shot out my tires for exposing his daughters to what he called 'smut.' That book was on the school curriculum and if there was anything distasteful, I couldn't see it. I looked it over closely to avoid making the same mistake. Sometimes smut is in the eye of the beholder."

I was tempted to ask the title but figured we'd get into a discussion that might distract Thelma. The rough road was cratered with potholes and a lesser ride might have left us with piles, too.

"There were other times?"

"Sure. A woman shot me off her property when a book she preordered didn't come in on time. She was *that* fond of the author. Another woman did the same when a book I recommended disappointed her."

"Seriously? Did you stop recommending books?"

Her kerchief swished a negative. "That would be dereliction of duty. You win some, you lose a tire or a windshield." After a quick turn, she added, "I did charge her to replace the book and requested a donation to the children's literacy fund. It made the point."

"Even librarians have war stories," I said.

"Very much so. I have a few that would curl your hair without rollers, but they're better told over a teacup. We need to keep our eye on the prize."

I couldn't see much of anything. One tributary lane looked just like another to me, but Thelma's eyes drifted up to the skyline, then to Keats and back to the trail. Her even breaths suggested she was confident she could get us out.

Keats mumbled what sounded like a correction but it was too late. The big vehicle was bumping down a lane that ended abruptly. It was a common trap in the maze of back country trails.

"Uh-oh," I said. "What now?"

"Now is where a country librarian shows her mettle. Anyone can drive a bookmobile forward, but can you reverse? At high speed?"

I grabbed the hand grip. "I can't even reverse my truck without stalling half the time. Guess I'd never cut it as a country librarian."

There was a clunk in the rear of the van as we shot backward. "Shakespeare," Thelma said. I thought it was her version of a curse word until she added, "Collected works. Heaviest book here and the most unwieldy."

There was another clunk and I suggested, "Chaucer?"

"Possibly. Never thought he was worth the work of figuring out Middle English."

"Me either. Has anyone ever borrowed those?"

She shook her head. "I reserve a bit of shelf space for the classics but they're the first to fall under siege. To see the covers, you'd think they got more use than they do."

A series of rapid clunks made her wince as she backed around the turn and shifted gears. "That's the Brontë sisters. I can tell by how they stick together."

"I love the Brontës."

Two more quiet clunks followed. "Anne Brontë," Thelma said. "Always felt she was overlooked."

The trail was very rough here, and roots threw the books up like popcorn. "The Americans," I suggested. "Vonnegut, Steinbeck, Fitzgerald, Hemingway."

Another one hit with a loud splat. "James Joyce's Ulysses," Thelma said, cackling. "Utter gibberish."

There was a gentle pitter-patter of romance novels as she hit a smooth patch, followed by a galactic swoosh of science fiction when she took the next turn too fast. While she was focusing closely, I imagined the genres mingling on the floor in ways the library filing system never allowed. This adventure could lead to unexpected mash-ups.

"Ivy, what's Keats saying?" she asked. "You're distracted."

"Sorry, Thelma. You know how I get around books and crazy things are happening back there."

"Don't worry. These are older, tougher copies. The best volumes stay in town." Reaching out, she gave me a sharp poke. "Have we lost our tail?"

I was so disoriented I heard the other spelling of "tale," until Keats grabbed my sleeve and gave it a little shake. His tone oozed disgust.

"Turn right, Thelma. We've got an advantage here."

It didn't look like it, at least at first. There was a small creek ahead of us that would have challenged the average van. Luckily, Thelma's benefactor had chosen the vehicle for hardiness. It glided down the bank slowly and then up the other side. We took out more branches, but the path cleared quickly and Thelma pounded the pedal.

"Do you hear that?" she asked, easing up a little. In the distance a frustrated engine wailed. It was a pickup truck, I guessed, but most people around hill country had one. "Stuck in the creek. Too bad, so sad."

I laughed and sat back, breathing a little easier. Then I pulled out my phone and texted. "The others are going to run into a trap if they don't stop."

"Gertie's van won't be any better than our pursuer's vehicle," Thelma said, turning onto the main road. "There's a lot to be said for a reliable bookmobile." She rolled up her window and turned to me. "I'll leave it to you to bring order to the chaos back there."

Keats mumbled a cheeky protest as he settled in my lap, but I grinned at Thelma. "It would be an honor and a pleasure."

CHAPTER SEVENTEEN

T he sun was low in the sky when I heard the crunch of boots on gravel in the library driveway and stuck my head out of the sliding door of the bookmobile. Keats left the garage with a bound and a flourish, leaving me to freeze like a possum beside a tipped trashcan.

"I can see you, Ivy," my beloved said. "Don't go hiding behind the collected works of Shakespeare, hefty as it is."

I pressed the big book to my heart. "Is it strange that I get palpitations because you recognize the collection?"

"I took a few undergrad English lit classes," he said. "But reading is a hobby for those with more time and less crime on their hands."

"Shakespeare will wait till you retire. I'm retiring him to the schoolhouse stacks now. Thelma said no one borrows this and it makes a mighty big bang when it falls off the shelf. Chaucer is going, too." I handed both volumes to him, mostly as a distraction. It would be harder to lecture me with literary greats in his arms. "Want to come inside?"

I figured he'd say no, but he set the books on top of a tarp in the garage and joined me in the bookmobile. "Nice wheels. Where did Thelma get that kind of coin?"

"Generous patron. She used to hand-deliver books to this guy's door every week, never realizing he was loaded. When the previous van broke down, he wrote a big check. But he still wants books delivered to the door."

"Huh. Interesting."

It *was* interesting and he would usually find it so, but I could tell his thoughts were elsewhere. Understandable, given the circumstances.

"Do you know if anyone captured the other swarms?" I asked. "No one's answered my texts."

He leaned against the shelves and stared at me. "You mean the two swarms of bees you and Thelma found while trespassing?"

"Yes, those swarms. Your best buddy Travis Wigg secured the ones on Pefferlaw land. Maybe he took his two firearms over to save the rest of the bees."

"He didn't get a chance. And we're not *that* close."

"Well, he knew I drove with a goat in the cab of my truck. Something only you saw."

"But others knew about, including your brother. Asher and Travis play hockey together and boys will be boys. It probably came up over a post-game beverage."

"Along with Ivy's other travels with pets. Glad I didn't mention the bee in the bookmobile."

He moved closer to the door. "Is she here now?"

"Off scouting. It's all work and no play for that girl." I rearranged the Brontës to profile Anne's books. "Such is the life of a worker bee. Did you know drones get tossed out of the hive in winter? The gals conserve energy and food to keep the queen warm and comfortable. No room for heat-hogging guys when new ones can be hatched in spring."

He practiced raising only one eyebrow. There was still hope of charming him with my quirky ways. It was one of the rare days I wished I'd worn makeup and done my hair a little. Obviously I wasn't one to squander feminine wiles but when stuck in close confines with a handsome cop who had the moral high ground, some eyeliner wouldn't go amiss.

"I know what you're doing," he said. "The vehicle smelled like dank books when I got in. Now it reeks of red herrings."

I ran my fingertips along the Brontë collection with gentle reverence. The only author to rival them in my heart was Jane Austen. Kellan was my own personal Mr. Darcy. But that didn't stop me from lobbing decoy fish at him. "I thought you liked learning about natural history."

"More so when there isn't an open murder investigation."

"But that's when I usually get educational opportunities. I'm thinking of setting up an apiary at the farm."

"For Bernice?" He looked pleased about remembering her name.

I shook my head. "She probably won't survive long enough to enjoy time with us."

"Why?" Both eyebrows were up now. "I'll get to the bottom of Tammi's death before too long and you can have your hive."

His concern made me smile. "Bees normally only live a month or two. But I do want to reunite Bernice with her beeple before she goes to the big flower garden in the sky."

"Beeple." He fought a grin and barely succeeded. "More red herrings and I snapped at them like a seal. Let's go back to how you were trespassing in this lumbering beast." He tapped a panel. "It's like a celebrity tour bus."

"Shakespeare was a rock star. Although some say he had a ghostwriter."

He lifted his nose. "Smell that? Fish facts."

"Whatever. You probably already grilled Thelma like a fillet of sole and found out Keats directed us to those extra swarms. My current mission in life is to get lost bees to safety so we went to take a look. I thought you'd be proud I didn't try to capture them myself."

"Only because you didn't have the right equipment."

"Maybe. Then Keats suggested we had company, so we left in a hurry and texted you. I felt bad leaving the swarms. It was a huge bee-trayal." I winked at him. "Get it?"

"Yup. I'm assuming there's a backlog of puns you'll fire at me with the red herrings."

"A few. But my point is we left on Keats' signal, just like we arrived. And it hurt to know we were leaving the swarms in peril."

"They're safe," he said, relenting, at last. "I've made sure of it. Turns out there are plenty of knowledgeable beeple around." He didn't leave time for me to respond before circling back. "Did you know the property where you were trespassing belonged to Kayla Ware's great aunt?"

"Don't forget the B in Kayla B. Ware. Did you know she has a display of crocheted animals in her shop that align with my living collection? It's remarkable."

"Did you know you're adding crafts to the red herrings? At least they don't smell."

"But they do lack flavor. And yes, Thelma mentioned that Binty Pefferlaw told her about BiBi Bouchard."

"Bibi is short for Bernice. In case you're wondering."

"Seriously? That's just weird. Kayla's daughter named a crochet bee after her."

"And you named a *real* bee after her. That's even weirder."

"Just a strange coincidence," I said. "It happens."

Keats was back from patrolling and offered a mumble of support. Strange coincidences did happen to us all the time. It was better not to examine them too closely.

"So you went over there with Thelma knowing it was risky."

"I was just worrying about the bees. Swarms don't fly too far. I thought there might be more, and there were. But we didn't see any sign of the rest of Tammi's hives. Did you?"

He shook his head. "Still looking. On the bright side, there's been no sign of them on major highways. Too much heat to take a chance right now."

"And what about Kayla? Did you double-check her alibi?"

"Kayla's whereabouts are accounted for at the time of Tammi's death."

"I couldn't see why she'd take the hives when she was getting them anyway, but I did wonder if she lost her mind over something and clobbered Tammi. Queen bees fight to the death, you see. When a bunch are hatching, the first one out will skewer the other babies."

Kellan winced. "Human queen bees have more social graces."

"As someone saddled with the nickname Flubby Flappers, I disagree. But I don't see why Kayla would kill Tammi when she was being handed the crown and scepter. She is the new queen bee, even if she doesn't have any hives now."

"The two women were good friends, by all accounts."

"Maybe. Or maybe they were more like frenemies."

He crossed his arms. "Did something come up when you were shopping for yarn? I was surprised to hear from Kayla that you were interested in stitchery as well as sneakery."

"Edna's been suggesting knitting for some time." That was totally true. "It's a useful hobby and she's made plenty of hats and mittens for bunker life, including some cute sets for babies."

He winced again. "We will not be raising a kid in her bunkers. None are fit for human habitation."

"How many are there, exactly? I've only seen two. Maybe three, but she moves them around to avoid being targeted."

"By zombies?"

"By cops." I grinned at him. "Sounds like you're a step ahead of her."

"Today. And you were telling me about your unauthorized visit to Kayla."

"You don't want me checking in with you every time I buy wool, do you? Or a new mattress?"

"A mattress? Well, that's different. But why are we talking about mattresses now?"

"There's a mattress and appliance store on the highway. When Jilly and I popped in, we found Nadia Reddy sound asleep. She's the third-ranked bee, in case you don't remember the pecking order of my high school years."

"I remember. You talked about it enough." He rubbed his forehead. "Those girls ruined a lot of visits to Clover Grove Gardens. You'd have to detox for an hour from their antics."

"True. And I'm sorry I let them take up so much real estate in my brain, let alone yours."

"If it helps, they got pranked for it. And not by me."

I nearly dropped the rest of the books I was holding. "Asher? Tell me more."

He shook his head. "I'm the chief of police. There's a rule about celebrating high school stunts."

"A rule applied at whim. You told me about drag racing with Asher."

"But no one knew. No one got hurt."

Pulling in an eager breath, I grabbed his arm. "Who got hurt? Tammi? Is that why you won't tell me?"

"No one got hurt. Not really. Other than wounded pride." He picked up some books and started filing them himself, carefully lining up the spines. "Always liked a good detective novel. Now, tell me about Nadia. We've already spoken to her, but perhaps you learned a thing or two, because you're old enemies."

"I didn't even have enemy status, Kellan. Frogs are not contenders in high school politics. I was out of the loop then, just like I am now. For example, I'd never heard that Tammi's husband strayed."

He continued to put books away without changing his rhythm. It wasn't news.

"Okay, so you already heard that," I continued. "Is there a

chance Tammi had a change of heart at the last minute about leaving, and Kayla took the hives by force?"

"The bees are valuable, but not worth life in prison."

"A crime of passion, then. Maybe Kayla blew a fuse over the lost throne. You can't promise social status and then jerk it away."

"Keep on guessing if you like. I know you enjoy a good story and we're surrounded by them."

I collected a few more books from the floor and handed them to him. "I know Eddy had an alibi, but doesn't his affair throw that into question?"

Kellan put a couple of Hemingway classics on a shelf, moving others around to make room. He was as skilled at this as he was at most things. At least, those that didn't involve farming and livestock. Of course, he was really just stalling as he decided what to share and where I might run amok with information.

Keats jumped inside with us to deliver a nip to Kellan's uniformed cuff. The dog was no fan of libraries in general and this bookmobile in particular. It provided too little scope for his talents and wily moves.

"I haven't entirely ruled out the husband. I think they were working things out."

I took a book from his hand to get him to look at me. "You think, or you know?"

"Hard to be sure of anything in situations like this. Tammi isn't here to tell her side of the story."

"And her friends likely aren't reliable. How about the other woman?"

He took the book back. The tug was sharp enough to let me know that I wasn't getting a slice of that information pie. "Ivy, no. You're not cornering an innocent woman with your cat and your dog."

"What about my bee? I bet Bernice could sting some facts out of her." I sighed. "Not that I would allow it. Worker bees have barbed stingers that don't come out and the bee dies. One and done for. Can't squander a life on a cheater."

"You don't know the full story."

"Well, tell me. Was Tammi cheating, too? I wouldn't put it past her. But then we'd have another tier of suspects."

"You mean, the police would. The extent of your work—as we mutually agreed—is animal welfare. Insects weren't even included in that arrangement."

"Mother Nature created complex creatures in the honeybee, Kellan. They have as much right to my aid as"—I scanned my mental catalogue—"mice, bats and foxes."

Going further back in my history might have impressed him more.

"Just stick to finding a home for recovered bees, Ivy. No more poking around on private property. And I've got bee rescue covered."

"Who's your bee rescuer?" I handed him the books back as I figured it out. "Seriously? You'll take Travis Wigg over my friends?"

"Travis is an experienced beekeeper. He had an apiary before he... Went away. But he probably can't host all of Tammi's hives. That was her full-time job and he's a busy man."

"Not too busy to talk smack about me."

He held up books to block me. "I told him nothing. As the chief of police, I don't gossip." Peering over The Great Gatsby, he added, "Unless it's with you, and even then I have misgivings."

"Fine. What's Travis' deal, anyway? I can tell he's hiding something."

"He's a good guy. A reliable craftsman with a great eye for detail." Surrendering the rest of the books, he gave me a warm enough smile to set the little library on fire. "But don't ask me. What does your genius dog tell you?"

Keats mumbled something long and involved that sounded like indignation over being used to get Kellan out of trouble. The dog was more than willing to be used to get *me* out of trouble, probably because he discovered that trouble in the first place.

"He didn't have an issue with Travis or Jay," I admitted, "even though they were rather heavily armed for bee rescue."

"Well, Gertie is rather heavily armed for breakfast, and I don't even want to know what Edna is packing. People are anxious these days. I don't like it, but I understand it. Maybe when we get the crime rate down, they'll ease up."

"Gertie's been carrying Minnie around since Saul died, and he wore a rifle before that. Same with Buckley. There was anxiety long before you and I came home and I doubt we'll be able to dispel it completely." Setting the books aside, I went in for a hug. "You know what would bring them peace?"

"Bees?" he asked. "Dogs? Cats, donkeys or alpacas? Wait, you're going for manure."

I leaned back and grinned at him. "Good guesses. But I was thinking of books, and more specifically, this bookmobile. It's heaven on wheels. You can request any story you like and it arrives at your door. Thelma hand-picks books for folks like a literary matchmaker."

He laced his fingers through my hair and kissed the top of my head. "That's a solution I could embrace. Book marriages for all."

"I'm glad you see the romance, because I had a great idea."

His fingers stilled in my hair. "Yeah? I worry when I hear those words. It usually involves either acquiring new animals or bending the law into positions that make me extremely uncomfortable."

"No need for either on our honeymoon. I was thinking we could borrow the bookmobile and take a relaxing tour of the region."

He practically blew a raspberry against my forehead. "I doubt I'd find it either romantic or relaxing to pilot this big ship of books around the region. You do know they already talk about us? Even beyond state lines?"

"But this would be good gossip. Bringing books and joy to the people."

"I normally find driving relaxing, but this thing is like a bus. Not what I think of for a holiday."

I buried a grin in his jacket. "Then I'll drive and you can sit with Percy and Keats in the passenger seat."

The groan blew up long strands of hair that he wiped out of his face. "Way to suck all the romance out of a honeymoon. All the testosterone, in fact. I'm not sitting with a lapful of pets while my lady drives me around in a bookmobile. Might as well take up crochet."

"Nothing wrong with a man who crochets. I hear it's very relaxing. You could make me my own gallery of stitched pets."

"Better than too many real ones, I suppose." After a moment, he added, "Are Keats and Percy really coming on our honeymoon?"

Keats mumbled an assertive yes from below. He was being generous in allowing me a nice moment with my sweetheart but expected the gesture to be returned in kind.

"Percy might choose to stay with Jilly, but you heard Keats. Crime doesn't take a holiday, and neither does he."

"There will be no crime on our honeymoon. And no bookmobile, either."

I hugged him hard. "Fine. It was just an idea. As long as you're there, anything will be romantic. And as long as Keats is there, I'll be relaxed enough to enjoy it."

His chin lurched forward and banged against my skull. Unromantic words shot into my hair, including, "Stupid cat."

"I guess Jilly's back with the others." I released Kellan reluctantly and we left the bookmobile. His handsome face was briefly obscured by orange fluff as Percy showed off his frontside shoulder-to-shoulder pass. "Think about what I said."

"You said a lot." His voice was muffled as Percy passed back. "There's no room on the shelves of my brain for all of it."

Scooping Percy off his shoulder, I started walking down the driveway to the schoolhouse library. "If you have trouble sleeping tonight, just think about crochet and which animal you'll stitch first. Super soothing for the stressed officer of the law."

"It certainly won't be a border collie."

Kellan's voice was fading a little and the words came in bursts. I didn't need to turn back to know Keats was creating an obstacle course for him.

"Keats!" I snapped my fingers. "Leave our fiancé alone. We've got bees to save."

CHAPTER EIGHTEEN

Leaving Gertie and Edna to visit with Thelma, Jilly and I drove over to Maud Gentry's to sit on the floor with the puppies. They were adorable and busy creatures, true to their breed and specific lineage. One of them managed to liberate my keys from the side pocket of my overalls and drag them under an ottoman. Uncle Percy retrieved both keys and pup with a few sweeps of his orange paws. Unlike the resident cat, Fanny, Percy was fond of the puppies and often climbed into their pen to give Frost a break. The pups curled up in his orange fluff and the cat kneaded the air, perhaps imagining a litter of his own that would never happen.

Jilly sat with her favorite, another female, in her lap. One girl was the mirror image of Frost, and the other of Keats—if Keats had two blue eyes. The male was darker, like Annie, and his eyes were a warm brown. Of the three, he was the calmest, which was likely why Wendel, owner of the sire, had claimed the male pup as pick of the litter. Maud had decided to keep both girls, at least till maturity, in hopes that they'd turn out to be good potentials for breeding. She was in no hurry, but her interest in furthering the lines of these magnificent dogs was reviving as she trusted in the support of her new friends. She had lost two dogs and both were now home, thanks to good backers. Frost's litter was a happy accident but the next would be well considered. Maud hated accidents, but she doted on the female who resembled Keats so much that Annie, the grandmother, grumbled complaints.

With our puppy love banks full, we surrendered the pups and left for home.

"I can feel you scheming," Jilly said, as we neared Clover Grove. "You want to make a last stop and can't figure out a way to do it without annoying Kellan."

"Are you a psychic?" The question was a bold move, because there were alleged psychics in Jilly's family and it unsettled her greatly. She didn't want to believe but inexplicable things happened when her cousin Janelle was around.

"It doesn't take a psychic to know you want to interview Tammi's husband and find out about the other woman."

Keats' mumble was short, like "Bingo."

"You're right, and I can't risk it."

She touched my arm. "Are you okay? What happened to risk-it-all Ivy? Was it the puppies?"

I nodded. "Those cuties temporarily suck all the defiance out of a person. More people need to sit on the floor playing with puppies. The world would be a better place."

"That's why we can't stay too long. We need our edge, my friend."

"Exactly. And since Kellan came by the bookmobile with a dose of romance, I'm doubly drained of my spark." I frowned. "This is what normal people feel like. The rule followers. It's pleasant but dull."

My phone pinged and then pinged again. And again.

"Uh-oh." Our voices overlapped. Multiple pings struck fear in our hearts. Six or more meant a family meeting and things would be neither pleasant nor dull.

Luckily, the pings stopped at three and all came from Mom. Jilly read the texts on her phone and shrugged. "Feel like dressing up?"

I snorted. "Please. I never feel like dressing up. Tonight, you couldn't pay me enough."

My best friend smirked. "What if I could pay you in clues about Tammi's unfortunate demise? What would you say then?"

"Well, that's obvious. I'd say, 'Can you lend me a dress and flat-iron my hair?'"

"And I'd say, you bet, and I'll throw in a full face of makeup because you're going to show those high school duds how a frog turns into a princess."

"Ugh, no. I'm not putting on a show for them. You tricked me."

"Not me. Kellan. Did he mention he'd given approval for a memorial gathering for Tammi?"

My fingers tightened on the steering wheel. "He did not. In fact, he encouraged me to get a puppy fix and have dinner with our Thistledown friends. Jilly, I've been had."

"Me, too," she said. "Asher told me he had a police function and not to wait up."

"That police function *is* the memorial," I said. "They're letting it happen because they're short on clues. Did they really think we wouldn't find out?"

"They hoped. But you've got to go a long way to pull the wool over Dahlia Galloway's eyes. When Asher came home to change, she wormed enough out of him to know we were being bamboozled."

Keats delivered a long and indignant monologue from Jilly's lap but Percy's meow was more sanguine. If I understood the cat, he was suggesting a subtle approach when I wanted to set the place alight.

"He's right," I said, not realizing I'd said it out loud.

"Who? Asher?"

"Percy. He's recommending stealth mode. We'll accomplish more that way."

"Got it. As long as we don't have to go in like frogs."

"Jilly Blackwood, you couldn't look like a frog even if you tried." I took the turnoff to the farm and pressed the pedal down. "And by the time your work is done, Kellan will be begging to honeymoon in a bookmobile with me."

JUST OVER AN HOUR LATER, we arrived at The Tipsy Grape wine bar looking like a million bucks. Or maybe a little shy of a million, given the pressure to get us both dolled up on a short turn-around. Jilly had lowered her usual "night out" grooming standards in favor of investing in me. Knowing that forced me to raise my heels, lower my neckline and resist the very strong urge to tie back my hair. I put on the diamond earrings and pendant Kellan had given me and polished my engagement ring to maximum glitter. If ever there was a night to pull out the stops, it was this one. Not because the focus should be on me, when the event was technically to honor Tammi Hickey. Rather, because my transformation from frog to princess would unsettle people and make them question their earlier judgement. Unsettled people had loose lips that might spill clues Kellan and Asher couldn't elicit. My flash and Jilly's charm would work differently, if not better, and we had our secret weapons in fur.

"Do you think Percy will get evicted?" Jilly asked. "People get so uptight about fluff in food."

"You used to be one of those people," I reminded her. "At one time you cared more about cuisine than crime."

"Yeah. My pride and prejudice have steadily eroded since I touched down in Clover Grove. Soon, I'll be wearing a poncho over camo." Her face crumpled. "How sad. I haven't even had kids and I'm giving up."

"Jillian Blackwood, you're stunning and you will never give up." The words could have come from me but there was a trilling takeover as Mom joined us. "I'm even more fabulous after producing six children."

Mom was trim and elegant in a sleek black dress with onyx jewelry. Unlike me, she'd forfeited flash for social propriety. Or so it seemed on the surface. By switching from her all-scarlet-all-the-time wardrobe, Mom actually attracted more eyes. She was stealth personified.

"Mom, why are you here?" I whispered. "This event is meant for friends and classmates. You barely knew Tammi."

"Then why did people invite me?" She winked at me. "Not one but three. How many invitations did *you* get, darling?"

Sometimes I wanted to shake my mother, but in this instance she had passed along the invitation, unlike my fiancé and brother. Luckily, secret weapon number two took over. Mom's all-black ensemble was a magnet for my warrior in fluffy ginger armor.

While Mom struggled valiantly to dislodge Percy from her shoulder, Jilly and I slipped into the small but growing crowd.

"I know you," someone said. The man was slight, with a thinning, frizzy afro and a scraggly beard. "You're Asher's wife. He did well for himself. Very well."

Jilly's fingers tightened into claws around her purse. "I'm Jilly Blackwood Galloway, yes. Have you met my best friend, Ivy Galloway?"

The guy reared back. "Ivy? Is that really you?"

Ah, the flatiron and heels were paying off already. "It's me, Scott. Good to see you again."

"Skiff," he said. "I kept the high school nickname. Did you keep yours?"

Jilly moved in front of me. "She did not. Ivy and I run an upscale inn together, Skiff."

The handlebars on his mustache twitched. "On a farm. How posh is that?"

"It's a little bit sweet and a little bit salty," I said. "The perfect blend. How's the cannabis biz treating you?"

"Made my first million before age thirty and doubled it the next year. Do you regret turning me down for junior prom?"

"I don't recall an invitation, Skiff. You must have gone through my brother."

"Everything ran through Asher. Or nearly everything. It was a relief when he graduated a year late. Or was it two?" Skiff stared at Jilly. "Did you know that before you said yes?"

Her smile amped up. "About all the time he spent as a volunteer football coach and mentor? Sure. Asher makes a wonderful cop, doesn't he?"

"Kellan, too," I chimed in. Standing on tiptoe, I looked for the tall men. "I don't see them, but you might think twice about passing weed samples around."

His smile was gone now. "It's legal where I come from."

"You come from down the street, Scott, and it's still not legal here. But there are other ways of honoring Tammi. What's your favorite memory?"

He stared up at a chandelier, thinking. "Once I bagged her groceries at the store and she said thanks. That was a big deal at the time. Later, she would have been bagging mine."

"And would you have said thanks?" I joked.

"Always. She was the prettiest girl in town." He paused and then went for it. "Until Jilly arrived, that is. Tammi's was-band was an idiot for cheating."

"Eddy Hickey is still her husband, Scott. Show some respect."

"That's not what I heard. Nadia keeps in touch with Jess Adcock, who said yes to me for junior prom when you said—"

"Asher said no," I interrupted. "And Jess said...?"

"That Eddy told Tammi he was done the very day she died. He was leaving and she was staying." He glanced at the door as Kellan and Asher walked in. "Don't know why Harper hasn't put the guy behind bars. Instead, Eddy and his girlfriend are both here and poor Tammi is gone. If Jess is right..."

Jilly and I leaned forward ever-so-slightly. "About the girl-friend?" I asked.

"I'm sure she was wrong. There's no way any dude would leave Tammi for—" He stopped abruptly. "Never mind. Jess says I talk too much."

"It's nothing the grapevine hasn't been passing along," I said. "I heard he was seeing—"

"Ivy, don't." Jilly cut me off before I could slander anyone, but I was just trying to bait Skiff out. "If it's true, the police will know, and that's all that matters."

It wasn't all that mattered for someone like Skiff, who still suffered so terribly from the slings and arrows of high school, including my supposed prom rejection. Asher had turned Kellan down a few times, too, but he persisted. Skiff would never have drag-raced for my hand.

"Ladies, you make sure your cops know this..." He folded the fingers of each hand into pistols and aimed them in different directions. "Tammi's was-band was stepping out with one of those girls. Or both."

"Women," Jilly corrected, staring from one to the other. "Rumor and nothing more, Skiff. There's no way Mandy McCain was seeing Tammi's husband."

He blew off the barrel of his righthand "gun" and then said, "Why not? Heard she dated that sleazy dogcatcher who died. Eddy's a step up." He stared at Mandy, who was helping the wait staff set out finger foods. "She turned me down for prom, too. Didn't answer me at all, just faded away." Hands dropping to his side, he tried to move in Mandy's direction, only to encounter a knight in shining fur. "Get your dog out of the way, Ivy. Mandy might just give me a different answer tonight."

In the past few months, Mandy had finally started to feel good about herself and it showed. Instead of watching the room for threats like a flight animal, she was immersed in arranging spring rolls in a large figure eight. It struck me as odd that she chose that number, since it wasn't significant for our graduating year. Bernice often flew in a tight figure eight and it was fast becoming my favorite number. Those closed loops felt safe in an uncertain world.

"Leave Mandy alone, Scott," I said. "She takes her catering seriously. If you really want to try again, go down to the store tomorrow."

"Forget it. I want the element of surprise on my side and you'll warn her by then."

"I won't, I promise." I angled my shoulders slightly so that he wouldn't notice Jilly tapping a message into her phone. Keats dove for Skiff's pant legs to keep him hopping. He didn't get a chance to see shock register on Mandy's face as she checked her phone and then bolted for the kitchen.

Skiff went after her anyway, and Keats let him go. The dog must have had other leads in mind, but I hoped it didn't mean going another round with Nadia, because she was standing beside her husband, wiping her eyes and honking into a tissue.

"Do we have to?" Jilly asked, eyeing Nadia, Skiff's option two.

We studied my dog, who was studying Nadia. His posture suggested he was no more impressed than the first time we met, but his hackles refused to convict her.

"I don't think so," I said. "Even if Nadia was involved with Eddy, she probably didn't take her queen out of the equation."

"Thank goodness," Jilly said. "She seemed so dedicated to Tammi."

I nodded. "It does happen in the actual bee world, though. Sometimes workers kill their reigning queen if she isn't performing well enough. It's called supersedure. First, they nurture new queens, and then they eliminate the original. They gather around her tightly and increase her temperature until she perishes. It's called 'balling.'"

"How gruesome!" Jilly gave a delicate shudder.

"Yeah, but apparently it's for the good of the colony to have a strong queen."

She frowned at me. "Can we change the subject? You're depressing me."

"Sure. Why don't we go over and chat to the faculty who dissed my family and get really depressed?"

Jilly didn't laugh, but Keats did. In fact, he was all for it, and herded us toward a table in the corner. Principal Gillespie was there, looking impeccable in a dark suit. School librarian Delsie Stubbing sat to her right with my former Spanish and math teachers. Both were in their seventies and looked it, with gray hair and clothes that said they didn't dress to impress anymore. Come to think of it, they never had. But aging normally didn't count people out as good leads in a mystery. Far from it. I got my best clues from our senior population and their long "corporate memory" of Clover Grove. They knew Tammi, as well as her family.

All heads were together as we approached and it was obvious they were arguing. Fiona's hands splayed on the table and she said, "It is going to happen. No matter what. There's too much at stake to stop now."

My feet slowed and I whispered, "What will happen? A bee club takeover?"

"Or delivery of the hives to the almond growers?" Jilly whispered back.

Keats gave me a poke and mumbled to hurry. "Let's get closer and find out."

Looking over her shoulder, Jilly said, "Abort. Abort. Incoming."

The missile in question was a bombshell of the masculine kind. Kellan had locked in on me with a look that didn't spell fun in a bookmobile. He was heading our way, but without a sheepdog to clear his path, it was slow going. Turned out my fiancé was the closest thing we had to a celebrity right now.

Still, he forged on. By the time Kellan got to me, however, someone else had gotten to me first.

CHAPTER NINETEEN

I moved away from the faculty table with Jilly and answered my phone in a quiet corner. "Hey, Finch. Two calls in one day. My head is spinning."

"Get your jokes out of the way, Ivy, because I'm not in the mood to laugh."

Was he ever? I couldn't remember seeing Finch truly let it rip. The odd smirk, a bit of a bark, but that was all.

"Did your brother find another swarm?"

"It's dark now, so he isn't looking. Besides, the police took over."

I looked around for Kellan and saw him closing in. Jilly tried to stop him, to no avail.

"What's going on then?" I asked. "You don't make casual calls."

"Something I try to avoid. And this one isn't about what we found but what we lost."

"Oh?" My chest got a little tight. Finch's voice was so strained that I feared it was one of their children. Why would he come to me, though? I didn't go anywhere near difficult situations with children, and luckily those were rare in our area.

"What's missing? Just tell me."

"Jaws. And Persephone."

The room seemed to go silent but it was just the roar in my ears and head. Finch was still speaking but I couldn't make out the words. "What? Both mastiffs are gone?"

"Yeah. Jaws was sitting on the porch at dinnertime and was gone when I went to let him in. Then Jay called from Thistledown and said Peeps vanished half an hour ago."

"Running away at the same time? What are the chances of that?"

His impatient sigh reminded me of Kellan, who was nearly in earshot. "Zero, Ivy. The chances of our dogs running away together when they've happily lived this far apart for over a year is negligible."

"I don't get it." The canine mumble at my side told me I *should* get it, but I didn't. Maybe it was the noise, the nature of the crisis, or my fiancé's hand landing on my shoulder. I understood Finch's dog was missing and that he wanted help to search. What I didn't understand was why he blamed me for it, when his tone suggested he did. "Spell it out for me. I'm at a memorial for Tammi and there's a commotion."

"Exactly. It's about Tammi. I took the risk of telling you where to find her swarming bees. My brother took the risk of allowing you on his property to rescue them. And now our dogs are gone."

Kellan's fingers tightened on my shoulder, so I pressed a button on the phone and crooked my finger for him to lean in. "Finch, Kellan is with me and I put you on speaker. Are you saying you think this double dog theft is retaliation for helping with Tammi's case?"

"That's exactly what I think. I'm sure you do, too, Ivy. You're annoying, but not stupid." There was a pause. "Sorry, Chief. If you're actually there and not one of Ivy's creative concoctions."

Kellan's lip twitched over the last part. "I'm listening, Finch, and I'm sorry to hear about Jaws and the other dog."

"Peeps," I said. "Persephone. She's a sweetheart."

"She is a sweetheart," Finch said. "Jaws will fight, but not Peeps."

Taking the phone from my hand, Kellan's gaze shifted to the middle distance as if watching pieces move around a mental chessboard. "Is there any actual sign of dognapping, Finch? I believe you, but—"

"There's a broken wiener in the garden near my porch. Pork, I presume. Jaws would only touch all-beef and even then, not when there's an intruder. You've seen my dog react to strangers."

Kellan's Adam's apple bobbed. He'd likely been stuck in his squad car with Jaws at the window. "A broken wiener suggests it was lobbed from a distance. How would anyone get Jaws in a getaway car?"

Keats pawed at my foot and when I looked down his warm brown eye flooded my heart with sadness. "Sedation. The only way you'd part a dog like Jaws from his people and property is medication. And if he didn't eat it, it was likely a tranquillizer dart."

"You may not have heard that," Kellan said. "Unlike a real gun."

The was silence on Finch's end. "Doesn't mean they didn't shoot him later. For real."

My dog pawed at my foot repeatedly with a clear message to deploy. The runs he put in my new hose were a reminder of the futility of dressing up.

"Finch, we're coming," I said. "We'll find him. If Persephone was the last to go missing, they're probably still in the Thistledown area. We'll start there."

Kellan rubbed a hand through his hair. "I can't spare officers. There's a murder investigation, as you both know. Drawing police attention away is a common tactic."

Finch groaned. "That's what I get for trying to help."

"What you get for trying to help... is help," I said. "I can gather a big team fast. Head down to your brother's place and we'll meet you there soon."

Jilly spoke for the first time. "Honestly, Finch, our friends are the very best people for this job. No offense, Chief."

"I can't leave my family." Finch's voice cracked and tears rose in my eyes at the sound. I knew only too well what it felt like to lose a dog.

Jilly touched my arm gently and then pointed at Keats. My dog was here. He was fine. Finch and Jaws could have that happy ending, too.

"Officers will be at your house in ten minutes," Kellan said. "That I can do. Go and find your dog. He'll only respond to you."

"I don't know about that." I took my phone back. "Jaws and I have been connecting lately."

"Ivy." Finch sounded exasperated. "Indulge your delusions after my dog is home safe."

"Aw, Finch, I thought we were connecting, too," I said. "But hang tight. This will all be over soon."

CHAPTER TWENTY

The great thing about Edna—one of many—was that the contents of the go-kit she stowed in my truck changed to suit the seasons. I was worried Jilly and I would have to split gear meant for one person but Edna had doubled up. The second set said a lot about Edna's evolving expectations around Jilly. At first, she'd dismissed my best friend as someone who wouldn't get her hands dirty. Now there were gloves and work boots in Jilly's size. The gear meant we could pull into an alley, change in the truck, and shave half an hour off our commute to Thistledown. When two beloved dogs were missing, time was of the essence.

"Thank goodness we brought Percy," Jilly said, maneuvering around both pets in the passenger seat to button her overalls. "We need all hands and paws on deck. Will Maud spare Frost?"

"Frost is excited," I said, patting my phone, which kept pinging as people reported in. "Annie is coming, too."

That was surprising. Frost was up for any challenge, even with three mouths to feed, but Annie disliked gatherings. For the sake of two dogs she'd never met, she was willing to put her reservations aside and join a formidable search and rescue team.

We traveled most of the way in silence, unless you counted the monologue from Keats. He knew Jilly and I detested walks in the hill country bush at any time, but especially in the darkness. The nights were still cold and it was windy, too. We were well equipped physically, thanks to Edna, but she couldn't do much about mindset. That's where Keats' pep talk came in.

"Oh, stop," Jilly said, patting him hard enough to set him off balance. "I'm never going to like this no matter what you say. It might be fun for you and your pack, but it's a unique form of torture for me."

"Ditto. It's the unexpected bunkers that worry me. I've fallen into enough of them. Impossible to see in daylight, let alone now." Keats mumbled what sounded like a reminder to listen to him during the trek. He knew the perils and pitfalls before I did. "Fine. But don't get caught up in competing with your sister or impressing your mother. Your focus gets a little scattered when there's ego at play."

He turned to cast a withering look with his blue eye. I just rolled my eyes back. Then I remembered how lucky I was to have him and reached out to touch his ears. He granted me a rare lick. It wasn't the time for bickering, even in jest.

"There's one upside," Jilly said. "Bees aren't active at night. Right?"

"That's right. All good bees are asleep right now, including Bernice."

Another mile passed and she said what we both thought. "I wish Asher and Kellan could come. Anyone who would steal two mastiffs is a maniac. They could take us down with a dart gun just as easily."

"Getting a good shot in the dark would be tough," I said. "Plus we'll be surrounded. Like Edna always says, armies make it harder to get picked off. By zombies or dognappers, I guess."

"Camo, too. We'll have the advantage over plenty of people, even at night."

I turned to her. "Jilly, do you think we're becoming crazy preppers?"

"The abundance of tinned beans in my pantry would say yes. The other day I had canned meat in my hand—the type that survives an apocalypse. A little voice in my head said better safe than sorry." She ran her hands over Percy and Keats. "It's tasty enough with spicy preserves."

I laughed. "In the old days, the voice in my head talked about climbing the corporate ladder. Getting a nice office and a nicer bonus. Now it tells me to watch my step and avoid bunkers."

"Let's do that tonight. We'll watch our step and let the dogs find the dogs."

Bright lights in the trees told us we'd arrived at the new meetup point about a mile from Jay Pefferlaw's house, in the opposite direction from the property Thelma and I visited earlier. We were starting there because Cori Hogan had boots on the ground before anyone else. She had found a pink collar on the shoulder of the highway with a tag that said "Peeps." There were no paw prints in the gravel, so it may have fallen from a passing vehicle, but Cori's border collie, Clem, had decreed it a good place to start the search.

Our team gathered fast, and it was all civilians. The Thistledown police force only had three officers—two more than a year ago —and they were still busy examining Bibi Bouchard Adcock's property where we found the swarms. One officer drove over with lights and orders about where we could search and then headed back to the station. Kellan oversaw their department now and had found them space in a former convenience store. He'd tried to deploy Asher down here but my brother kept declining the "promotion." They cobbled support together with neighboring jurisdictions, making the best of a challenging situation.

"It's about time," the tiny trainer said as Jilly and I jumped out of the truck. She was dressed all in black, but there were neon orange bands on her arms that matched the middle fingers of her signature gloves. "We couldn't start without you. Or more specifically, Keats.

Clem has been restless but there's a lot of ground to cover and he needs backup."

I shook my head, watching Keats swish around Cori. He adored and respected her and showed it with enough play poses to irk me. Frost, who arrived a few minutes later, greeted Cori and Clem with similar enthusiasm. Only Annie ignored the trainer. Instead, she came over to me, nudged my hand and gave me a searching stare with startling blue eyes in her dark face. Just two months ago, Keats and I had followed a fox's lead to find Annie imprisoned in terrible conditions. Ever since, she'd made a point of quietly greeting me and making sure I was okay. Annie had little patience with her fur kids. Keats and Frost were focused and driven, but enjoyed every adventure. Annie took life more seriously.

That gravitas was on display now as she walked over to Clem and shouldered him out of the way. The expression on Cori's face would have made me laugh in different circumstances. Two proud and reserved men were here grieving lost pets and it wouldn't pay to laugh over canine politics. But Cori always knew how to read a room, even if that room was a clearing and the VIPs were dogs.

"Annie's on point," she said, after exchanging nods with Maud Gentry. "Fall in, Clem. Keats and Frost, you're with Ivy if we need to split up."

The words were really for the humans, because the dogs already understood, even without Cori's vibrant hand gestures. The sheepdogs were all brilliant and I had no doubt they'd find the mastiff siblings if they were in the vicinity.

Keats and Frost flanked me and there were mumbles, some higher, some lower. "What are they saying?" Jilly asked, on the other side of Keats. "Can you catch it?"

"They want to get going. Annie's on a scent, no question."

"Edna," Cori bellowed. "Are we organized?"

There was a scuffle in the shadows and Edna came into the light dragging Buckley Brackens by one arm. "Yeah, we're good. Everyone's been assigned a buddy or team, but Brackens here isn't cooperating."

"I'm a team unto myself," he said. "But I'll take one of the dogs if you're sharing."

"We're not," I said.

"You don't need two," he grumbled, waving his rifle in my general direction.

"Oh, she does," Edna replied. "If anyone needs two dogs to keep her out of trouble, it's Ivy Galloway."

A laugh rippled through the crowd and even Finch managed a weak smile. "I'm changing teams," he said. "I'm with Ivy and the wonder twins."

"No switching," Edna said. "It's not a democracy."

Keats overruled her. He went over and rounded up Finch, Jay and another man to join me. I didn't recognize the guy at first, because of his deerstalker hat, and when I did, I frowned. "Hey, Travis."

"Hey, Ivy. Heard you ratted me out to your fi-an-cé." He dragged out the syllables to make it sound ridiculous. "Oh, Chiefheart, Travis was so mean to me."

I glared at him. "I don't need you reminding Kellan about past adventures, thank you very much. How about you stop teasing me and focus on getting the Pefferlaw dogs back?"

He started to speak again and got nipped for his efforts. One in each leg, as Frost joined Annie in defending my honor. "What the —? Call these two off."

"It only gets worse from there," I said. "Each dog has a signature move that brings a deadbeat to his knees. Just so you know."

"Travis is not a deadbeat," Jay said. "He's saved our bacon a couple of times. That's why he had to—"

Travis made a slashing gesture at his throat. "Let's roll, folks."

Cori walked over and stared up into Travis' face. He had a full foot on her and well over a hundred pounds. "I don't like your energy, dude. We have two dogs missing. We have four brilliant dogs on the case. Do you think I have time for"—her fingers flashed up and down, like he was a mannequin on display—"playground antics? Step up or step out, Travis. And yes, I know who you are and why you just came back. Got it?"

"Yeah." His voice sounded higher. Like some testosterone had leached out of him. "Happy to be here, Ms. Hogan."

"Better," she said. "Now, deploy. Typical search formation. Constant text communication."

A team of nearly 20 set out from the clearing but it wasn't long before Keats and Frost wanted to split off. We were well behind Cori already, so I texted to let her know. The search party divided, too, and Jilly and I ended up with Gertie and Poppy, in addition to the three men. The little hitch in my breath as I heard Edna yelling orders up ahead reinforced how much I'd come to depend on her. Gertie was equally awesome in different ways, but Edna liked to do some of my thinking for me and that was often a nice break.

"Why are we leaving the others?" Finch asked. "That bossy trainer and the black dog seemed to know what they're doing."

"They do," I said. "Can't say for sure but I'm guessing Jaws and Persephone split off. Or were taken to separate locations." When the human grumbles died down, the canine mumbles seemed to confirm it. "I can't imagine the dognapper carried either mastiff too far. They must weigh a ton."

"Jaws is a hundred and thirty pounds and Peeps a little less," Finch said. "Why isn't there a broken trail? No one could carry them, and it sounds like they were doped."

Gertie motioned with her rifle to get everyone to fan out. "Line up in a row, no more than three feet apart. We don't want to miss an inch or a clue."

"She's bossy, too," Travis muttered. "Like we don't know how to search for a dog."

I turned to glare at him, but the effect was likely lost in the wavering beams of flashlights. "If you had it covered, Finch probably wouldn't have called for backup."

"I appreciate the help," Finch said. "But we wouldn't have been in this position if not for you. That's what I get for telling you about the swarms. For being a team player."

Edna would have torn a verbal strip from his heavy brows to his possibly hairy toes. Gertie merely swung Minnie around to aim at him and that didn't fluster Finch one bit.

"Oh, stop it," Jilly said. Her expression was more imperious than Principal Gillespie's, although the fact she was clutching a cat baby undermined the impact. One day, my best friend would bring order to our kids so that I could go shovel manure in the barn. "Finch Pefferlaw, you came to us because you cared about the lost, swarming bees. That's commendable, but good deeds don't often go unpunished in this region and you know it. So don't blame Ivy for stepping in both times."

"Yeah, back off and focus," Poppy said. "Leave my sister alone. She's done more for animals than the entire population of Clover Grove. And I bet she'll find your dog, too, you ingrate."

I appreciated Poppy's support all the more because she'd been avoiding me since my first text from the market. She might not trust me enough to confide in me, but she was still there when the chips were down.

I directed my phone light at my sister and found her staring from under the brim of an oversized purple faux fur hat with a purple striped tail hanging down the back. She was wearing fuchsia plaid pajama bottoms tucked into work boots. "It's okay, Pops. Finch is just worried about Jaws."

He swept off his hat and churned his hand through thick black hair. "I am. If he's— Well, my kids will lose it. There's never been a better family dog."

"Peeps, too," his brother said, sounding equally disconsolate. "Do you really think they're out here, Ivy?"

"Doesn't matter much what I think. When four sheepdogs agree, all we can do is believe. Each in turn has done remarkable work. Together, they could likely fly a space shuttle."

"Build it, too," Gertie said. "So just simmer down and follow their lead. Eyes on the ground to avoid landmines." Jilly squeaked and Gertie added, "More specifically, caves, bunkers and other hazards."

We did as she suggested, walking in proper formation. Finch was on my left and after about 10 minutes of tough walking, he said, "Sorry, Ivy. That was uncalled for."

"It's okay. I know how you feel. I lost Keats once, too, remember? But I got him back. And Frost helped. Their mom and Clem are here, too. You're in good paws."

Pulling a branch aside for me, he sighed. "I love animals. It's people I hate."

"Hey," Travis said, from my right side. "Better add a caveat."

Finch's laugh had a slightly bitter edge. "Most people. With notable exceptions."

"Better," I said. "I hope I'm one of them. We've come a long way since you threatened to shoot me off your land while I searched for my pig."

"I don't recall a gun, but I do recall that you basically accused me of murder. Don't forget that."

"Oh, right. I did forget. Don't take it personally. I've basically accused half the town of murder by now."

"True," Poppy called. "Even her own family."

Travis turned his light from Poppy to me. "She looks just like you. Only cooler."

"Ask my Chiefheart about Poppy if you think she's so cool," I said. "Let's just say she has a checkered past mixed with plaid."

"Can we talk about our missing dogs?" Jay asked, from down the row. "What's the end game? Why hasn't this guy asked for ransom?"

"We don't know it's a guy," I said. "Edna and Gertie are quite capable of getting big dogs moved."

"Bodies, too," Gertie added, with a cackle. "But this was ambitious. Those two brutes would be unwieldy."

"It feels like more than retaliation," I said. "The most obvious conclusion—which isn't always correct—is that Tammi's murderer wants us distracted. Or maybe he wants you and Jay silenced. Do you know anything more?"

"Nothing." He stomped forward, breaking branches with loud snaps. "Not that I can think of now, anyway. Ask me again when the dogs are safe."

"Okay." For the next quarter mile, at least, we walked in silence. Finch held many branches aside for me and helped me cross a couple of small gullies. Whether he'd admit it or not, we were on the same side now. One thing coming home to Clover Grove had shown me repeatedly was that you couldn't just put people in boxes and decide you knew everything about them. At some point your enemy might become a friend and vice versa.

Life here had a lot of gray area, but my feelings about walking in the woods at night never faltered.

I hated it.

Granted, I hated it less now with so many friends surrounding me, but still, there was a pervasive sense of menace in the thick trees and heavy darkness.

Feeling suddenly alone, I reached out mentally for my dog. Where was he?

Far ahead, as it turned out. A sharp yip told me to watch my step.

Finch reached out and tapped my shoulder. "What—?"

He never got to finish his question because his hand slid down my arm, clutched my hand briefly and then fell away.

A moment later, I fell after him.

CHAPTER TWENTY-ONE

Finch Pefferlaw was a man of few words but the ones that spewed out of him now were extremely colorful.

No one sanctioned him for language because he was in a bind that would make most people swear.

I wanted to fire a few off myself but I was afraid to open my mouth in case swamp water got in.

Finch and I had toppled into one of the sinkholes that pocked farm country. I'd landed in others and it was as bad, if not worse, than falling into a bunker.

It was certainly colder at this time of year. My extremities prickled as blood rushed to my core. On the bright side, if there was one, the water usually smelled far worse in summer. Or maybe my chilly nose just didn't work.

"Ivy? Ivy!" Jilly's pale face loomed over the side. Percy had left her arms, like any sensible cat around a sinkhole.

"Don't panic," Gertie called, kneeling beside Jilly.

I was one flutter kick from panicking. "There's no bottom!"

"Of course there's a bottom." Gertie flipped off her backpack. "Otherwise you'd fall through the earth's core, which would probably be warmer."

"Just get her out, Gertie," Jilly said, texting. "Jay, Travis, you help. Poppy and I will keep lights steady."

"I can't swim," Jay said. "Finch can't either."

That jacked up the tension considerably. I didn't like where I was one bit, but slicing scissor kicks with my work boots easily kept my head above water.

"Get Finch first," I said. "I'll swim laps."

Poppy laughed a little but I couldn't join her because Finch smacked me in the face as he thrashed. There wasn't enough room for laps. The sinkhole was maybe eight feet across, but the sides were slick mud. That didn't stop Finch from raking at it with frenzied fingers.

While Gertie unfurled a rope, Travis swung from a large, bare branch and broke it off, snapping off smaller sticks to avoid poking us. Kneeling, he placed it across the sinkhole with plenty of room to spare on each side. "Finch, hold on. You, too, Ivy."

Only one of us did as we were told and it wasn't Finch. When the flashlights hit his face, I saw the glazed look of the feral animal. He was beyond reach of logic.

Jilly saw it, too. Instead of texting or phoning, she raised her voice in a rare bellow. "Edna! 911! Edna!"

Clutching the branch, I called, "Gertie, throw me the rope. Poppy, help her tie it off and I'll catch Finch."

The big man was floundering and scraping on the other side of the branch. Would I have to go under water to reach him?

"Hold up, Ivy," Travis said. He lifted the branch so I could scoot under and then lowered it again. I held on long enough to grab the rope, but then I needed both hands to circle Finch's waist. If I could manage to avoid—

He smacked me in the head again. Entirely by accident, but it still hurt.

"Finch. Settle. I am getting you out but don't kill me first."

My words or my tone calmed him enough that I could reach

around him with the rope, while scissor kicking hard. Now all I had to do was stay afloat long enough to tie a good knot. If it slipped, this plan would fail, because my fingers were already stiffening.

Everyone was quiet while I focused, but the second I called "pull" there was a flurry of activity. I tried to hold Finch's belt to get hauled out, too, but he was kicking too hard. I fell back and grabbed the branch.

"Coming, Ivy," Poppy called. "Cut the rope, buddy. Cut it! Give me that knife."

Travis actually laughed. "Ease up, would you?"

"I will not ease up. That's my sister drowning."

"I'm not drowning. I'm freezing but not drowning." My eyes searched the area above me, looking for black and white in the wavering glow of the flashlights. "Jilly? Where's my dog?"

My voice hadn't given me away before but there was a quaver in it now.

"He's here," she said. "Ivy, I'm sorry. It's water. You know how he is. Shaking. Moaning."

"For pity's sake, Keats, really?" I called. "I could go down in slime here and you're just going to shake and moan?"

There was a whoosh above me and then a splash. I thought my dog had found his nerve, but the hero who joined me in the sinkhole was mostly black and her blue eyes caught the light in a doubly eerie way.

"Annie, it's okay. I'm okay. Get out."

But now the dog was stuck, too, with the slick sides providing no purchase for claws, either.

There was another flurry of bodies above us and someone called, "Dagnabit! Doesn't anyone know how to lasso? Gertie Rhodes, you should be ashamed of yourself."

"Save your prepper shaming, Edna, and throw a loop for the dog."

She did, and a few minutes later, Annie was safe.

Meanwhile, Travis and Poppy dropped to their bellies and held out their hands. My hands slipped out of their grip twice but neither shied away from slime and gradually, they inched back and hauled me out.

Jilly enveloped me instantly in a shiny silver blanket that crackled. "We need to get you home and warm."

"Keats," I called. "Annie, where is he?"

Annie shook hard, sending flecks of muck flying, and then raced off. "Follow her," I said. "I hear Keats. He's found something."

Whether I heard him with my ears or my heart was the question. He had raced some distance away and now there was a craggy hill in between. Travis and Poppy helped me over, while Edna and Gertie did the same with Finch, behind us.

Jilly was in the lead with the cat at her side, bellowing again. "John Keats Galloway, you show yourself. Now!"

He didn't. Nor did Annie. But Percy showed everyone. The orange cat pushed through a dense copse of trees, and let out a yodeling wail.

"Is that good or bad?" Travis asked.

"Both," I said. "He's found something good and probably something less good."

Jilly changed places with Travis and let him force a path through the bush for us. On the other side, Keats was waiting in a point.

I was resigned to finding a cave or bunker. Instead, there was a pup tent. Hearing a whine from inside, Edna didn't bother with the zipper and speedily sliced it open to reveal Jaws.

He tried to get up and fell back, too sedated to coordinate his limbs. His head lolled but his whine grew stronger when Finch fell on his knees beside him. I gestured for everyone to turn so they could have a moment. The last thing I saw was Jaws aiming a sloppy lick at Finch and hitting Keats by mistake. My dog grumbled in disgust and came back to my side.

"Serves you right for letting me drown," I said. He mumbled

something back that was saucy, apologetic and proud, all at the same time. My fingers found his ears, which sent warmth through me that the blanket Jilly tried to wrap around me again couldn't provide. "I'm good," I told her, reaching for Annie. "Two great dogs and another reviving."

"Such a relief, but what about Peeps?" Jay said. The glow from his flashlight showed tears gleaming in his dark eyes.

I released Annie and Keats. "They know. We'll go after them."

Poppy and Edna stayed behind with Finch and Jaws, while the rest of us followed the sheepdog mother and son. The feline hero rode on Jilly's shoulder, which she didn't usually allow.

When we found the second pup tent, the third member of the brilliant trio was already waiting. Frost was crouched and poised to attack, as needed.

She didn't move until Gertie slashed that tent to reveal Persephone, passed out cold.

Jay hugged the mastiff's big, floppy body and cried. "How are we going to get her out of here? She needs a vet."

Travis shone his light around. "They got her here somehow... That's it." An old brown sedan sat near a mere hint of a road leading out of the bush. He walked over and looked inside the vehicle. "Good thing I know how to hot-wire a car, because someone else already did."

CHAPTER TWENTY-TWO

The next morning, when the phone woke me before dawn, I felt very much the worse for wear. There was a swampy smell in the bedroom that I wanted to blame on the dog, but couldn't, since he'd kept his white paws on dry land. Despite a long shower with a variety of scented products, I must be the one stinking the place out. Luckily, I didn't need to see many people today.

Glancing at call display, I fumbled for the button. "Sutton? It's five a.m. The rooster hasn't crowed."

"Sorry, but I need you."

His voice was anxious, almost pleading. What had that kid gotten himself into now? But this was my blood and there was only one answer. "Okay, I'm coming. What's wrong?"

"Don't get mad."

"If you're in jail, I'm going to get mad. Fair warning. And I will tell your mother."

There was a huffy sigh at the other end. "I'm not in jail."

I put the phone on speaker and turned down the volume so it didn't wake anyone else. Setting it on the bed, I started opening drawers and pulling out clothes. "What then? A car accident? A fight?"

"No and no. You're so dramatic."

I slid out of flannel pajamas and into overalls and a long-sleeved T-shirt. "I'm dramatic? Who called who before sunrise?"

"It's not that big of a deal, but Asher can't come through for me."

I stopped with one sock still in my hand. "Asher wrote this situation off and then you came to me?"

"Well, yeah. Don't take it personally. He's a cop. Exactly what I needed for the job."

I put the sock on, hopping a little. "What job did Asher decline?"

"He was supposed to come for Careers Day. Every Thursday someone brings a guest to talk about jobs and community. It's my turn and Uncle Ash cancelled. Iris turned me down, too."

Sitting on the side of the bed I glanced at Keats and found his mouth hanging open in a pant-laugh. "So, your supposedly favorite aunt is third choice for career day."

"Well, you don't really have a career. At least, not one you can talk about in class."

"Sutton, I own an inn. That's not nothing."

"But Jilly pretty much runs it and does the cooking." There was a pause. "Asher told me I couldn't call her. She's tired after last night."

"I fell into freezing swamp water last night, pal. I'm tired, too. But I got up and dressed because I thought you needed me."

"I do need you. This counts for 10 per cent of my grade in my Individual and Society class and I'm nearly failing."

"How can that be? It's a bird class."

"You mean a boring class. Especially career days. I already know I'm going to open a car repair shop with Weston. But I still want to pass, because Mom will punish me by restricting access to everything I love."

My hair was a lost cause after going to bed with it wet, so I started braiding it. "Good thing you're not planning on a sales career because your pitch needs work. I've got a dozen other things to do today. How about asking your grandmother? She's a skilled barber and has a thriving clothing design business on the side. Plus, she owes you for taking her out driving when she's unlicensed."

"First, Dahlia is crazy and I never admit we're related. Second, you owe me, too. Remember how I faked sick to get you into school? I even ate an old tuna sandwich in case I legit needed to hurl." When I didn't respond to his manipulation, he added, "Are you telling me there's nothing else you could do at school today for your unofficial investigation?"

So, he wasn't a terrible salesman after all. I was very curious to know more about what Fiona Gillespie got so heated about at the memorial gathering. "Fine. I'll do it because of the tuna sandwich. If you belatedly die of food poisoning, your mother will restrict access to everything I love. By killing me."

"Great, thanks. Let's talk about what you can talk about."

I got up and snapped my fingers at the dog. He jumped down so I could make the bed, whereas Percy doubled down and made me work around him. "I know how to give a talk from my corporate days, Sutton. I don't love it, but I'm a capable speaker. What's more, I think I have valuable experience to share. I have a dozen HR awards but chose to come back to Clover Grove."

"It would be totally great if you talked about HR. Maybe bring one of the awards along."

I fluffed a pillow and tossed it down. "Don't even know where they are. Nowadays, I'm a happy innkeeper and even happier hobby farmer."

"Aunt Ivy?"

This must be important because he almost never called me 'aunt.' "What?"

"Just don't be weird, okay?"

I grabbed another pillow and shook it hard. "Since when did you care about my being weird? You said you want to be like me."

"Ivy the vigilante, which Kellan won't let you talk about. The farm stuff is... weird. You get a strange look when you talk about manure." He paused again. "Please don't talk about manure."

"Do you want to write a speech for me and I'll just read it?" I threw the pillow down hard enough that Percy cracked open green eyes accusingly. "How about that?"

"You know I can't spell. That would be even weirder."

"Honestly, Sutton, you're making me nervous. I think we should find someone less weird. Because I am who I am and there's a reasonably good chance I'll talk to my dog in front of your class. And worse, that he'll respond."

Finally, Sutton laughed. "I know. That's why I went for Asher, even though you're way cooler, Aunt Ivy. My class won't see the cool part."

I perched on the edge of my bed holding the phone. "Aha! There's a girl, isn't there?"

"There's no girl. And I wouldn't want to be with one who didn't think you're cool. But people already talk about us a lot. I can only take so much before... you know."

"Spray painting the school walls."

"Or worse."

I thought about asking what was worse but decided to bide my time. If this week had told me anything, it was that high school brought a huge amount of tension that was bound to blow at some point. When this talk was over, I'd probe more and make sure he was safe.

"I'll do my best to avoid an open discussion with Keats but I make no promises about manure. I've got a good side hustle with fertilizer and many of your classmates' parents either use it or want it."

"Manure will never be cool. But how about I teach you to hot-wire a car? That is cool."

"Might come in handy. I suppose Asher taught you that?"

"Learned it in shop class, too. Only good thing Sever did for us after he started volunteering. But I'd already taught myself from an online video when I was ten. Took Mom's car down to buy ice cream." He paused. "Don't mention that. It went fine, obviously."

Setting the phone on the bed, I pushed the heels of both hands into my eyes. Never had I needed a coffee so badly. "Don't tell me these things, Sutton. It puts me in an awkward position with your mother, who's basically my mother, too. Is that weird enough for you?"

"Yeah. Don't talk about that today, either. And Ivy?"

I got up and reached for the doorknob. "What now?"

"Don't wear overalls."

———

I WORE OVERALLS. Not to embarrass Sutton, but because the outfit suited the theme of the talk I developed while doing morning chores. I did put on a fresh pair before leaving. Talking about manure was one thing, smelling like it another. At least the swamp bouquet was fading.

"I'm not going in there to fake it, boys," I said, walking up the front stairs of the school with Percy on my shoulder and Keats by my side. "I want to be authentic and show kids they can succeed while being authentic, too. We need to keep more bright, hardworking young people in Clover Grove to revitalize it, and they won't stay unless they see good options for making a living. Many of them would be happier cobbling jobs together here than parking their butts in concrete towers. We can show them that."

I was afraid the talk would be in one of my old classrooms, but Sutton met me at the front door and led me to the school library.

"You had to bring the cat?" He scanned me with thinly veiled disgust.

"I've seen that expression before. On your grandmother's face."

"Stop it." He gestured to the full chairs in the gathering space in the library. "These are my people, remember?"

"These aren't your people. Well, maybe one or two of them are your people but the rest... You'll try to forget most of them."

"Bitter much?"

He tried to grab the cat off my shoulder and got a clawed swat for his efforts. Keats added a nip for good measure. It was important for pups of the human persuasion to know their place.

"Family, Sutton. Good friends like Edna and Gertie. They're your people."

"Edna and Gertie are not my people." He shuddered. "The camo? The poncho? No. Just no."

"They'd save your life without a second thought, pal. Can you say the same about the kids slouched in those chairs?"

He rubbed his forehead and pushed back unruly dark hair. "Can we not talk about this? It's giving me a headache."

"Fine. Let the show go on." I strode ahead of him into the library, introduced myself to the teacher and pumped Delsie Stubbing's hand. They both looked a bit nervous, probably because Percy was puffed and restless. Something had irked him, and it seemed like an overreaction to what Sutton had done. Keats, on the other hand, was mumbling happily. He liked mingling with a group now and then. A border collie craved new and different experiences.

This certainly was new to me. I had never spoken to a class before. Two classes, as far as I could tell. There were more than 50 kids by the time everyone got seated, and the teacher kept bringing in more chairs. Finally, she closed the door and locked it, leaving some kids outside, faces pressed to the glass. Were students coming to hear me by choice? That was unexpected, and it jacked up the pressure even more.

Keats herded me with a strategic nip onto a low platform at the front. There was a chair for me, and a table that held a pitcher full of water. I poured myself a glass and chugged half of it. Then I moved the chair aside and perched on the edge of the table. Jumping down from my shoulder, Percy stuck his paw into the pitcher and then licked it. Repeatedly.

Everyone laughed and it was a good opening.

"That's what working in Clover Grove is like," I began. "You come hoping for peace, calm and dignity, and you get a dog steering you around with nips, and a cat churning things up in a public setting. And you get more variety and freedom than you could ever find in a city job. Today, I want to talk to you about second chances and makeovers. Because I left this school with a single-minded plan to succeed in business. I got a scholarship to a good college, graduated with distinction and worked my way up the corporate ladder till it was time to make a jump to a new ladder and start climbing again. Instead... I came home. I bought a farm. I launched an inn. And yes, I helped put a killer or two behind bars. I bet that's why you're here, but my nephew says I can't talk about that. So, let's talk instead about being authentic. About figuring out what will make you happy in life before you spend ten years on the wrong ladder and have to climb backward or make perilous leaps. It's possible to make a good living right here in Clover Grove or nearby towns. You just need to get creative. That's what I'm going to talk about today, with a sincere attempt not to embarrass Sutton. He already knows what he wants to do with his life. But many of you won't, and I hope when you're filling out college applications, you'll think about this talk. About me in my overalls with my rude cat and nippy dog. It took me a long time to become this person—a happy person—and if I give you a few shortcuts today, I'll be well satisfied."

I grabbed the water glass and took another sip before Percy could churn that up, too. In the pause, someone muttered quietly. It was a scornful jeer and girlish titters followed. Scanning the room, I found my nephew staring at a pretty girl with blonde hair and dark roots. No one in this generation seemed to care about roots. That must be freeing.

Keats took his cue and skulked toward the jeering girl with his belly brushing the stained industrial carpeting. She was an unruly sheep who needed to be schooled.

"Would you care to leave?" I asked the girl. She was probably 16, like Sutton, and wore a short white skirt, identical to the ones her friends on either side wore. "I see your legs are bare and—full disclosure—fang marks sometimes scar."

"You shouldn't be bragging about a dog who bites," she said, pulling her feet up. "My mother will report you to animal services. She says you're nuts."

I studied her features and made the connection. "Wait, you must be Kayla Ware's daughter. You make those adorable crocheted farm animals. I loved the pig so much! It's Linzy, right?"

"That's my little sister." Her face practically burst into flame. "I'm Tamlyn and I definitely do not crochet."

"No shame in textile arts. Your mother's made a career out of serving crafty people, which illustrates my point beautifully. You can do what you love in Clover Grove, with hard work and some ingenuity."

Tamlyn tried to kick Keats with a white sneaker and lost a shoelace for her pains. The dog shook it like a rodent and flung it in the air with a flourish. "Look, Tamlyn." I pushed off the table. "I know you're probably grieving your Aunt Tammi and you have my sympathy. But that doesn't give you license to kick a dog. Any dog. This one's a hero, by the way, who's saved lives a dozen times. Keep it up and I'll leave." I glanced around. "Show of hands, please. Who wants me to leave?"

Tamlyn's hand shot up and her two friends followed suit. In the second generation of queen bees, Kayla's offspring automatically got top billing since Tammi didn't reproduce.

The teacher stepped forward to intervene but I motioned for her to stand down. I had more life experience now. Teenagers weren't much worse than Wilma or Drama Llama. "Okay," I continued. "Show of hands. Who wants the dog-kicker and her buddies to leave?"

At least two dozen hands shot up and waved. Another dozen followed more slowly.

Keats sat in front of Tamlyn and I motioned to Percy to join him. "It's okay, girls. You can stay. One day, we're going to be friends."

Tamlyn tossed her backpack at my pets and missed. "Never. Gonna. Happen."

"Maybe not if you go to a city. But if you stay here, it'll happen. You'll need help one day and my barn door will be open to you." I smiled at the teacher. "Let's carry on."

I talked for another ten minutes, giving concrete examples of local success stories and tips for getting ahead without going anywhere.

The applause at the end was loud, but nothing was more satisfying than seeing Sutton's incredulous expression. I'd exceeded his hopes for Iris, if not Asher.

Tamlyn waved her hand and I thought she had a question. Instead, she was showing a video on her phone. "Have you all seen this?" she called. "Farmer lady and her nephew were doing some lame kung fu moves after tagging the school wall. My mom reported the graffiti, too."

"There was no tagging. As for the lame kung fu... guilty as charged. Sometimes a farmer lady needs to let off steam."

The phone started circulating and Sutton's face turned as red as Tamlyn's had been earlier. He tried to snatch the phone, while shaking off Percy. The cat was scaling my nephew's leg with single-minded determination.

Suddenly, I understood Percy's mood, but it was too late to do anything about it.

One of Sutton's ferrets came out of his collar and jumped into the air to escape the cat. It was sheer luck and coincidence, I'm sure, that the frisky mustelid happened to land on Tamlyn's lap.

The session ended with screams, chaos, and ultimately, tears.

Tamlyn's, not mine.

CHAPTER TWENTY-THREE

I sat in the reception area outside Fiona Gillespie's office with Delsie Stubbing. A smile that was not HR approved flickered onto my face as I realized it was my first summons to the principal's office. I'd never had the guts to do anything out of bounds until fairly recently. My head injury had blown my scruples to smithereens. As a teen, I would have been terrified to face Mrs. Gillespie. Now, the only authority figure who scared me was Kellan, and when he heard what happened today, he would laugh.

Keats was already laughing. He gave a happy pant, tossed the piece of shoelace, and repeated the sequence. Percy was in his carrier because the ferret was still at large. The faculty refused to believe the cat and dog would be an asset in locating it.

"Why on earth did Sutton bring that thing in here?" Delsie said, literally clutching her pearls. I was surprised she could afford such a nice string on a school salary, but maybe it was an heirloom. Personally, I wouldn't risk showing off my jewels here, and had propped my rings on with a rubber washer from my bathroom faucet. It would slow a young thief down until Keats took her out.

Tamlyn's face had come to mind but I had no reason to think she was a thief. Just a bully with the audacity to punch above her weight.

I gave her points for courage but still hoped to be gone when she left the restroom, where she was washing off mascara and ferret cooties.

"No idea," I said. "I'm sure Principal Gillespie will inquire. Maybe Sutton thought my talk would bomb and he'd release a distraction." Or maybe he did it often and this was his first accidental disclosure. I wouldn't put it past him. It was ironic that after asking me not to be weird, he'd outdone me.

"It didn't bomb," Delsie said. "Far from it. I think you delivered an important message to these kids. Something no one has said before, and we've had twenty speakers."

"My senior friends have long lamented how our best young talent leaves Clover Grove. I guess I've been thinking about how to make them want to stay. Some of my friends would give great talks. Like Teri Mason and Mabel Halliday, who do well selling their art. All kids seem to hear about is how hard it is to make a living here. It doesn't need to be true."

"I agree. Tamlyn Ware had planned to bring in Tammi Hickey to talk about beekeeping. Tammi's business was growing like crazy and big apiculture outfits were knocking at her door. Her designer queen bees commanded a good price and I hoped to get in before they were out of my budget." She gave me a sly look through the thick lenses of her glasses. "Did Tammi's queen nursery survive the robbery?"

I shook my head. "Didn't know there was such a thing. How is it different from a regular hive?"

"It wouldn't just be sitting in her yard, for starters. Queens are valuable in today's market. Of course, they'd be worth less now. Tammi was breeding for calm colonies and queens that weren't quick to swarm. I hear many of hers did."

"That was different. Those bees were rattled and probably wanted to go home. You can't blame queen quality in these circumstances."

"Don't worry about it, Ivy." Delsie shrugged. "I was just curious.

They've probably died by now. Or killed each other, as competing queens do."

At that moment, an insect flew in the open door of the waiting room, did a quick figure eight, and buzzed out again. It seemed Bernice was making her rounds, and that made me sit up straighter. "The animal kingdom is fascinating, isn't it?" I said, rubbing my hands together.

"Except for ferrets, I suppose. It's too bad your talk today ended on that note. All anyone will remember is the ferret."

I got up and paced around the room. The large reception desk was vacant, as it had been the other day. Maybe they'd downsized staff again. I ran my fingers over the dark oak. This was the kind of antique Jilly would love at the inn. Dad could refinish it and repair the locks. There was room to store most of my ceramic figurines in the drawers.

Perching on it, I smiled at Delsie. "Animal stories grab attention. Phones were out and I bet videos are already circulating. I wish Tamlyn hadn't flailed so much and let the ferret into her sweater. I know how uncomfortable that feels."

The librarian's hand moved from her pearls to her fine, wispy gray hair. "Those twins are something else. Worse than your sister ever was."

A spark flared in my chest and Keats mumbled advice not to let my temper ruin an opportunity. It was hard to hang around and play nice with Delsie when she'd said harsh things about my family, but I couldn't call her on them. "I'm sure Daisy was a model student."

"Not Daisy. Poppy." She tapped the chair I'd left. "She was sitting here countless times, accused of truancy, plagiarism, vandalism, theft, fighting..." Her voice drifted off as she searched for more violations, and then finished strongly with, "Illegal substance use, and possibly distribution, before Skiff took over."

"That's quite a list. I never heard about anything other than truancy."

"She was expelled after a significant incident. Confidential, of course." Delsie folded her hands in her lap and stared at them. "I always felt bad about it."

"Don't. She finished school eventually. Some would say it was meant to be." Not me, of course, but I had to tamp down my temper like tobacco in a pipe.

"I suppose," Delsie said. "But Poppy had a creative gift and if things had gone well, she could have ended up like Mabel and Teri. The art teacher of the day advocated for her but other voices were louder. And now look at the poor girl, with her blue hair and desperation."

"Purple hair," I said. "At least yesterday. And Poppy is good at a lot of things, including working for me."

"She wasn't meant to be a farmhand. The art teacher never fought like that for another student."

"Which teacher was that?" I asked. "Art was never my elective."

"Judi Morrell. Nice enough lady, if a bit flighty. What happened to her wasn't fair, either."

Keats nudged my foot to make me dig a little deeper. "What happened to Mrs. Morrell?"

Delsie's knuckles whitened in her lap. "It was one of those scandals that plagues all schools if you're around long enough. Worse in those days."

"An affair?" As an HR rep, it was always the first place I went, before moving on to drink and drugs. "There are few scandals I missed in my corporate job, Delsie. I doubt a school could rival a big company for trouble like that."

In my experience, affairs never ended well. Usually someone was forced to leave for the wrong job at the wrong time. Careers were scuttled and the relationships seemed to fail anyway. I'd categorized them under "not worth it."

"Well, this is an old story and long over. I only mention it because Poppy might want to track Judi down."

"She might," I said. "Is Mrs. Morrell still teaching?"

"Retired. Has a studio near Dorset Hills and does very well, from what I heard."

Keats weighed in with a mumble and I hopped off the desk. "Gotta run. The blacksmith is coming to the farm." It was true, although Dad would handle the visit.

"Ivy, you can't run away now. The principal asked to see you."

"We've been waiting for fifteen minutes. Please tell her I'm sorry about the ferret. I'll speak to Sutton about it, and I'm sure Daisy will, too."

"Maybe Fiona wants to thank you personally." She touched her pearls again, suggesting otherwise. "We're not used to such—uh, lively—visits."

"That's me. Lively." After rooting around in my pocket, I handed her a dogeared business card. "Fiona can scold me by phone." I bent to pick up Keats' prize and handed it to Delsie. "And I'll replace the shoelace, as required."

I SWUNG by the grocery store to collect Jilly on my way to Dorset Hills.

"Should you talk to Poppy before cornering her former mentor?" Jilly asked, after I filled her in on my morning. "She might not like you poking into her secret, arty past."

"She probably won't but I've been trying to pin her down for two days. Weston took two of her farm shifts and she's giving one-word responses to my texts. The only person more slippery than Poppy right now is—"

"You?"

"Ha! I was going to say Mom. Guess the trait runs through the family on the Swingle side. Even without the satin skirts she loves, Mom's slippery."

Jilly laughed. "She is. But now I'm sliding down a slippery slope with you. I don't want to upset Poppy more. Remember how supportive she was last night when you were stuck in a sinkhole."

"I remember. But once I was safe, she ignored me again."

"Hardly. You and I got a ride out while she walked back through the bush with the others and looked for clues. Who got the better part of that deal?"

"I still smell like swamp, don't I?"

She sniffed. "Vaguely. It's been worse."

"Anyway, I'm hoping this visit will give us information to make Poppy feel better. Delsie Stubbing said Pops got a bum deal at school and I want to know more. Something's keeping her from dealing with it or even talking about it."

My best friend ran one hand over Keats and the other over Percy. "Well, the boys want to go, so I guess something will come of it."

Changing the subject, I asked, "Do you think the class reunion will happen? The memorial ended early because of the dognapping."

"I can't see Kellan agreeing to it. They're no closer to figuring out what happened to Tammi, at least according to Asher's insomnia. Found him on the couch watching sports reruns this morning."

"Comfort TV," I said. "Kellan's check-in was super short last night so I think you're right." I turned onto the bypass that would take us to Dorset Hills. "I guess I don't need to worry too much about the reunion, but I still worry about Poppy and figure talking to Judi Morrell can't hurt." Pressing down on the gas, I tossed Jilly a smile. "I need you to deploy the Blackwood velvet punch. It seems like there was an illicit romance that got this teacher fired from Clover Grove High."

Jilly's fingers stilled, her hands hanging above the pets. "Why do we need to bring that up when we're going there to figure out what happened with Poppy?"

"It's an icebreaker. Once we spring that on her, she'll be eager to change the subject to Poppy and spill everything."

"Affairs are never icebreakers. They're the iceberg that takes down a conversation and tears people apart under the surface." Her hands landed in fur. "I got a lot of work finding people new jobs after affairs. So much heartbreak and professional upheaval."

"Delsie said this one is long over, though. Hopefully Judi's moved on and found a good man."

"Or at least channeled the emotion into her art."

I took a winding road into the hills and before long, we pulled up to the quaint studio. It was a single story, with large windows and a spectacular view of the valleys and Dog Town below. On this sunny morning with the hillsides turning green, I could see how the landscape would inspire any artist. Surely this was an upgrade from the stale and sterile high school that evicted Judi years ago. She must have done well to own the place, and her name was the one stenciled on the door. We were within regular studio hours, although that wouldn't have stopped me anyway. Not when Keats was pawing at the door. Percy elected to loll in Jilly's arms. He always played cat baby when our goal was to lower someone's guard.

The woman who opened the door was almost a cliché of the artist, with a paint-smeared smock, a messy bun with drooping tendrils of gray hair, and a distant look in her gray eyes. "Good morning. Would you like to— Oh. Ivy, it's you."

"You remember me? I didn't take art classes at school."

She stepped back to let us pass. "I know. It was all academics for you. But you were hard to miss, winning all the big awards. And not showing up to collect them. Seems like you got sick at the end of every school year. Mononucleosis, vertigo, gastroesophageal reflux, ocular migraines... Always something creative."

"Reflux!" My face grew very warm for a cool spring day. "Obviously, Mom improvised when she called. All I said was that I was too sick to go to the final assembly."

Keats gave a happy ha-ha-ha, while Jilly turned to stare at me. "You didn't collect your awards?"

"And be an even bigger target for the bees? No way." I turned back to Judi. "I meant Tammi and her attendants."

"I know. There was always a Tammi. When one graduated, another moved into her place." She led us through the front hall and into the main gallery. "Usually they stop queening after high school, but Tammi exceeded a normal lifespan." Her face seemed to get hotter as mine cooled. "Just in terms of insects."

"Three to five years for a normal queen bee," I said. "That's a good showing for high school."

"Speaking of showing..." Jilly formally introduced herself and then tried to steer the conversation into safer territory. "Judi, your gallery is gorgeous and your art is... well, familiar."

It most certainly was familiar, and not because I had seen Judi's work before. The walls were lined with bright and cheery watercolors of farm animals. Cows, sheep, goats, a menacing pig, llamas, donkeys, an old saggy-backed mare and a sweet brown alpaca.

In short, *my* farm animals.

I turned to Judi. "Have you been to Runaway Farm?"

She nodded, her cheeks redder than ever. "Once, and before your time. I was a fan of the online show, The Princess and the Pig. I knew Hannah Pemberton and worked in an arts collective with her mother, Mavis." Following us around the barnyard portraits, she continued, "I've been working on new pieces since you and your animals started getting accolades for your work helping police."

Accolades was the wrong word. There were no plaques coming from the police or the mayor, and the news coverage was rarely favorable.

Reading into my silence, she added, "I suppose I should have run this by you, first."

I shrugged. "It's okay. You're not the only artist who's been inspired by my animals, and I can't complain about that."

Keats mumbled a decided complaint, perhaps because his handsome face was missing from the collection.

"I didn't include the dog, of course," Judi said. "Or the cat. That would feel intrusive, especially after all you've done for the community."

Reaching the end of the exhibit—a trio of jaunty hens—I couldn't help smiling. "This feels a little bit like the school's awards assembly, Mrs. Morrell." I touched my throat. "I think I have tonsillitis."

"You got your tonsils out in eleventh grade," she said. "According to your mother. We'd take bets in the faculty lunchroom over what ailment she'd devise next. It wasn't just you. Several Galloways were frequently absent. I figured she kept a list by the phone."

"Never too late to learn about your family." I was somewhat dismayed to find I was the butt of jokes among teachers, when I tried so hard to keep a low profile.

Jilly and Keats flanked me to offer support. "There are worse things than boycotting awards," my friend said. "She didn't show up in person to collect HR awards either. Ivy's never needed that kind of validation."

That was true, but mostly, I just hated being the center of attention. Keats nudged me and mumbled something encouraging. It was time to turn this conversation around—and maybe even my perspective.

"Maybe we could consider your exhibit an award," I said. "Although my animals are the real prizes. Seeing them in your beautiful work suits me far better than a certificate or plaque." I cleared my throat. "Two tonsils agree."

The artist stared at Keats and Percy with a hunger I recognized from the faces of treasure hunters and antique collectors. "Would you mind if I sketched them? I couldn't do them justice till we met."

I shrugged. "Ask them. Keats never sits still for long. Percy's easier."

She earned points from me by doing just that. Keats rumbled a gracious assent and Percy just flicked his tail idly before deciding to jump down. They sat side by side in a ray of sunlight that hit their eyes just right, while the artist scrambled to find a sketchbook.

Perching on a low stool, she began capturing their image with bold strokes of her pencil. It was like Jilly and I had left the building.

I seized the moment. The best time to make inquiries was when someone was preoccupied by something they loved. "Mrs. Morell, I—"

"Miss, Ms., or just plain Judi. I never married." The pencil sailed toward the right corner, perhaps capturing a fluffy tail. "Not for lack of trying."

"I heard there was someone at school, at least for a while."

The pencil stopped and her eyes came up with a piercing stare. "Oh?"

Oops. Too much, too soon. I was bringing my B game.

"Delsie Stubbing mentioned it today when I was waiting to be reprimanded by Principal Gillespie. My nephew released a ferret during my career talk."

Her pencil resumed its graceful sweeping. "I don't want to discuss my love life, Ivy. But I could use a ferret on the walls."

"I'm sure I could deliver a model. They're very social."

Jilly gestured for me to stand down. She'd been right about the affair being an iceberg. "Judi, we're really here to talk to you about Ivy's sister."

"Poppy?" Judi didn't look up. "She was the only Galloway who enjoyed my class. How's she doing?"

"Fine," I said. "She had a rough few years where I didn't see much of her, but seems happy working at the farm, now."

Jilly took up the baton again. "As a former headhunter, I'd say Poppy never quite found her calling."

Judi's eyes darted from Keats to the page and then back. "I

would think not. Her calling was art but I couldn't get her to hear it. She's one of my lost girls."

"Lost girls?" Jilly asked. "What does that mean?"

"Lost kids, I should have said. Maybe once in a cohort there's a student with a lot of raw talent. Poppy was that kid. Her drawings were incredibly vibrant." She flipped the page in her sketchbook and started something new. "So many monsters. A real taste for horror. But she lacked confidence. Commitment. It's like catching butterflies without a net at that age. I did try but she eluded me."

"I remember sketchbooks at home but they disappeared. She must have outgrown them."

Judi shook her head and her messy bun loosened. "You don't outgrow a talent like that, but sometimes it gets pushed underground for a long while." Her lips curled into a smile. "One day you might find her decorating the barn walls."

"I'm sorry to hear Poppy gave up her art," Jilly said. "Lots of us don't find ourselves till our thirties."

"I sure didn't," I said. "That's exactly what I told the students today."

Lifting the sketchbook, Judi turned it toward us to reveal a charcoal portrait of two women standing shoulder to shoulder—one in overalls and a braid, the other more polished, with flowing curls. Jilly and I had been photographed often but this was different. We looked older. Natural. Authentic.

"Beautiful," the artist said, smiling at us. "Women at peace with themselves and their actions. Even if others complain, sometimes."

I laughed. "It's like you know my fiancé."

"Better than you might think. Kellan was in my class for two years, and I noticed he had a good eye for art, as well as character."

Tempting as it was to explore Kellan's gifts, there was a gifted dog putting his talents on display. I gestured to a closed storage unit, where he stood, pointing. "Keats is very interested in your cabinet, Judi. Are you hiding liver treats?"

"Just art supplies." She got up and opened both doors. Percy took over from Keats by scaling the shelves and dropping into an open cardboard box. On the side it read, "Clover Grove High."

"I'll get him," I said, reaching up for the box. The cat scrabbled around inside, making the most of his mischief.

Judi motioned for me to set the box on a table and Percy jumped out, looking satisfied. The artist moved things around and stopped. "Wait. I think I have one of Poppy's sketchbooks. You could return it to her. Maybe it'll stir things up, like the cat did." After a few minutes, she found what she wanted and flipped the pages. "See? Monsters. Poppy had worries and here's where they came out to play."

About midway through the book was a sketch of the reception area outside Principal Gillespie's office, where a zombie-style creature jumped out of a box, arms outstretched. The monster was spitting symbols, including dollar signs and letters. Lemons and other fruit also dotted the page.

"How... interesting." Jilly struggled to find words. "What's next?"

On the following page was a trashcan, out of which my sister's head emerged, complete with spiky hair and piercings. More symbols appeared, most of them teardrops.

"That was it," Judi said. "She was expelled, and I supposed that's how she viewed the situation."

My stomach did unpleasant gymnastics and delivered a legitimate case of gastroesophageal reflux. I swallowed hard to get rid of the acid. "You mean, that's how she viewed *herself*. As garbage. Taken out to the curb by the faculty."

"Not by everyone," Judi said. "I wanted to give Poppy the art award and I defended her on several occasions, including this last incident. Someone broke into the secretary's desk and stole a lockbox that held about two thousand dollars from a fundraiser. Because

Poppy was called in twice that day—for truancy and then graffiti—everyone assumed she was the thief. There was no proof."

I flipped back and forth between the two sketches and Keats mumbled a commentary. "She felt helpless to do anything about it. Mom probably didn't fight for her."

"Actually, she did. No one took her seriously, I'm afraid. So, Poppy was expelled. She came to say goodbye and left this behind."

"She left town right after that," I said. "Didn't see her again till I finished my first year of college."

"I left soon after, too," Judi said. "I wasn't fired, although you may have heard that. I definitely made a poor choice in men. He broke my heart and drained my bank account, but after substitute teaching for a few years, I inherited this place from my aunt. I got the fresh start I craved."

"I can see why you retired from teaching," Jilly said. "This is a wonderful life for you."

Judi put the box back on the shelf and closed the doors with a clang. "I still teach classes, but the pressure is different. In the school system, I took the responsibility for influencing young minds seriously. Seeing Poppy drop out and give up on herself was more heartbreaking than losing— Well, never mind." She brushed at her smock, as if the old paint stains weren't permanent. "I won't say his name in my happy place."

Keats was getting restless so Jilly squeezed Judi's arm. "That's all behind you now. What's ahead?"

The artist walked us to the door. "I suppose I'll be adding some key players to my farm hero series. Maybe I'll do a grand opening. Would you come?"

I clutched my abdomen. "I think something's about to rupture in there. Appendix? Spleen? Where's my gall bladder?"

Tugging me out the door, Jilly laughed. "Probably with your tricky tonsils. But if attending the opening means business for the inn, we'll be here with business cards." Keats mumbled his two cents and Jilly added, "Don't forget Ivy's taken up public speaking."

"For youth only," I called back to Judi as we headed for the truck. "Ferrets entirely optional."

CHAPTER TWENTY-FOUR

I was driving to Thistledown with Keats to visit the puppies that afternoon when Jay Pefferlaw texted to tell me there were two more swarms of honeybees near his property. Travis Wigg was willing to give them a home but he wasn't available to collect them today.

"What do you say, buddy?" I asked the dog. "Do we know enough to tackle this alone? Edna left beekeeper gear in the back."

He delivered a scathing retort that you didn't need to speak Keats to translate.

"Fine, whatever. I think I only saw one hive box, anyway. We can't put two colonies together without an epic battle of the queens. I'll call an expert." Pressing a number on my phone I hit speaker. "Hey. I need your help. Not in a my-life-is-in-imminent-peril sort of way. More like regular, routine help."

"Excuse me? Who is this?"

"Very funny. Last time I checked"—I held up my left hand and angled my jewels to catch the light—"I was your betrothed. Still have the bling, so if anything's changed you'd better send your repo squad."

"I'm a gentleman, Ivy. I'd never reclaim the bling. But I also don't believe you're calling for regular, routine assistance. Anything so basic would have been done already and I'd hear about it in a few weeks when it crossed your mind again."

"He knows me well." I glanced at Keats, whose mouth hung open in his happiest smile. Fiancé banter was the best banter. "But maybe he's wrong this time."

"I doubt it," Kellan said. "You know I'm working an investigation, so you'd better call in your backup squad for routine tasks. Unless it's a routine task related to that very investigation."

I directed my next comment to Keats, too. "He's very sharp. We were lucky to convince this guy to propose to us and the entire sixty head of livestock. Sometimes we need to do the right thing in case he realizes he made a mistake."

"Up to seventy now, I believe," he said. "Should have put a ceiling in the agreement."

"Unlimited critters and offspring. We'd better get a move on it with the latter. A drive in a bookmobile would surely put us in the mood."

He laughed. "Okay, you've got my full attention. What is it you and Keats are doing? I don't hear anyone else in the truck with you."

"That's exactly the problem. I'm on my way to visit the pups again and Jay told me there are swarms of bees near his property. Since they aren't technically *on* his property, I thought you might give me a hand to nab them."

"Me! Swarm nabbing is not in my job description. It'll never be in my hobby description, either."

"Never say never. The more you learn about the complex life of bees, the more you want to get into the game."

"No thanks. Don't try slipping that into your vows. You're quick with a quip, even with a hostile teen audience."

"You heard? It was a tough room, but I agree with Sutton that busting out a ferret is a great way to defuse tension. Bet they're still looking."

"It was recovered, no thanks to you or your canine sidekick. Fiona Gillespie said you beat it before you got called in."

I rolled my eyes so hard the truck veered. "Tell me the principal didn't rat me out to the cops."

"She did. But I was there on another matter." He felt the question coming and hastened to add, "I can't discuss it."

"Then I can't discuss what Ms. Morrell said about you, either."

There was a bit of dead air and then, "Judi Morrell? The art teacher?"

"Okay, twist my arm. She said you had a good eye for art and character."

"She's half right. And why was she weighing in anyway? Did she hit you up for fertilizer?"

"Turns out my farm has been fertilizing her muse for some time. She has a whole exhibit of watercolors of livestock."

"Huh. Didn't you say Kayla Ware's kid is knitting little animals based on the farm?"

"Crocheting, but yeah. Her other kid's dreadful, but one out of two ain't bad."

I could hear him tapping on a keyboard and then, "There was some other homage to Ivy and menagerie, wasn't there? I feel like I'm missing one."

"Thanks for noticing, Chiefheart. That's Travis' nickname for you, by the way."

"Travis Wigg? Seriously. We'll have another talk."

"Don't worry. Cori ripped into him and he helped pull me out of a sinkhole last night, so I'm cutting him a break for now. Anyway, thanks for keeping track of my tributes. You did miss one and I'll give you a hint. People used to smoke in this gallery. And call out insults as I passed. Like Froggy Flappers."

He tried to hold back a snort and failed. "Right. The school graffiti. But still, the obsession with Ivy Galloway is gaining momentum. Not quite sure how I feel about that."

Keats knew how he felt about it and said so with an elaborate mumble. As much as he enjoyed attention, too much of it meant we'd lose the anonymity we craved.

"Did you hear that?" I asked.

"Hard to miss. Sounded like he leaned right into the speaker. I take it Keats wants to keep a lower profile."

"We both do, and so far I don't appear in any of the fan art. The animals are the stars. I'm just an anonymous attendant, like the nurse bees who look after the queen."

"Let's keep it that way, okay? I'd like to avoid a spotlight on your unorthodox methods of assisting local law enforcement." His voice got a little quieter, as if others were listening. "Some call it 'vigilantism.'"

"Only Sutton calls it that. Typical teenage hyperbole. I don't like the term and it's not what I'm seeing in these... well, exhibits. The art I'm seeing shows a love of animals and that can only lift people up. Maybe even educate." Keats mumbled something and I added, "I'll speak to Judi about that. As a teacher, I'm sure she'll be open to doing more with her work."

"So you're saying I just have to get used to the idea of spending my life with a celeb?" His tone lightened.

"That's exactly what I'm saying. Keats' star has been on the rise for ages. He's the true queen bee of our lives and we're lucky to be his attendants."

Finally, Kellan found another laugh. "It's come to that, has it?"

Keats added his mumbled opinion that it had ever been thus. Indeed, my life had pretty much revolved around him since the day we met in the yard with the sunflowers and skull.

"Did you know beekeepers trap extra queens in little cages?" I asked Kellan. "Otherwise the queens fight to the death."

"Sounds like a brutal regime."

"If there's a strong queen in place it's all good. She lays a thousand eggs or so a day and releases pheromones that keep workers happy and producing honey. It's quite a system."

"Definitely."

Keats gave a pant-laugh. I had lost Kellan to whatever task he faced. Bee dynamics fascinated me, but they were a tough sell for a cop on a case.

"The experts say it's always better to start with two hives. You can compare behavior and output and start to improve your lines. Tammi divided opinion, but everyone agrees she had the best bees. Do you think I could keep the swarms we find today?"

"Nope. They're only housed with Travis temporarily."

"Well, why can't they be housed with me temporarily? I have room for hives."

I had his full attention again. "Because someone might come after them. And then something might happen at the farm that upsets you. Wait for your bees, Ivy. Yours will be happy and healthy and way better than Tammi's. The honey will be the talk of the community."

He sure knew how to make a girl feel special. "I'm here," I said, turning into Jay Pefferlaw's lane. "Ready to go swarm chasing."

"Stay put. I'll send the best bee guy I know."

My brow furrowed, ultimately dragging my entire face into a scowl. "Travis is busy. Jay already said so."

"I know. But there's someone better. You'll see."

CHAPTER TWENTY-FIVE

The junior Pefferlaw brother seemed glad to see me, and Persephone, the mastiff, was even happier. She was barely conscious when we rescued her last night but perhaps she knew we smelled like safety. Now fully recovered, she was exuberant and looking for fun. Keats very rarely wanted to play and never when there was a job to do.

"Where's the bee team?" I asked.

"Coming. The chief didn't give details. He just said—"

"Stay put?" I asked, smiling.

Jay smiled back, proving again he was the softer brother. "Yes, and to make sure you stay, too. I'm supposed to tackle you if you get frisky."

"I'll have a word to say about that," Binty said, coming out with the kids.

Jay's permanently tanned skin flushed. "Not like that. A no-contact citizen's arrest."

For the moment, the only one frisky was Persephone, and she was getting in Keats' space. If the mastiff didn't calm down, I'd have to put Keats back in the truck before he did something I'd regret. Today, I trusted Peeps more than my impatient border collie. His mood had shifted on the ride down until it mirrored Kellan's. Now the dog was wearing his chief canine badge and it made me ponder. Finding more bee swarms wasn't that big a deal. Had I missed a clue? Was it something Kellan said about the case?

Keats mumbled a warning that seemed equally directed at Peeps and me. A "settle down and focus" sort of sound.

The mastiff walked over to me and we did as we were told. I stroked her pointy ears and silky back, marveling at how different dogs could feel. I'd only ever been owned by one, and now my entire notion of dog was mid-sized, furry and fast. And mouthy, in more ways than one.

He turned his blue eye on me and then cocked his ears toward the lane. A familiar truck pulled in and Keats walked over with his tail up and fanning slightly. It wasn't the full-on swish reserved for Jilly, Mom and Asher, but it was close and getting stronger all the time.

Turns out the best bee guy Kellan knew happened to be my father. And his attendant today was also a relative, specifically Poppy.

Dad hopped down from the truck, gave me a nod and walked over to shake Jay's hand and wave at the rest of the family. There were no introductions. Somehow, they all knew each other. I wondered how my hermit father knew another hermit. They lived far enough apart that they wouldn't run into each other in the normal course of a day. Keats stared at me again and I gave it up with a shrug. There was a club for everything in hill country, possibly even hermits.

Jay came to the back door of the truck but my dad shook his head. "Just give us a rough idea and I'll find them. Wouldn't be the first time." When Jay protested, my mild-mannered father gave an assertive wave. "Chief's orders. You've been through enough this week. My turn."

Kellan didn't deploy my father often. Nor did our other chief,

Keats. Calvin, as I still normally thought of him, didn't much like leaving home or barn. Specifically, *my* home or barn. He had his own home—a big one—but spent most of his time tending my livestock, building or mending fences, and sleeping in the loft with his posse of barn cats. This seemingly small life was working wonders for him because he looked younger and healthier than when he arrived home after his long absence from my life. He was steadily and quietly present, giving me the space to build my menagerie and my trust. There were more pens and pastures than I knew what to do with but they always filled. On top of that, he'd acquired the former Harlow property, recently the source of much contention, and made that available to my animals, as well. For the moment, I wanted bad memories of that land to fade but eventually we'd "launder" the energy with goats and perhaps bees.

"Let's roll," Poppy said. "Dad promised swarm chasing."

He shook his head as he slid behind the wheel. "No chasing. Always calm. Always friendly. These bees are homeless and stressed."

Jay had given us a rough idea where to find the swarms. Dad must have known they were on the abandoned Bouchard property, because my company in the back seat was a rifle. Keats had elected to ride on Poppy's lap in the front and I decided not to take it personally. Poppy wasn't his favorite Galloway girl. She was unpredictable and occasionally combustible. He could only handle one twisty sister and that was me.

"How will you know where they are?" I asked.

He tapped his glasses. "Wore the trifocals for a change. Normally I'm too vain."

Poppy and I laughed. Dad was many things but vain wasn't one of them. He was as married to his overalls as I was and sleeping in the loft didn't leave much room for primping. Jilly had designated one of the downstairs bathrooms to him, however, and he came and went without fanfare.

Looking over her shoulder, Poppy said, "Don't fall for that. Keats is navigating."

"Makes more sense. Did you bring all the gear?"

Dad nodded. "Don't need much."

"I've watched the videos online. You're supposed to have a suit and a smoker and some tools, too."

He pulled into the Bouchard lane and drove toward the old house. "Those are good for newbies, but when you have experience, it's rarely necessary to suit up. Swarms tend to be docile."

"I did see a lot of people letting bees climb all over their bare hands."

"They don't want to sting. It's all about work for a honeybee. They just want to get their job done and serve the queen."

"And not die," I pointed out. "Maybe they know that stinging is a one-off."

"They're complicated, but probably not quite that evolved." He opened the door. "You girls stay here while I take a look."

After he walked away, Keats grumbled and I followed suit. "Girls? We haven't been girls in a long time and have proven we can take care of ourselves."

Poppy flicked my complaints away with her fingers. "Cut Dad some slack. He works harder around the farm than the rest of us combined."

A twinge of guilt mixed with irritation ran through me. "I know that. I'm just saying we could help with the bees. I want to learn more."

"He's protecting us from getting stung. I, for one, appreciate that."

"And I find your tone annoying, Poppy. Especially when you've been avoiding me all week. What gives?"

"Nothing. Just busy, that's all."

She refused to turn and as I was sitting on the passenger side, all I could see was her hair. It was normally pretty close to my shade but after a year of going natural, she'd added colorful highlights this week. A more cynical person would think that had something to do with the reunion she refused to discuss.

The only person more cynical than me was Jilly and she wasn't here, so I decided to pass the time by pestering my big sister. Keats looked around the seat and mumbled. He thought I could do something more useful.

"You had time to get your hair colored. You could have called from the salon."

"And get dye on my phone? Not again."

"I guess you wanted to look good for the reunion. Can't blame you for that. Too bad it was cancelled. Or at least postponed."

Now she gave a quarter turn. Just enough to show her chin jutting. We all had the same chin, but hers looked a bit witchlike in that moment. "Mom wanted me to go to the reunion. I didn't."

"No? Your hair says otherwise. Purple screams, 'I want to be noticed.'"

That got me a half turn and enough of one eye to know I was asking for trouble. I wondered if my hazel eyes fired off little sparks like hers did. "Just drop it, Ivy. I wasn't the golden girl in school like you, with the scads of awards you didn't collect. Maybe Gillespie will rent a trailer and haul them to the reunion."

"I doubt it. I'm not in her good books after riling up the students this morning. But I didn't care about any of those awards. Didn't want them then, don't want them now. How do you feel about flipping the bird to the school art award?"

Her face turned far enough that I got the full effect of both eyes. The section of purple hair that hung over her face had a red slash underneath. "What arts award?"

"The one Judi Morrell would have given you. She said you had incredible talent and sent me away with your sketchbook. Kept it all these years, probably hoping you'd seek her out."

"Why would I do that? She's a loser."

"A loser! Far from it. She's running a gallery near Dog Town and featuring an exhibit of farm animal portraits."

"So, she's successful and likes cows. Still a loser."

"Judi Morrell is not a loser." My voice sounded brittle. Poppy always knew how to push my buttons. I couldn't shake it off the way I did with Asher, but I guess it went both ways. "She thought you were gifted and that is good enough for me."

"Raise your standards a little. She was dating Mr. Sever, an even bigger loser."

I thought about it. "She could do better, I agree. But a lot of people make poor relationship decisions and it doesn't pay to write them off entirely. My love life hasn't been without challenges and yours hasn't either."

Our father happened to open the driver's door just then, and closed it again quickly when he got the gist of the conversation. Keats pawed at the glass to get me to follow.

I jumped out of the back seat, and called, "Need help?"

Keats ran over to him and delivered what sounded like a plea not to get stuck with Poppy and me.

"We've got a few minutes," Dad said. "Finish your conversation with Poppy."

My sister stayed in the car and Keats kept me from going back. He'd had enough sisterly bonding.

"Anything more and she'll punch my lights out," I told Calvin. "Poppy's strung pretty tight right now."

He led me over to a buzzing, fluttering swarm of bees. "The school reunion brought up old memories. You know she was unfairly accused of theft just before graduating?"

"I didn't actually know what happened until school faculty mentioned it today." I stayed well back from the bees. "She told you about it? You weren't even here."

Sticking his arm out, he let bees land on his hand and sleeve. "Not Poppy. Others who were around at that time."

Most of my anger over Dad leaving us had faded but there was just enough venom left to hurt now. "It's a bit annoying that you knew more than us, when we were here the whole time."

He leaned closer to the swarm. "I don't feel good about it."

"The bees?"

"Not the bees." He bent even closer and I reached out to pull him back. "But also the bees."

The family drama could wait. "What's wrong with them?"

Crooking his finger, he called me closer. "Hear anything different from the previous swarms?"

I listened and then nodded. "They're louder. Agitated."

"They call it the queenless roar. We have at least fifty thousand subjects and no leader. Without a queen, the colony will weaken and die. They have no purpose."

Something drew my eyes up and I saw Bernice doing figure eights over me, faster and tighter than ever before. Was this her hive? Was her queen gone?

Backing away, I tapped my father's shoulder. "I was reading up on bees and learned the workers can replace a sick or missing queen."

He nodded. "Happens all the time. But they need the raw materials to do it. If they've lost their comb, their brood, their honey stores and their queen... Well, it's just a matter of time before this group dies off."

"Can't we put them in a new hive with brood from somewhere else and let them get busy?"

"Possibly, but they've taken a big hit already. Normally bees only swarm with optimal conditions. With so many colonies leaving, the hives must be uninhabitable. Maybe it was too wet, too warm or poorly ventilated."

"Well, then, let's get these gals rehomed and buy a queen. I saw some for sale for less than fifty bucks."

"You get what you pay for. It sounds like Tammi Hickey wasn't a nice lady, but she knew bees. I visited the hives at Travis' place and they're sweet as puppies. Takes work and sound breeding to get a temperament like that. Happy bees make for a happy beekeeper."

"How about Finch Pefferlaw? He cares about their welfare. I bet his bees are nice and he might be able to spare a queen for a good cause."

"Worth a try," Dad said. "But keeping extra queens takes work. Bigger apiaries sometimes have a nursery." Stepping back, he caught my eye. "Ivy, some loss is inevitable in farming."

My heart sank. I knew this was a "fact of life," and I'd been very lucky so far. But the longer I was at Runaway Farm, the more inevitable loss would become. It was part of the package, but I didn't need to like it.

I looked up again to take my cue from Bernice, and saw her repeating a flight loop between Dad and me. It reminded me a little of Keats' sheepdog love knot.

"I'll find a queen," I said, more for Bernice's sake than Dad's.

"Go for it. But sometimes they won't accept an imposter."

"And they ball her?" I asked.

"They do, and it's tragic. Spells their own demise if they can't accept her. But there are strategies for making it work."

My father pulled out his phone and started texting. Apparently, the message was directed at Poppy, because she got out of the truck and brought over the hive boxes. "Ivy, just so you know, I didn't appreciate your talking to my teacher about me today."

"Are you telling on me?" I asked. "Because I only wanted to help. If you dyed your hair purple, it means your heart's bruised."

Keats gave Poppy a little nip and mumbled something along the lines of, "Family. We're in this together."

Dad unpacked the equipment and tossed each of us a suit and veil. "Don't get stung, girls. Especially by each other."

"We're not girls," Poppy said, as we put on the gear. On that point, we agreed. "We aged out of that label long ago."

There was a third suit but Dad ignored it. Maybe he was that confident, or maybe he just wanted to get this over and done faster. "I know. And I'm sorry I missed that stage."

Keats' mumble seemed to suggest it was no great loss.

"I'm serious," Dad said, as if he understood Keats. "There was so much I could have taught you." Readying the boxes, he grinned at us over his shoulder. "Not about surviving high school, I guess. I left early to marry your mother."

I gasped as he plunged his bare hand into the swarm and nudged gently until it dropped into the box. The bees began climbing the frames, but their hum was louder than ever. They were disoriented and waiting for orders from a leader who'd vanished. "What now?" I asked.

He grabbed a plastic bottle and spritzed the bees, before putting the lid on the box. "A little sugar water to keep them fueled on the journey." Gesturing ahead, he grabbed the other box. "Keats has a bead on the second swarm. We'll load them and drive them down to Travis' house where they'll be safe—at least from thieves."

Dad let me help the next time, and while I wore my veil and suit, I eventually took off my glove and let the bees coat my fingers. There was a strange hypnotic quality to the buzz and the vibration. I found myself drifting away mentally, until a sharp yap shook off the trance.

"Ivy, what's the first order of beekeeping?" Dad asked, looking up from the hive box.

"Bee prepared?" I quipped.

"Bee aware," he said. "You could have been dinged a hundred times over. What were you thinking?"

His tone was milder than his words, and I sensed he really wanted to know.

I backed away slowly. "I wasn't thinking. I guess I was just—"

"Bee-ing," he supplied, with a grin. "Let's go deliver the colonies."

"Can you drop me back at Jay's and go on to Travis' place without me?" I asked.

"He's a good guy, Ivy," Poppy said. "Don't go making your snap judgements."

"There's no snap in my judgements." There was some snap in my voice, however. "He's a little full of himself, that's all. Doesn't mean he isn't a perfectly good beekeeper."

Dad looked down at Keats and shook his head. "Girls. Women. I don't understand them. You?"

The dog delivered a brief soliloquy that sounded like fatherly advice. It made Dad and me smile. Probably Poppy, too, but her helmet hid it.

My smile faded as I carried the "roaring" queenless hive box back to the truck. There was a note of desperation in the sound and a sensation that went straight up my arms to my heart. What happened to this hardworking colony wasn't fair. I couldn't bring back their queen, but I could do my very best to give them a new purpose in life.

Bernice stuck with me every step of the way, flying in slow circles as I slid the box into the bed. I slipped out of the white suit and the lone bee finally came in for a landing on my shoulder, where Percy normally sat. It was the first time she'd touched down on me.

Dad reached out to brush the bee away but I stopped him. "That's Bernice. She's my friend and tour guide through the world of bees."

"Your friend?" he asked.

Poppy pulled off her veil and rolled her eyes. "See what you missed, Dad? Weirdness."

I glared at her. "I wasn't weird back then."

"Please. Who fakes a gall bladder attack to get out of receiving awards?"

"Someone falsely demonized for having flabby feet, that's who. I wasn't walking up on the stage to give people a better view."

Dad scurried around to the driver's side, as if he could actually escape us. "Ivy, you'll go straight home after we drop you at Jay's?"

"Sure." I got into the back seat. "Might stop for a sweet treat. I've got that late afternoon blood sugar low."

Dad looked back at me and then at the dog, now perched in my lap. "Is she lying, Keats? I wasn't around enough to know the signs."

Keats rumbled more advice as we drove back to Jay's, but I knew he wouldn't spoil his own fun by giving too much away.

We were going in search of a queen and the less anyone knew about that, the better.

CHAPTER TWENTY-SIX

I followed Keats and Percy right up to Tammi Hickey's front door and knocked. The police tape was gone, but I wasn't sure if her husband had moved back in. He probably wasn't free to leave for the city until the case was closed, but staying there with all their memories would be painful. I didn't necessarily buy that there had been infidelity. The day we met in the farmer's market, Tammi seemed happy to be shaking off the dust of Clover Grove. If she felt misgivings about Eddy, it didn't show. Sure, the wronged spouse was sometimes last to know, but with Tammi's list of enemies, someone would have wanted to tell her and smash the image of her perfect life.

Keats poked my leg twice, which felt like encouragement to knock again. I did, and then a third time, just to be sure. I even peered into the mottled glass on either side of the door to see if there was any movement. No one could blame the man if he wanted to keep a low profile in these stressful times.

Once we'd ticked off all the boxes of polite behavior, we did what we'd wanted to do all along. Hopping off the porch from the side, the three of us walked around the back of the house. Well, I walked, in case anyone happened to be watching. Keats and Percy ran like the wind.

By the time I turned the corner, my furry vanguard had dropped to the grass, or what was left of it after vehicles churned it up. I glanced around the large yard and found it had been entirely cleared out. There was little to suggest it had ever been an apiary.

My search for a queen here was going nowhere fast. If Delsie was right about Tammi's royal nursery, that must have been moved to another local beekeeper. There were eager takers for lines like Tammi's.

At first, I thought Keats and Percy had dismissed the place as boring, but when my eyes dropped to tell them to leave, I saw they were anything but bored. Percy's tail had the restrained twitch of a cat on the hunt, and Keats' hackles were slightly raised.

"What is it?" I whispered, kneeling beside them.

Percy got up and clawed at the damp earth where he'd squashed some of the remaining grass. A little clump came out with a litterbox sweep and released something small and round. A coin, perhaps.

Pulling my penknife out of my pocket, I prodded the object until some soil dropped away and allowed it to catch the last low rays of sunset.

Gold.

Not a coin, a ring.

A wedding ring, to be precise, and it had been on Tammi's hand at the market. I recognized the twisting strands of yellow, white and rose gold. That was uncommon for wedding rings of our generation and didn't match her engagement ring. They were probably family heirlooms. Before Kellan proposed, I rarely noticed such things. These days, I checked out other rings because they made me love mine even more.

Hooking this one with my blade, I wrapped it with a tissue and slipped it into my pocket for the police. Either they missed this bit of evidence or it arrived later.

Keats gave me a penetrating stare with his blue eye and mumbled a quiet warning.

We weren't alone.

I sat back on my heels and looked around. There was no place for anyone to hide but behind a tree or in the utility shed.

The shed. Of course. Since the double doors were wide open, I hadn't been concerned. Now, I sensed someone inside. Or more specifically, I sensed my pets sensing someone inside. The big question was whether the person inside sensed us right back.

"What now?" I mouthed the words to Keats, although he was already telling me what I needed to know. His hackles were in the exact same position and his ears were forward. Percy sat, too, wrapping his tail around his grimy front paws. That he didn't clean them suggested our dirty work was not done.

I tried to still everything so that I could hear, but my heart was pounding. What's more, there was a persistent buzz overhead. Bernice was back on her home turf and had plenty to say about it with busy wings and intriguing flight formations. Skywriting would have been a big help but it wasn't in this talented bee's repertoire.

Finally, I heard the whispers. Plural. Two people in the shed were locked in a heated argument. Or at least as heated as whispering allowed. One voice was male, the other female.

What was my best move? A cheery neighborly callout? A creep and peek? Or direct ambush with flashlight? The light had all but vanished as a bank of clouds smothered the setting sun.

Keats mumbled a negative to all three, and for good reason. There was a rustle and scrape of footsteps and two people appeared in the doorway.

The failing light was on their side but they didn't seize their advantage to look around for intruders. Instead, they glared at each other, and I took that opportunity to slump slowly to the earth. I tried my best to disappear and the pets crouched, too.

"If not here, then where?" the woman asked.

"I don't know. She didn't talk to me about those things." There was a pause and a shift in the atmosphere. "Or if she did, I never listened."

"Don't bother getting maudlin now," the woman said. "Way too late for that."

"It's not too late for regret. I'd be a monster, otherwise. We were married for sixteen years. Some of them happy, at least until you got in my head."

"Not just your head," the woman said. "And trust me, I have regrets, too."

I'd expected Tammi's husband, Eddy. After all, he still owned the property. What I didn't expect was to find him cracking open his guilty heart to Kayla B. Ware. Apparently, the stories about an affair were true. Had Kayla and Eddy teamed up to eliminate the middle-woman?

Too easy. It was a thought in my head but also the merest hint of a mumble from the grass beside me. If Kayla and Eddy had killed Tammi, the police would very likely know already. What I found out by sheer happenstance would have been easily discovered by a dozen diligent cops. Even if they didn't have evidence—say in the form of missing wedding and engagement rings—they would have generated enough suspicion to keep these two from meeting. If Eddy and Kayla weren't too worried about being seen together at the scene of the crime, they likely weren't behind the murder.

Still, they could have met anywhere to argue. They were here for a reason, and if I could stay quiet long enough, chances were good they'd say something incriminating. Hopefully they'd continue to discuss what went missing and it would point in the right direction.

"KK, come on. You know how I felt about you. Always did, always will."

Kayla let out a huff of annoyance. "Tell it to your other girl, Eddy. Maybe she cares."

"It wasn't like that," he said. "You were special."

His words sent a ripple of revulsion down my back. Not only

had he cheated on Tammi with Kayla, he'd cheated on Kayla with someone else.

"So special you hooked up with Nadia? Forgive me if I feel like the filling in a trash sandwich."

"It wasn't a hookup. Nadia and I had dinner a few times, that's all. I needed to vent to someone about Tammi."

"You vented plenty to me, but you needed extra ears?"

"Actually, yeah. As the move got closer I felt like I was going to explode. I didn't want Tammi to come with me, but I couldn't see a way out. I needed to talk to someone who understood. You're always so busy with the kids and your business. Plus, I wanted to get other perspectives."

"Was Nadia's perspective different from mine? Or was she just more available?"

He sighed. "It wasn't that different. We all felt the same. So lucky to have Tammi, at first. Proud she chose us. Then gradually wearing down but not knowing what to do about it. I finally got up the nerve to leave, fully expecting Tammi to say no, because she couldn't take her bees. I dreamed about living separate lives until she pulled someone else into her web and offed me."

"But she was the one offed. And while the cops may have cleared you, public opinion hasn't."

"The only thing I'm guilty of is wanting to get away from a toxic marriage and handling it badly. That isn't new or criminal."

"Playing me off Tammi was criminal. You should have stood up to her. You were the only one who could."

"That's just it. I couldn't. You had your own life but I was trapped."

Kayla gave a bitter snort. "I haven't had my own life since I handed it to Tammi in sixth grade. She was the sun and I was just a planet, orbiting her."

"Tell me about it. I was Jupiter, the largest planet. You were Saturn. And Nadia was Uranus."

There was a pause before Kayla said, "I guess it could have been worse. How did we end up this way? How did *she* end up that way?"

"You've met her family. They're awful. Turned her into a bully." He rested a hand on Kayla's shoulder and she didn't move away. "Tammi was starting to realize that. Thought about it a lot when she was out here working with her hives. I guess that's why she agreed to give up what we had here. To get away from her past. Start over where no one knew her but me."

His chin tipped up as he stared at the sky. I hoped he didn't see Bernice on her strange celestial path. Especially since it was nightfall, when all good bees should be in their hives.

"I didn't blame Tammi for wanting that," he continued. "I just... didn't want to be part of it. Too much damage to reverse. Easier to start fresh as the bereaved husband. Could be worse."

"It is worse... for me," Kayla said, shrugging off his hand. "Every time someone comes into the store they stare at me, wondering if I might be the 'other woman.' Or worse yet, the killer. Businesses shipwreck on rumors like that, Eddy."

"They'll find the killer soon and you'll be off the hook."

She rubbed a hand over her eyes. "Never fully. I was the one she threw her rings at. Nearly blinded me. Why did you tell her about us?"

"I don't know." His chin dropped to his chest. "When I saw her packing up her apiary and crying over leaving her bees, guilt got the best of me. I decided to turn off the security cameras and do the right thing. Tell her the truth and let her stay. I warned you as soon as I left."

"I was already on the way over and walked into a tornado of angry bees. It's like they picked up on her fury and attacked. I got stung a few times and then ran." She touched her derriere. "Tammi hit me in the face with the rings and the bees went straight for my bum. At least the police didn't investigate that closely."

Kayla *was* the filling in a trash sandwich, I decided. Even if she hadn't killed Tammi, she'd taken her husband and planned on taking her beloved bees, along with her social status.

"I've been stung a few times. They're very protective." He chuckled. "Gives me some satisfaction to know they die after they do it, whereas we'll keep on going, KK."

"Like I said, I'll be paying for this a long time. With four kids, I can't just pack up and move like you. I've got to suck it up till the story fades. Clover Grove has a long memory."

She was right about that, and in this case I was glad. I hoped people would remember the downfall of their colony, and vow to keep a similar regime from rising again.

"The story will fade. Always does," Eddy said. "It'll happen fast if you take over as the premiere beekeeper. You'll gain respect."

"I lost all the hives and the police said they're not coming back. I'll be starting from scratch without Tammi's stellar lines unless we can find those queens."

My hand came down on Keats' back but the dog didn't move a muscle. *Stay cool.* I couldn't tell if his command was a mumble or just in my head.

"I thought Tammi stopped production coming up to the move," Eddy said.

"She did, at first. To increase demand. No one's been able to get a Tammi queen for ages. But then she bred a lot of them to pave my way into the beekeeping community. Said they should go for at least eight hundred a pop, and there were dozens of them."

There was another shift in the atmosphere as Eddy understood what was at stake. "That's a lot of money."

"It sure is. And it's also my silver bullet to shoot down the naysayers who don't want me swanning into the club. I deserve those queens, Eddy, and it's starting to look like someone took them."

"If someone took them, the person wouldn't keep coming back. I've seen a shadow on the security camera three times and the cops can't identify it."

Kayla heaved a sigh of relief that the queens were still around and I echoed it more quietly. "The queens will die in a few days if we don't find them. The stolen colonies might die, too. Tammi warned me about the fragility of the bee ecosystem. Change one thing and their world crumbles."

"We'll find them," he said. "You'll start over and I'll start over. We'll forget Tammi ever happened."

Kayla's quiet laugh sounded hollow. "She shaped my whole life. I don't even know who I am without Tammi."

"You already have a family and a thriving business. She didn't give you that."

"She did, actually. Tammi set me up with my husband. Then she bankrolled my store because he wouldn't, and clients found me because of her. But then she wanted to control everything, and she didn't even like crafts." Kayla stepped down from the shed and I eased onto my belly in the damp grass. "Tammi cast a long shadow."

"Yeah, I was always 'Mr. Tammi,' and she backed my franchise with honey, too." He stepped down beside Kayla and tried to put his arm around her, but she slid out from under it. Perhaps she saw him as a drone, now, easily replaced and therefore dispensable in a hive. "We have plenty of time ahead, KK. Don't give up."

"Let's find those queens, Eddy. They'll go a long way to helping me heal from this." They left the shed and walked toward the house. "The problem is that no one will ever know what it was like. Abusive. Controlling. And yet, we benefited, too. It was hard to walk away."

"But we're walking away now. We'll find those valuable bees. She owes us."

"Owes *me*," Kayla said. "You'll profit from the insurance."

"Let's just find them and take it from there. She was pretty clever about hiding things."

As they walked away, Kayla grumbled, "We couldn't figure her out before. It's probably a bust."

For them, it probably was a bust. For me, maybe not. Keats' muzzle had come up, sniffing and perhaps watching Bernice fly around. Then my dog got up and pointed.

Unfortunately, the bee wasn't the only thing buzzing. My phone vibrated in my pocket and it was loud enough to make Kayla and Eddy turn quickly.

"Did you hear that? The thief is back," Eddy said. "Stand watch, KK. I'm getting my gun."

"I'm not staying here to get picked off first." Kayla's voice was shrill as she ran up the back stairs. "Are you trying to lose every woman you've ever—"

The last word cut off as the door closed behind them and I was glad about that.

Still, they'd soon be back with a gun and my little crew would need to work fast.

CHAPTER TWENTY-SEVEN

There was just enough light left to follow Keats and fluffy beacon Percy away from the house and into the trees. It was a good thing I'd parked down the road and in the brush. My thought at the time was to avoid detection by nosey drivers who might call my fiancé. Now, I'd already texted my fiancé about the cheaters and just wanted to buy myself enough time to test a theory. Kellan thought I'd headed to safe haven and by the time he arrived, it would be true.

For the moment, I was pushing my way through prickly brush and hoping the boys could lead me back to where we found the murder weapon. The rain last night would have rinsed the smell of a smoky killer away.

We walked out into a meadow that looked vaguely familiar in my phone light's beam, but nothing stood out.

Well, nothing except Keats' white paw. I shone the beam on the dog and then scanned the area around him. It was just the usual rocks and scrub. I'd hoped to find another shed that served as a castle for the queen bees Tammi wanted to keep safe. Her hives were prized and the young queens perhaps more so. Their "street" value might be initially less, but their potential far greater. They could lead to generations of pollinators and honey producers who had the disposition of puppies. My research suggested only an apiarist at the top of her game could breed queens of this caliber at volume. It took great care and the right conditions. They couldn't be too hot or too cold and they most certainly couldn't be housed together. That said, in their little tubes or cages, they wouldn't take up much space either. A shed would be far more than was needed. One online guru used a fishing tackle box filled with pine needles to transport his ladies.

"Think smaller," I told myself. "She wouldn't put the bees in the ground. Too cool, unless she had an incubator. But then she'd need a power source."

Keats had his nose down, exploring the area, but this time it was Percy for the win. He meowed from overhead and when I flashed the light up, I saw him sitting atop a large birdhouse set in the crook of an oak tree. The house was covered in faux bark and had a hinged door at one end. It would be plenty big enough to hold a tray of bees. He gave it a few sweeps with his paws to let me know we'd struck gold-and-black. Then he went to work in the gap between the tree and the birdhouse.

Unfortunately, the bee refuge was nearly 15 feet from the ground, meaning I'd need to get up there somehow. What was easy for Percy was less so for me, and wouldn't be a smooth ride down for the lady queens, either. How had Tammi navigated the challenge?

I regretted leaving my backpack in the truck. There was rope in there and even a set of spikes for climbing. But that still wouldn't have kept the queens comfortable on the way down. If I wanted them to arrive at Travis' home ready for colony building, I needed to treat them like fragile treasures, even though they were hardy creatures capable of laying nearly a million eggs in a lifetime. The thought of all those bees made me a little dizzy as I stared up at Percy and the birdhouse, so I lowered the light and then turned it off to save battery while I pondered. I'd expected to recharge the phone before now.

That was reason enough to text Edna and put up with her chiding over leaving the backpack behind. Besides, she knew where to find us, at least the general location.

I needed help and moral support. My heart had never settled back into a regular rhythm and now I had to worry about Eddy. Tammi's husband owned a taco franchise and maintained multiple affairs with women. It was unlikely that he spent much time on target practice, so if he decided to take a shot at this trespasser, he'd probably miss me. The bigger risk was that he'd hit one of my pets by accident. Or the birdhouse holding the bee queens.

The feeling of unease deep in my core grew quickly. If I chose to turn on the light, I'd find hackles on high alert. Keats confirmed it by moving his prickly ruff under my fingertips. There was just the faintest hint of a growl to tell me we were in trouble.

A second later came a crackle no more than 20 feet away. Just that. No more and no less than a single stick breaking. The sound was loud enough to suggest a heavy foot.

It could be Tammi's husband, here to defend his property. If so, he'd come without Kayla, because I was quite sure she wasn't done chastising him. Never would be done. She'd followed Tammi's lead all her life and named her daughter after her, before violating her trust. Then Eddy had done even worse by connecting with Nadia, thereby rendering Kayla's treachery worthless. No matter what came of the bees, Kayla would never get over what happened. She'd handed over her identity in childhood, tried to take it back recently, and found nothing but a void within. She'd be howling about that for a lifetime.

So, the person crackling near me was either Eddy alone, or someone else with bigger feet than mine. Travis Wigg, perhaps. He was on my suspect list, partly because he had secrets but mainly because he was unlikable.

Another man came to mind. Someone else who appeared to have a genuine interest in bees but lacked Tammi's skills and passion. Anyone who truly cared about bees would have found somewhere safe to store the hives. They'd have settled in their new home. Instead, he distressed them so much that many colonies risked everything and swarmed.

If I was right, he'd committed this crime not for passion, but money. Many of the bees, like Tammi, wouldn't survive his greed.

And now he was back for the precious queens.

Well, he wasn't going to get them.

Because I had a pretty good idea who he was, and if I was right, I had a personal bone to pick, too. Turning, I held my phone screen close to my chest to dull the light. I pressed Kellan's number and SOS before sliding the phone into my pocket.

My first priority was saving the queens. I owed that to Bernice. Then I could challenge this villain on his other, less deadly crimes. Tammi may have been his first murder victim, but he had ruined lives in other ways.

Could I hold the fort until Edna and Kellan arrived?

Keats grumbled a quiet reminder that it wasn't an "I" but a "we." And further, that we'd faced situations before that were equally dire and come out on top.

Or at least alive.

He meant it to be encouraging, but in the moment, it felt ominous. The situation was just as bad as other times we'd encountered a murderer, but we were more isolated than was often the case. It would be tough even for Edna to locate us in time.

I took a deep breath and smiled. The intruder couldn't see it but hopefully he'd sense the defiance in my tone. "Good evening," I called out. "Are you lost?"

There was a long pause and then, "I think you're the one who's lost. Finally and forever this time."

"Oh? It sounds like you know me. Have we met?"

"A while ago, and I never liked you."

"Ditto. But there was nothing I could do about it then."

"There's nothing you can do about it now. Let's be clear on that, Ivy."

"We'll see. I'm not the person you picked on back then. But I suppose people like you made me who I am now."

"You're welcome," he said. "Glad I passed you over for the science award in eleventh grade."

"Wouldn't have collected it anyway. I believe I had a splenectomy that year."

He tried to gulp back a snort and it turned into a snuffle. "It was always something. You didn't deserve awards if you refused to show up."

"I didn't *want* awards from a school administration that enabled bullying from the top down. What meaning would a certificate have when I was afraid to use the restroom for fear of attack? Tammi and crew burned people with cigarettes, you know. We called it the bully brand. Lots of people coming home for this reunion have a scar. Too scared to complain, of course."

"Don't know anything about any bully brand. I wasn't the type of teacher who got involved. To me it was just a job, not a calling, like some think."

"Judi Morrell, for example. That's why she dumped you, Mr. Sever." I paused and then delivered the verbal punch. "Well, that and draining her nest egg to fund your gambling addiction."

I had hoped to startle him enough so that I could shift position and it worked. Keats herded me slowly and carefully away from the retired science teacher. I didn't want to leave the tree with the stashed queens, but at some point, one of us would turn on a flashlight and he'd see the birdhouse. I had no doubt that's why he was here. From what Tammi's husband said, he'd tried before and come up empty. By now, he was probably feeling desperate, because the queens' days were numbered.

Desperate people did terrible things. Piled on top of other terrible things.

"You don't know what you're talking about," he said. "Judi didn't say anything about gambling, I'm sure of it."

"Maybe not, but others did." A little bluffing never hurt anyone. Or it did, but sometimes it was necessary and worthwhile. What wasn't worthwhile was getting Judi into trouble. There was a chance Clint Sever would escape tonight and I couldn't risk his former sweetheart being harmed. Judi was well rid of him and hopefully we could put him away for good.

All I needed to do was get him to confess.

And get him hogtied.

It was a tall order for a hobby farmer and her pets, standing in a meadow in the dark. Like Keats, I knew we'd dealt with some equally bad situations before. Only then, we always seemed to have an ace in the hole. A little secret we could pull out... and shazam! Murderer, detained.

Not tonight. All I had were the pets and my wits.

Plus an old wound that wasn't done healing.

"Come over here before I shoot you," he said, finally turning on a flashlight. He looked different from when I saw him in the school library, but the shadows probably weren't doing me any favors, either. The pistol in his right hand made it hard to focus on anything else, but I was pretty sure he wouldn't shoot me if he thought I knew how to find the queens. Like it or not, my escapades with animals were becoming common knowledge.

"You can shoot me just fine from there if you want," I said. "But first, there's something I want to ask you about."

"Unless you have a gun or a badge, I've got nothing to say to you."

"Honestly, it'll just take a minute."

"I don't have a minute. You don't have a minute. And the queen bees you're protecting don't have much time, either."

"See, that's the thing. I need to take them to the hives you stole and make them queenright."

"What do you know about bees? You can't go shoving queens into hives at random. There will be mutiny. A massacre."

"I know all about balling," I said, trying to bait him with science facts. "I was more interested in biology than you thought. Based on how you treated those colonies, it seems like you're the one who needs educating."

"Please. I've been raising bees for decades."

"So you know all about the queenless roar I heard yesterday rescuing a swarm."

His next snort was less amused. "If you're looking for another award, you won't get it. Sometimes loss is inevitable in farming."

My father had said exactly the same thing but hearing it now infuriated me. "Other times it's very much avoidable. You've probably killed several colonies. A costly blunder when a hive's worth thousands in the almond trade. At least a dozen have swarmed."

"I was clumsy," he admitted, and the pistol's muzzle dropped for a second. "And I couldn't find a big enough space on short notice. Should have had a backup plan."

"Not fair to the bees, but we were able to rescue some of the colonies and they're safe for the moment."

"My loan shark thanks you for that. I'll collect them from Travis Wigg once I get the queens you're hiding. Tried last night when he left to search for the dogs. Big brutes. Strained my thumbs dragging them."

"Ah, the stolen pet diversion," I said. "Oldest trick in the book."

"Those Pefferlaws are full of themselves. Happy to knock them down a peg, but I didn't want to take it out on the dogs."

It was the only kind thing he'd said so far, but that didn't make him redeemable. "That was nice of you. And if you promise to leave their dogs alone, I'll get you into Travis' bee yard.

My dad went down this afternoon with more colonies."

He thought about it and then bought it. "Fine. I'll take you with me. First, we get the queens."

"First, you tell me why you framed my sister."

"Who, Poppy?"

"Did you frame any of my other sisters? I have four."

He made a little circle with his gun barrel. "That's old news. Ancient. Can't recall a thing about it."

"I can." I thought about my sister's old sketch book. The letters floating around weren't parts of words but chemical symbols. They tagged Clint Sever, the zombie. The dollar signs defined the crime. He'd stolen the lockbox containing funds raised by students during car washes, and other events. "You took the money from the school secretary's desk and blamed it on Poppy because she was conveniently there."

"Conveniently delinquent, you mean. So, she was pegged for a crime she didn't commit and got away with some she did. It all comes out in the wash."

"That's a convenient justification. Poppy knows what you did and that no one would listen. Judi Morrell stood up for my sister. Believed in her talent. Yet you kicked Poppy in the teeth. She finished school against the odds, but she's never recovered, Mr. Sever. Isn't that a violation of the teacher's oath?"

"There's no oath and the only credo I believe in is every man for himself."

"It sounds like you are alone, now. You lost a good woman who was so demoralized she left teaching because of you."

"I don't care about any of that." He motioned with the gun. "All that matters is the bees."

"You mean all that matters is the money you can make off them."

"Pretty much, yeah. So shut your gob and get them down here." He flicked his light toward the tree with the birdhouse and walked over to it. "I saw where your dog was looking."

Luckily, he had not seen my cat, who had climbed much higher and was likely only detectable to the trained eye. "How do you propose getting the queens?"

"I just proposed it. You'll get the bees for me. You seem to care a lot about them so you're the gal for the job."

"Why would I help you? You burned my sister and killed Tammi Hickey."

"Like you gave a crap about Tammi. Everyone hated her, especially you, Froggy Flippers."

"Flappers," I corrected. "And while she wasn't kind to me—or most people, from the sounds of it—she was kind to bees. As an advocate for all animals, and let's include insects, I say Tammi deserved better than being clubbed with a smoker."

"She wasn't supposed to be there, but when I drove up, she was hysterical. Crying about some stupid thing."

"The end of her marriage. Not so stupid."

"Explains the diamond ring I found," he said. "But I didn't have time for a heart to heart, because my driver was coming. I gave Tammi a chance to run but she came at me with a J hook, instead. So, I smacked her with the smoker and she caught a bad angle."

"You hit the back of her head. Creeping up behind is always a bad angle."

"I acted in self-defense. That's my story and you won't be around to say otherwise."

"The evidence will say otherwise. I don't need to be around to see you put away."

He jerked his head to the tree. "Get climbing. And be gentle with those queens."

"I'm not doing your dirty work, Clint."

"Mr. Sever. And sure you are." He made a figure eight with the muzzle of the gun, and I reconsidered making that my favorite number. "Otherwise, I'll test drive my new gun on your dog." He offered the most sinister chuckle I'd ever heard. "Still think I'm nice, Ivy?"

A cold front started in my heart and blasted in all directions. I almost fainted from the blizzard in my brain. Warm ears arrived under my fingertips to thaw me.

When I didn't answer, Clint barked, "Faint and you're both gone. Got it?"

"I'm fine," I said. "Totally fine. Let's do this."

CHAPTER TWENTY-EIGHT

"So, about the tree, Mr. Sever. I can't climb it. You've scared me to death and my legs are shaking. What's the hormone? Cortisol?"

"And adrenaline. Plus epinephrine. It's the stress response."

"Exactly. And there's no way I can scale that tree without falling and smashing the queens to bits. How much will they be worth to you then?"

He thought about it. "A few might survive. I'm willing to take the risk."

"Gee, thanks. But I don't have any equipment and I'm not Wonder Woman."

"That's not what I heard," he said. "There are tributes to your superpowers springing up all over. I don't hear you whining about that."

"Let's stick to brainstorming how we're going to get the queens down."

"Fine, I'll give you a boost. Don't think I won't strangle you with my bare hands if you try any funny business."

He stuck his gun in his coat pocket and I walked over to the tree.

I had to get the bees anyway. It might as well be from a boost by Tammi's killer.

Keats wasn't so sure about that. All his flags were flying and his fangs showed as he escorted me to the teacher's side. Clint Sever backed away. His head turned this way and that and I stared at him. He'd looked strange from a distance, not unlike the zombie my sister drew. Now I saw why. His entire face, including his ears, had been stung repeatedly. All the many bumps came together in a craggy range that must have burned like fire.

"Your face," I said. "What happened? This is recent."

He turned away. "Little ingrates came after me when I was trying to shift some hives last night. The old hunting lodge where I stashed them is falling apart and the guy I hired flunked out on me after... what happened."

"After you murdered Tammi, you mean."

He pulled his hat down over some vicious welts. "Nothing anti-histamines won't fix."

With the gun out of the way, I thought about making a run for it. Keats would lead me through the brush and Percy would catch up. But that would mean leaving the queen bees unattended. And in my brief moment of peering up at Percy, I saw a tiny speck on the bird-house. I was as sure as I could be that it was Bernice, bravely standing guard and ready to add one more sting to this man's ugly mug.

That would be Bernice's one and only sting. I couldn't let her sacrifice her life to Clint Sever, murderer of one former cheerleader, many bees and countless high school dreams.

"Bend over," I told Mr. Sever. "Please."

"Take off your boots," he said. "I'm not sixteen anymore."

"I'm not taking off my boots. If I fall, I could break my foot."

"If you fall, you could break my neck. And your back. Not that it matters what happens to you, now. Once I get the queens and the hives together, I'll be done with you. So, take off your boots or lose the dog."

I took off my boots. Then I put my foot into Clint Sever's cupped hands and accepted a lift up the side of the tree.

The trunk was too wide to circle with my arms, but I grappled as best I could with clawed fingers and socks. There was no way I could climb it.

"Higher," I said, stretching and falling far short. "Can't reach."

Clint braced himself against the tree with both hands. "Step onto my shoulders. Carefully."

I did as he said, setting one foot on each of his shoulders, gradually inching my way to a standing position while continuing to grip the tree in a terrified embrace. He groaned underneath me and I grumbled, "I'm not that heavy."

"And I'm not like your prepper friends. This week's done a number on my sciatica."

"Don't make me laugh," I said. "I'm about to grab a bunch of queen bees. You know they can sting as many times as they like and never die."

A shudder ran through him and up my feet and legs. "Grab them. Now."

Seeing a light bobbing toward us in the distance, I grabbed something else. Percy had been poking at it earlier. It was a rope that Tammi had tucked between birdhouse and trunk. It was tied off to the tree and painted the exact shade of the bark.

"Bernice," I whispered, "stay calm. I got this."

I didn't have this at all, but I hoped the bee wouldn't pick up any of the stress hormones I was throwing out.

Gripping the rope loop tightly, I found my balance and twisted the latch on the birdhouse door.

Locked.

"Uh, Mr. Sever? The birdhouse is locked and I have no idea where Tammi hid the key."

My human stepladder let out a string of curses. "You'd better not be joking."

I was afraid to look down. Afraid to see his fury between my stocking feet. Afraid to see my dog, helpless and hopeless.

Luckily, my dog had more faith in us, and his little whine told me to hold on. A meow from above said the same.

The light in the distance might not make it soon enough. I couldn't see it at all now. Maybe it wasn't Edna or the police, but Tammi's husband.

"Might be another way in," I said. "Hang on." Standing on tiptoe, I pushed at the roof of the birdhouse and then pried at the wood. All with one hand, while clinging to the rope loop. "Wait. Wait. I think I've got it."

The birdhouse wasn't anywhere close to giving up its royal stash, but what I did have was assurance that friend, not foe, was heading our way. The light stopped about five yards from the clearing and as I watched, it began to zip in a brisk and exaggerated figure eight. It was Bernice's signature move coming from a camo package. Other than Jilly, only Edna and Gertie knew about my winged friend's flight patterns.

"Have you got it or what?" he grunted.

"Yeah. This time I really do."

That's when I freed the rest of the rope, hoisted myself up and then kicked Clint Sever hard in the head with both heels.

CHAPTER TWENTY-NINE

"Dagnabit, Ivy!" Edna charged into the meadow waving her flashlight in one hand and pepper spray in the other. Gertie was close behind with Minnie trained on Clint Sever, who was lying on the ground screaming blue murder.

Attached to his left earlobe was a 48-pound dog-shaped earring. There was a piercing in session.

I dangled and swung from the tree, catching a flash of orange fluff whisking past me down the trunk in reverse. Percy did not want to miss out on the action.

"Edna, help! Get me down," I said.

She did just that, with Gertie standing guard. It wasn't an elegant descent by any means, but my socks eventually landed on rocks, sticks and damp grass.

"Guess you couldn't give up your cheerleading dreams, Froggy," Edna said. "For the record, while your feet *are* big, they're within normal range based on my medical experience."

Mr. Sever fired off more colorful language. My feet had obviously felt like flappers to him, but he didn't get a vote. Percy punished him by raking off the man's hat and giving his scalp a double smack.

"Can you tie him up and then break into the birdhouse, Edna?" I said. "There's a bunch of queen bees in there that need to be rescued."

"Can you just rope the killer and grab the killer bees, Edna?" She repeated my request in a singsong voice. "Do it all while I stand around in my socks and shout orders."

"Snippy." I pulled out my phone and spoke into it. "Kellan, if you're listening, maybe *you* could tie up the killer and break into the birdhouse to get the queens. Clint Sever was just saying he isn't as tough as my prepper friends, but maybe I've worn them out."

"Maybe so," Gertie said, smirking as I called Keats and Percy off. "Probably not."

She rolled Clint onto his belly with one boot and let Edna secure his wrists and ankles.

When she was done, Edna nudged me rather rudely out of the way and walked to the tree. As I suspected, she was not going to let the police chief best her.

Heaving her backpack off her shoulders and dropping it, she pulled out spikes and a harness. In no time, she'd scaled the trunk, and tied herself off.

"Bee veil," she called down.

Gertie shoved the white helmet into a bag and tossed it up. "Can't be too careful, old friend. You don't want to look like this sad excuse for a man."

"No, I do not." Edna put on the helmet and gloves before pulling bolt cutters out of her pocket. The lock snapped and she opened the door gently. Her voice softened and she almost purred as she shone a light inside and greeted the bees. "Hello, ladies. Hope you've had a nice vacation up here, because it's time to get to work creating pollinators and honey makers. Hill country needs you."

Tammi had fittingly chosen a large, professional makeup storage box to hold her queens. It was well ventilated and secured by yet another lock that Edna broke.

"Wouldn't it be funny if there was just makeup in there?" Gertie called, as Edna tentatively lifted the lid.

"It wouldn't be funny at all," I said. "A queen bee died for these actual queens."

Edna closed the lid quickly. "Palace and royals secure. Three dozen queen cages or more. Tammi left a gorgeous legacy."

"All in the eye of the beholder," Kellan said, coming into the clearing. "I see you have the site secure, Miss Evans and Mrs. Rhodes."

"Very much so, Chief," Edna said, rappelling down very slowly with the queens. She offered him the rope. "You can have a swing if you like, since the hard work is done."

He shook his head. A smile fought a scowl, and as police flooded into the open space carrying lights and equipment, the scowl won. "Ivy? A word, please."

It wouldn't just be one word, but a torrent, I knew. If not now, in front of his staff, then later. "I'm sorry, Kellan." I tried to preempt the lecture. "I just wanted to reunite Bernice with her colony and make them queenright."

He wanted to stay on track but couldn't stop himself from asking, "Queenright?"

"That's the term used when a colony has a queen. A hive won't survive without one, and that's what happened to Bernice's family. Mr. Sever implied other colonies are in the same state." I tried to slow down but the words kept coming. "I think he owed people a lot of money. Did you know there's a secret casino in hill country? People have dropped a few hints."

His scowl and rising eyebrows battled for control of his expression and it was a toss-up. "I knew about half of what you're saying." His lips pressed together so I figured I wouldn't hear which half. At least, not right now when he was angry.

My best strategy was continuing the information dump until I hit on something that would distract him. "I came to ask Tammi's husband if he knew about the queen nursery. Delsie, the school librarian, had mentioned it and I wanted to find a new leader for Bernice's colony. Keats led me around back where Eddy and Kayla were arguing, like I texted. You know the rest."

The scowl came back. "When you put the phone on speaker like that, it leaves me feeling frustrated and helpless. I don't want a single beep to give you away, and I can't teleport. There were no officers closer tonight."

"I know and I'm sorry. But Eddy told Kayla someone had come around a few times likely looking for the queens. Kayla wanted the queens, too."

"I know. I found them bickering on the driveway about which way to go. They were easily apprehended."

"You arrested them with the gun?" My voice had a lilt. "Awesome."

"Detained for questioning. Both of them lied earlier and their stories are still so garbled it'll take time to untie the knots." His scowl intensified to a glower. "So you knew Eddy was getting a gun and still went after the queens alone?"

"Yeah." I scuffed the ground with a sock and regretted it when a sharp stone grazed my sole. "I counted on Keats and Percy to find them fast, and they did. Unfortunately, the bees were out of reach."

"What about Clint Sever? Did you know about him?"

This was the key question that would save me from getting expelled from crime-solving. Luckily, I had a good answer. "I didn't know Mr. Sever would be here and didn't suspect till he arrived that he was the killer. Did *you* know?"

"He was near the top of my list. I knew about his chronic gambling debts and he was in the bee club so he knew the value of Tammi's apiary. But he had an alibi and we couldn't find where he stashed them."

I told him about the decrepit hunting lodge where Clint Sever had housed the bees in such miserable conditions that they fled. It was heartbreaking to know so many loyal workers had lost their lives by stinging him. Karma should have delivered an allergic reaction, or at least an infection from the venom. Instead, my former teacher was yelling insults and obscenities at Gertie and Edna. Asher came over and ushered my friends away, like the gallant gentleman he was. Perhaps Ash didn't realize the spicy octogenarians were goading the teacher on with quiet commentary about his deficiencies. I was getting better at lipreading every day. It was a good skill for a sleuth.

"Sever got Poppy expelled in high school for a theft he committed," I said. "Judi Morrell was the only one who backed her, and she gave up teaching because of unfairness within the administration. They shamed her over a relationship with Clint, whereas he stayed and made students miserable for years to follow."

"Until he was fired with cause for something else," Kellan said. "His actions caught up with him."

Hearing that helped. A lot. "Really? What did he do?"

"Another theft to pay off his loans. There wasn't enough evidence to convict so they let him off with a spanking and reduced pension, which only increased his desperation. He was always on the make for more money."

"But Fiona still let him volunteer in shop class," I said. "That's not right."

"Far from it." Kellan's voice was heavy with disapproval. "On the bright side, my investigation exposed some nasty business to stamp out." He looked down at my feet. "I wore boots for that."

"Always a good choice," I said, smiling as Keats left Clint's side to bring me a boot. He normally didn't waste his talents on retrieving, but probably sensed numbing toes put me at a disadvantage with Kellan.

I took the boot and leaned against a tree to pull it on.

"I was bushwhacking when you and Clint were arguing, so could you tell me how you happened to be bootless?" Kellan asked.

"He insisted I take them off before boosting me to the birdhouse.

Just as well since I ended up standing on his shoulders." Keats brought the other boot and dropped it, giving Kellan a sheepish swish. The dog knew we were still in trouble with the law—at least Fiancé Law. "Do you know Mr. Sever had the gall to call me Froggy Flippers? Everyone knows it was Flappers."

Kellan turned slightly away to watch his staff. "Don't try to make me laugh, Ivy. I'm annoyed at you." He aimed an index finger at Keats. "You, too. Leading her into the bush in the dark after bees was sheer recklessness."

Keats started to mumble something cheeky but stopped when his orange sidekick took over. The cat hit Kellan's midriff and made a show of scaling to the chief's shoulder. This was nothing new or onerous for my athletic cat, but he worked the climb hard for heroic value.

"Percy, must you?" I asked. "The chief has a lot on his mind."

"I do," he agreed. Once the cat was settled between us, however, Kellan couldn't easily bore into me with his serious cop eyes. "Perhaps we'll continue the discussion at the farm."

"Good idea." The worst of his ire would dissipate by then, based on experience. "I'll run down and drop Bernice and the queens with Travis. Time is of the essence in getting the queens properly situated and introducing them to the hives that are—"

"Queenwrong?" Kellan interrupted. It was the first sign my fiancé was cracking through the chiefly veneer.

"I haven't seen that term in my research, but I like it."

"You're humoring me." He leaned forward to peer around Percy's puff of fluff, but the cat leaned, too, happily obstructing justice. "Where is Bernice, anyway? Shouldn't she be tucked safe in her hive?"

"Absolutely, and thanks for worrying about her. Once the queens were in good hands, Bernice repaired to my pocket."

"Your pocket? What if you forget, and—"

"She's not going to waste her one precious sting on me when it's needed to protect her new queen." I touched my jacket outside the pocket and felt a gentle vibration within. "I do want to reunite her with her family. It's been a rough few days."

"For all of us." Kellan blew fur out of his face and then sneezed. "So many of them are, lately."

"On the bright side, we're human with years ahead of us. If we were worker bees like Bernice we'd only have about six weeks of hard labor before shoving off to bee heaven."

"There is that," Kellan said, signaling for us to walk back to the others.

Clint Sever was now face up and it wasn't his good side. The stings would fade but his inner monster would always show. I couldn't help but think he warmed up to murder by destroying young people at a vulnerable time. Poppy wasn't his only victim, I was quite sure of that. More hands would rise when this news got out.

Kellan squeezed my arm, staying well away from my pocket. "Be careful. I'll send a police escort."

I shook my head. "I've got a prepper escort. Imagine if I'd had that in high school."

Finally, he laughed. "Probably would have brought you even more trouble, but it's fun to imagine."

Looping my arm through his, I smiled. "So fun. I'm afraid Edna would have been the one delivering bully brands. With her father's pipe."

His eyes glazed for a second, likely trying to imagine it. Then he jumped. And then I jumped.

A sheepdog was bullying our calves, signaling that it was time to buzz off.

CHAPTER THIRTY

I expected to hate every minute of the school reunion, but instead, I enjoyed it. The new planning committee, comprising Jilly and my sisters, changed the scope at the last minute and opened attendance beyond my graduating class to anyone who cared to come. They also doubled the price of a ticket, both to cover the cost of the larger location at the Palais Royale in Dorset Hills and to gather money for a worthy cause.

The fundraising idea came directly from the hill country school board, who wanted to salvage their reputation. Fiona Gillespie was a no-show at the reunion. It turned out she was at a conference in Florida and looking for a retirement condo by the beach. A cross-country move would be far easier than facing down the alleged corruption under her regime. I wasn't sure how much she knew about Clint Sever's actions, but her rapid departure without any kind of public statement was a red flag. For the first time, I was grateful to Justine Schalow, who'd tracked Fiona down and published photos of the principal looking windblown and disheveled beside the pool at a cheap motel. Leave it to Justine to expose someone's bald spot.

I hoped Fiona would keep Justine busy a little longer. It had been nice to get through an adventure without the so-called press dogging my every step. I was only interested in one dog, and regrettably, he was a no-show tonight as well.

"Sorry I was late," Kellan said, taking my hand and leading me to the dance floor. "There was more cleanup than I expected after this debacle."

"Any chance you were avoiding the tribute to Tammi?" I asked. "I tried, but Jilly made me come on time." I moved back a little to show him my new stilettos. "She also insisted I buy some glittery shoes to claim my nickname."

"Your feet are perfect, Cinderella, and you are nobody's frog." He swept me into his arms and spun us into the crowd. "You're the most beautiful woman in this room, hands down. Make that feet down."

"Spoken like a true prince." I squeezed his shoulder. "I'm glad you made it tonight because Keats and Percy stayed home."

He leaned back to stare at me, eyebrows morphing into question marks. "By choice?"

"They didn't protest or pout, so I guess that's a yes."

"There must be too many busy feet here for their comfort." Kellan moved with his usual grace while I tried to get my new shoes to cooperate. "Too many for mine," he added. "I don't enjoy crowds anymore."

"That's because we know too much," I said. "Someone in this room is probably planning something awful, or about to be the victim of an awful plan."

He had to sigh pretty hard for me to feel it in all the commotion, but I did. "I knew policing here wouldn't be easy, but it's like juggling fireworks and grenades."

"I'll distract you with a bit of family news." I stared over at my sister, who was at a table with my mother, Jilly and Asher.

"About Poppy? She looks... well, happy. What happened?"

"A letter of apology from the school board, for starters. They also secured a scholarship to an art college. Judi Morrell had a hand in that, of course. She offered Poppy part-time work at her gallery and better yet, her mentorship."

"And then there's Travis," Kellan said, as the tall, bearded man led Poppy to the dance floor. They bumped into us deliberately and then laughed as they moved off. "Did you set them up?"

"Nope. Figured you did."

He shook his head. "Wouldn't do that to Travis. He's a good guy."

"And my sister isn't?" My voice was indignant. In my view, Travis hadn't proven himself good enough yet for family. However, his impressive stewardship of Tammi's hives went a long way. He'd worked with Dad to introduce one of the queens to Bernice's colony and so far, so good. If Travis treated Poppy equally well, I could put up with some teasing.

"It's Poppy," Kellan said. "She hasn't always shown the best judgement."

"Because she has trauma." Now I sighed. "Maybe with all the changes, she'll end up looking that happy for years to come. Anyway, Keats likes Travis. Can't argue with that."

"Oh, I can argue with Keats and plan to do it often. Just not about Poppy's love life."

I decided to change the subject. "I've submitted a proposal to the school board to tap into the funds they're raising."

Finally, I'd managed to surprise my mostly shockproof fiancé. "For what? Fertilizer apprenticeships?"

"Yes, but think bigger. I'm pitching a Youth at Work project, where we'll invite guest speakers from around the region to talk about career options. Including you, by the way. I want to show teens there are options for satisfying work here at home. That also means volunteer opportunities or internships. We ship our best and brightest off to the city for college, expecting they'll never return. That can change. Often, it's better for them to be near family and community."

"Better for the crime rate, too, I would think. You might need the mayor on board."

"Copied her on the proposal and asked for her backing. Figure she kind of owes us, after what happened a few months back. You know, the corruption incident."

He nodded. "Hope she sees it that way. I suspect she views corruption as part of the package in politics and policing."

"Don't tell the kids that. The message is life is good here in Clover Grove. Despite everything."

"Do you wish you never left?" he asked.

"Maybe. That fifteen years feels like a waste, considering how happy I am now. But it wouldn't be this way now, if I hadn't gone. I wouldn't have met Jilly. I wouldn't have Keats and the farm." I grinned at him. "You may have fallen for public opinion that my feet are too big."

"Never. But I'm happy we both came back." He spun me around so I could see the family table. My sister Daisy was trying to hold Mom back from confronting Nadia Reddy, but luckily Kayla and Eddy hadn't come. "Are you worried about your nephews?"

"Definitely. They could so easily cross to the wrong side, and I want to keep a close eye on them. That means I'll probably back their new entrepreneurial idea."

This time his sigh turned into a gusty snort. "Can't wait to hear."

I rested my forehead against his shoulder to gather strength. "They want to use my sheep for a lawn care business. The goats, too."

"What? I don't understand."

"It's the latest thing for environmentally conscious businesses.

So, the mayor, theoretically, could hire my sheep to mow the lawns at city hall. The boys heard about it and want to give it a try."

"You trust them with your sheep?"

"Of course not. Sutton ate an old tuna sandwich on purpose this week. He can't take care of himself let alone the sheep. But if I want to support youth, it starts at home and I need to figure something out."

"Oh, Ivy. You know this probably won't end well for the boys, the sheep or the clients."

"I'm hoping they'll forget about it when they see how much work it is. They have the attention span of gnats."

He gave me a hug, right in the middle of the dance floor, under the mirror ball. "Let's talk more about your youth project. I love seeing you fired up for a cause other than animals for a change. Can I be on your think tank?"

"Would you?" My heart buzzed with the power of a billion bees. "With you on board, no one could say no."

"They say no to me all the time. But together we'll have a better chance of twisting their arms to do the right thing. For their kids, and eventually ours."

My inner bees sent heat to my cheeks. I loved talking about our future children even if the prospect of delivering and raising them scared me to death. "And the next generation of our nieces and nephews. I figure you and I thrived *despite* the school system here, not because of it."

"Wouldn't change a thing, given how well it turned out."

We were spangled with light from the mirror ball and surrounded by friends and family. Back in high school I could never have imagined my good fortune. It was the crucible that made me what I became and attracted the wonderful people and animals I loved.

Edna and Gertie were keeping us all safe on the perimeter so that Kellan and Asher could enjoy some well-deserved downtime. Minnie had stayed in the van with Gertie's poncho, but I was confident Edna had stowed what she needed somewhere handy. She was no stranger to the Palais Royale.

Asher finally managed to liberate Jilly and they joined us on the dance floor.

"Hey, brother," I said. "There's something I need to ask you."

"If it's about Travis, forget it," he said with a wink. "Bro code."

I released Kellan's shoulder and caught Asher's arm. "It's about Tammi and her crew back in their heyday. A little bird told me they got pranked and you seemed to keep a running list of the best."

He sucked in his lips and looked up, pretending to scour his memory. "I do recall hearing something about that. The squad had this habit of staking out restrooms, and one of my girlfriends was scared to use the facilities." Pausing, he kissed Jilly's cheek. "She was just my starter girlfriend. The one where I made all the mistakes."

"Carry on," Jilly said. "We're listening."

"So they ambushed this girl in a cubicle one day and threatened to do something despicable with a cigarette."

"Branding," I said. "Narrowly avoided it myself."

"Like I said, it was despicable. And I spoke to the principal about it myself, the very next time I was in her office on another matter."

"Detention," Kellan supplied.

"The reason isn't important," Asher continued. "The point was that Gillespie dismissed it as myth. That was her word. Yet the starter girlfriend's sister had an actual burn delivered by Tammi herself."

I spun my hand. "Get to the prank, Ash. At midnight our limo turns into a pumpkin."

He wanted to drag it out longer, but Jilly poked his chest to hit fast forward. "So, one day, when the big three were at the mirror fixing their makeup, someone in disguise carried in a big bucket of the foulest swamp water you could ever imagine and dumped it right over their heads. There was enough to douse all three."

"From Huckleberry Swamp?" I asked. "It's the worst."

"Maybe," he said. "It was thick and green and stunk to high heaven. At least from what I heard. Some said there were tadpoles in Tammi's hair."

"Aw, the poor baby frogs," I said.

"See, that's why I didn't want to tell you," Kellan said. "I knew you'd get emotional over the frogs."

"Oh man, she ruins everything." Asher rolled his eyes until they twinkled with light from the mirror ball. "That story is classic."

"It was a great story," I told Kellan, as he whisked me away. "He was probably embellishing with the tadpoles."

"Probably," Kellan agreed. "Story works just as well without them."

We took one more turn around the floor and I said, "Life is good, and I can only think of one thing that would make it even better."

"A honeymoon in Thelma's bookmobile?"

I was legitimately shocked that he guessed what I was going to say. "Am I that transparent?"

"Far from it. Not with your advanced degree in sneakery. But when it comes to books, well... you're an open book."

"You think you're so smart."

He raised my arm to spin me around before we left the dance floor and I whirled so many times there was a very real chance of falling off my new shoes. But then he caught me, like he always did.

"Smart enough to catch you," he said. "And smart enough to enjoy a dance when there are no pets around to trip or bite me."

"Good point." I let him twirl me again. "But don't get used to it. Your future is all about fur and fun, Chiefheart."

He opened his arms wide and I scooted in for a hug. "I embrace it," he said. "Whatever comes."

When a music concert leads to murder at the fairground, Ivy's nephews—and her sheep—land in a heap of trouble. Join the team on their next crime-solving adventure in **Sheep with One Eye Open**.

Interested in hearing more about my writing and my dogs? Join the Ellen Riggs newsletter at **ellenriggs.com/opt-in**.

Runaway Farm & Inn Recipes

Beekeepers' Honey Rice Bubble Slice

Ingredients

2 tbsp honey
1/3 cup brown sugar
1/2 cup butter
4 cups crispy rice cereal

Instructions

1. Add honey, brown sugar and butter to a large saucepan.
2. Melt on the stovetop until bubbling around the edges.

3. Remove from heat, add rice cereal and mix well.
4. Pour into a lined 8-inch square baking pan and spread out. Chill in the fridge for one hour, or until set.
5. Cut into squares and enjoy!

**Courtesy of esteemed editor, Serena Clarke.

More Books by Ellen Riggs

Bought-the-Farm Cozy Mystery Series

- A Dog with Two Tales (Prequel)
- Dogcatcher in the Rye
- Dark Side of the Moo
- A Streak of Bad Cluck
- Till the Cat Lady Sings
- Alpaca Lies
- Twas the Bite Before Christmas
- Swine and Punishment
- The Cat and the Riddle
- Don't Rock the Goat
- Swan with the Wind
- How to Get a Neigh with Murder
- Tweet Revende
- For Love Or Bunny
- Between a Squawk and a Hard Place
- Double Dog Dare
- Deerly Departed
- Think Outside the Fox
- Mouse of Ill Repute
- Bee All and End All

- Sheep with One Eye Open
- Roo the Day
- Till Death Zoo Us Part
- Hit the Road, Quack
- One Horse Open Slay
- Beg, Burrow or Steal

Bought-the-Farm Mysteries - Boxed Sets

- Bought the Farm Mysteries - Books 1-3
- Bought the Farm Mysteries - Books 4-6
- Bought the Farm Mysteries - Books 7-9
- Bought the Farm Mysteries - Books 1-10

Dog Town Series

- Ready or Not in Dog Town (The Beginning)
- Bitter and Sweet in Dog Town (Labor Day)
- A Match Made in Dog Town (Thanksgiving)
- Lost and Found in Dog Town (Christmas)
- Calm and Bright in Dog Town (Christmas)
- Tried and True in Dog Town (New Year's)
- Yours and Mine in Dog Town (Valentine's Day)
- Nine Lives in Dog Town (Easter)
- Great and Small in Dog Town (Memorial Day)
- Bold and Blue in Dog Town (Independence Day)
- Better or Worse in Dog Town (Labor Day)

Mystic Mutt Mysteries Paranormal Cozy

- I Want You to Haunt Me (Prequel)
- You Can't Always Get What You Haunt
- Any Way You Haunt It

- I Only Haunt to be with You
- All I Haunt Is You
- Do You Haunt to Know a Secret?
- All I Haunt for Christmas
- I Haunt You Back